THEY LOVE, FIGHT, AND RISK THEIR LIVES IN A TOWN CALLED ABILENE!

LUKE TRAVIS: Abilene's tall, rugged lawman is famed for fighting the most dangerous gunslingers in the West. But with petite, hot-headed Bethany Hale in town, he's in for a new kind of trouble . . .

BETHANY HALE: The Philadelphia beauty is traveling the West to spread her message against the evils of liquor. But when people start dying of poisoned whiskey, the law starts looking into her past . . .

CODY FISHER: As quick with his fists as with his heart, Travis's deputy is out to break up a ruthless whiskey war. Then Bethany Hale starts showing a preference for his brother, Judah, and Cody starts seeing red . . .

REVEREND JUDAH FISHER: Judah is captivated by the spitfire from Philadelphia. But when Bethany asks him to play the part of a drunk in a morality play, it strikes too close to home . . .

KERMIT BARLOW: The lean, sharp-shooting pig farmer runs whiskey as a side business. But when a big company tries to take over the trade, Kermit knows the value of his still—and how to turn it into

Books by Justin Ladd

Abilene Book 1: The Peacemaker
Abilene Book 2: The Sharpshooter
Abilene Book 3: The Pursuers
Abilene Book 4: The Night Riders
Abilene Book 5: The Half-Breed
Abilene Book 6: The Hangman
Abilene Book 7: The Prizefighter
Abilene Book 8: The Whiskey Runners

Published by POCKET BOOKS

JUSTIN LADD
ABILENE

Book 8

THE
WHISKEY RUNNERS

™

Created by the producers of
**Wagons West, Stagecoach,
White Indian, and San Francisco.**

Book Creations Inc., Canaan, NY   Lyle Kenyon Engel, Founder

POCKET BOOKS

New York   London   Toronto   Sydney   Tokyo

This book is a work of fiction. Names, characters, places and
incidents are either the product of the author's imagination or
are used fictitiously. Any resemblance to actual events or locales
or persons, living or dead, is entirely coincidental.

An *Original* Publication of POCKET BOOKS

POCKET BOOKS, a division of Simon & Schuster Inc.
1230 Avenue of the Americas, New York, NY 10020

Copyright © 1989 by Book Creations, Inc.
Cover art copyright © 1989 Gordon Crabb

ISBN: 0-671-66993-1

First Pocket Books printing June 1989

10 9 8 7 6 5 4 3 2 1

POCKET and colophon are trademarks of
Simon & Schuster Inc.

Printed in the U.S.A.

THE
WHISKEY RUNNERS

Prologue

A BITTER AUTUMN WIND WHIPPED AMONG THE BUILD-
ings of Abilene. The night was clear. The moon and
stars shone brightly, but the silvery illumination was
cold. Abner Peavey could see where he was going as he
stumbled out of a ramshackle saloon on the western
edge of town. The saloon he was leaving sold only the
cheapest whiskey, like the amber liquid sloshing
around in the half-empty bottle he was carrying. He
was drunk but not so far gone that he did not notice
the moonlight. Anything that helped him find his way
was a blessing.

There were no boardwalks in front of the buildings
in this part of town, so Abner did not have any posts
to hang on to for support. He lurched into the street,
hunching his shoulders as the bitter wind hit him and
penetrated his thin cloth coat.

Isn't a fit night for man nor beast, he thought as he

staggered along. Had it not been for the liquor warming his insides, he knew he might freeze to death before he reached the abandoned cabin on Mud Creek that he claimed as his own.

Abner Peavey had been a great many things in his forty-odd years. He had punched cattle and eaten dust on trail drives; had tried to scratch a living from the ground as a farmer. He had driven freight wagons and worked as a blacksmith and for a while had even clerked in stores. But the very best thing he did was drink.

Nobody's better than I am at that, he thought with a chuckle as he lifted the bottle to his lips and took another long swallow.

The rotgut burned as it trickled down his throat, just as he knew it would. The fire that had been kindled in his belly blazed even higher as he added more fuel to it.

Abner blinked his watery eyes and peered around him at the dark, empty street. *Where is everybody tonight?* Sure, it was cold and windy, but that was no reason for folks to hide inside. Abner did not like to drink alone. He had forgotten that when he left the saloon a few minutes before; some peaceful solitary boozing had been the only thing he had had in mind.

He staggered over to a hardware store that was closed for the night. Pounding on the door with his free hand, he called, "Anybody home?" No one answered.

Abner was about to raise his voice to shout even louder when a warning in his alcohol-fogged brain made him stop. If he made too much of a ruckus, somebody would call the marshal, and then Luke Travis would haul him off to jail.

Abner frowned and pondered that for a moment.

Getting tossed in the hoosegow might not be so bad. At least it would be warm there, while his ramshackle cabin would be icy cold. Maybe he would start a fire in the little stove, but it would take most of the night to warm the place up.

In jail, however, his bottle would be taken away from him. Travis would never let him keep it and finish it off in a cell. Abner had paid good money for that bottle, and he intended to polish it off when he got home. Nobody would take his whiskey away from him, he decided.

Lurching back toward the middle of the street, he peered into the deep shadows, trying to remember the way to his cabin. A moment later, he picked a route and began shambling along.

He had taken three steps when a fiery pain flared up in his gut. Gasping, Abner pressed his free arm across his middle and doubled over. The savage pain made him tremble. Beads of sweat broke out on his forehead, making the bitter wind blowing in his face seem even more frigid.

Slowly the spasm eased. Abner gulped deeply and straightened. He had no idea what was wrong, but it had been bad. He did not want to go through *that* again.

"Best take another drink," he muttered to himself. That would fortify him, give him the strength he needed to make it back to his cabin.

He lifted the bottle to his lips and guzzled some more whiskey. Satisfied for the moment, he wiped his mouth with his coat sleeve. Then jamming his battered felt hat down on his head, he started walking again.

A moment later fresh pain wracked him again. An agonized groan escaped from his lips. Abner forced his head up and opened his mouth several times before he managed to croak, "H-help . . ."

But no one was around to hear him. With the bitter weather and late hour few people were stirring in Abilene tonight.

Somehow Abner moved his feet. He moaned again as the pain stabbed at his insides. He had gone only a few more yards when his strength deserted him completely. His knees buckled, and he collapsed. The almost empty whiskey bottle slipped out of his fingers, bounced in the street, and rolled away. Abner doubled over, trying to curl his body around the agony inside him. When that brought no relief, he twisted and writhed in the dust.

The sound of hoofbeats pounding the street some distance away reached his ears. He lifted his head and looked out into the darkness. A few blocks away a lone horseman crossed the street from an alley. Forcing his lips open, he wheezed, "Help me."

But the rider never looked around. He was going about his business, his body hunched against the cold. The chilly wind whipped Abner's desperate plea away before it could be heard.

Abner saw the man disappear into the shadows, and then another convulsion gripped him. He tried to retch, but nothing came up. Suddenly he realized he was going to die. Less than five seconds later, he did.

Being a devoted lawman is one thing, Marshal Luke Travis thought, *being a dad-blasted fool is another.* Nobody was going to make any trouble on a night like this. Folks were too busy trying to keep warm.

It was almost midnight, and Travis was taking his final turn around Abilene for the night, just finishing his swing through the old west end. He paused in front of a particularly disreputable saloon and peered through the filth-streaked glass of the window. A few men stood before the makeshift bar—rough planks laid across empty barrels. No tables were scattered around the long, narrow room; this was not a place for playing cards or seeking the company of women. Men came here for only one reason—to guzzle moonshine and escape the hardships of their lives in the oblivion of the fiery brew.

There was no need to step inside, Travis decided. The saloon was quiet, like all the others in town. The first real cold snap of the season had depressed everybody.

The tall, broad-shouldered man in a dark suit and flat-crowned hat moved away from the window. Luke Travis's face was lean, his eyes quick and intelligent. A sandy-colored mustache drooped over his wide mouth. A walnut-butted Colt Peacemaker rode in the well-oiled holster belted around his hips. He had been a frontier lawman for a long time, and he moved confidently through the shadows as he turned away from the saloon. Abilene was his town; he knew its ins and outs, knew how easily trouble could crop up unexpectedly.

But not tonight—the weather was just too nasty for anybody to have mischief in mind.

Travis began to think about the stove in his office and the pot of coffee that was staying hot there. He started back toward Texas Street. But some instinct made him pause and turn to stare back the way he had come.

In the glistening moonlight he noticed something lying in the middle of the street. As he watched, the wind caught the object and whipped it around for a few feet. Travis finally recognized that it was a hat.

So someone had lost a hat. The town marshal did not need to concern himself with something so minor. Nevertheless, Travis grimaced and strode quickly over to it. He had been around too long to ignore a nagging feeling that something was wrong. It was his job to find out what.

He picked up the hat and, frowning, turned it over in his hands. In the moonlight he could see it looked like Abner Peavey's. Abner had spent quite a few nights in Abilene's jail, sleeping off drunken binges. Along with big Nestor Gilworth and a few others, Abner was one of the regulars in the cellblock.

Squinting into the wind, Travis peered up the street and spotted an odd form lying several feet from one of the buildings. The lawman started toward the sprawled shape. A few steps later, he broke into a run.

As Travis drew near, the huddled figure resolved itself into something human. The marshal's eyes darted around, his hand hovering near the butt of his Colt. He had plenty of enemies, and this situation might well be a trap.

Warily he approached the figure and dropped to one knee beside what he now could identify as a man lying curled up on his side. Grasping his shoulder, Travis carefully rolled him over on his back. The moonlight shone harshly on Abner Peavey's distorted face. The marshal gasped. Seldom had he seen anyone's face twisted in such agony. With the back of his hand he touched Peavey's cheek. It was cold, too cold to be chilled by the wind alone. Abner Peavey was dead.

From the looks of it, Peavey had been dead for half an hour or so. Travis drew a match from his coat pocket and struck it, but the wind blew out the flame before it had a chance to reveal anything. The marshal found another match and scratched it to life. This time he cupped his hand around it and quickly scanned the body. In his hasty examination Travis did not see any wounds.

That did not mean much. If Peavey had been killed, he might be lying on the bullet or stab wound that had taken his life. Travis let the wind blow out the second match and tossed it into the dirt. He slipped his hands under Peavey's arms and straightened up, pulling the body with him. It was a thoroughly unpleasant task, but Travis wrestled the body over to the shelter of a small porch that fronted a nearby building. Then he went to look for Abilene's undertaker.

Cyrus Worden had already turned in for the night, but since he was the town's undertaker as well as the Dickinson County coroner, he was accustomed to having his sleep interrupted. The balding, fussy little man pulled on his clothes, then lit the kerosene lantern that stood on his front porch. Clutching his coat closer to his thin body, he walked with Travis toward the spot where Abner Peavey's body lay. In his high-pitched voice Worden complained about the bitterly cold night, but Travis sensed that he was just grumbling to have something to say.

"He was in the street when I found him," Travis said as Worden knelt and examined the body by the lantern light. "All I did was move him over here out of the wind. What do you think, Cyrus?"

Worden grunted. "No sign of injury. Of course I'll have to examine him more thoroughly to be sure. But right offhand, Marshal, I'd say this man died of natural causes. Abner Peavey, isn't it?"

"That's right." Travis turned up his coat collar. It seemed as if the wind was getting even colder.

"He was a heavy drinker, wasn't he?"

"Right again."

Worden stood up and brushed his hands together. "There you are, then. The man drank himself to death. He probably did so much damage to his internal organs that they simply wouldn't function any longer."

"At first I thought he might have frozen to death, but it doesn't seem cold enough for that," Travis commented.

"I agree with you, Marshal, although the exposure he suffered may have indeed contributed to his death. When the human body gets cold, it has to work much harder to warm itself. This man simply couldn't keep that up."

Travis nodded. What Worden said made sense and fit with what he knew of Abner Peavey. Wearily Travis said, "I'll help you get him back to your place. Go ahead and check him over, just to make sure we didn't miss anything, and then I guess you can bury him at county expense. I doubt Abner had any money."

"Very well. Why don't I go get my wagon? That'll save us having to drag him over to the undertaking parlor."

"All right." Travis pushed his hands deeper in his pockets and watched Worden hurry off into the night.

Standing alone in the bitter wind, he began to pace, both to put some distance between himself and the corpse and to ward off the cold.

He had not known Peavey well, but he hated to see anyone die so needlessly. Travis liked a cold beer on a hot day and a bottle of good wine from time to time. He even enjoyed a shot of whiskey under some circumstances. But Abner Peavey had always been drunk. Every time Travis had run into the man he had been intoxicated to some degree. It was a waste, he thought disgustedly, but there was nothing he could do about it.

Staying close to the body, Travis strolled aimlessly in and out of the moonlight. Suddenly his foot bumped against something that was lying in the long shadows cast by a building. He bent down to pick up whatever it was he had kicked, his fingers groping in the dirt. Finally they closed over smooth, cold glass. As he straightened, he stepped over to a patch of moonlight and frowned at the liquor bottle in his hand.

It had no label, which was not unusual; a lot of the rotgut served in Abilene came in unmarked bottles such as this. He lifted the uncorked neck to his nose, sniffed, and recoiled slightly as the pungent odor of cheap whiskey assailed his nostrils. If he had had any doubts about the cause of Peavey's death, this discovery laid them to rest.

Travis crossed to a trash barrel that stood at the entrance to an alley and tossed the bottle into it. Abner Peavey would no longer need it.

Chapter One

AT DAWN THE NEXT MORNING DEPUTY CODY FISHER awoke in the small room next to the cellblock. The first thing he realized was that the bitter wind of the night before was no longer howling. Yawning, he rose from the bunk and ambled sleepily to the side door of the jail to bring in the bucket of water he had left outside. As his fingers touched the cold metal handle, he shivered at the chill that ran up his arm. A thin layer of ice floated on top of the water in the bucket. Now as he carried it into the warm office, he saw the ice begin to melt.

Cody shoveled the ashes out of the stove and added some kindling and small logs to the glowing coals that remained. Then he washed up, fetched more water, and started a pot of coffee brewing. There were no prisoners in the cellblock, but the deputy knew that when Luke Travis arrived he would be ready for a cup of hot coffee. At this hour, Cody wanted one, too.

While he waited for the coffee to finish perking, he went to the front door of the office and stepped out onto the boardwalk. Drawing a deep breath of crisp air, he stretched and then leaned against one of the posts supporting the awning above him to gaze at the shops and saloons housed in the two- and three-story frame buildings that lined Texas Street.

He saw that the saloons were closed, as they ought to be at this hour. The Bull's Head, almost directly opposite him, and the Old Fruit Saloon, located on the corner to his left, were dark and quiet. But diagonally across the street to his right he noticed a flicker of movement as someone opened the curtains at the Sunrise Café.

The sky was a clear, bright blue, and Cody could tell that the day would be pleasant once the sun had a chance to warm the chilly air.

Abilene's deputy marshal was a clean-shaven, dark-haired man in his mid-twenties. Lounging lazily against the boardwalk post, he struck a deceptively casual pose. But anyone who had spent much time in the West would spot the alertness in his eyes and the habitual way his right hand was poised inches from his pearl-handled Colt.

In repose, his handsome features had a grim cast, but that would be relieved by one of his frequent smiles. His boots were worn but well cared for, as were the holster and shell belt that were strapped around his hips. The denim pants, work shirt, and cowhide vest might have marked him as a cowboy had it not been for the badge pinned to his vest.

Cody Fisher was handy with a gun and in his earlier

years had come awfully close to riding on the wrong side of the law. He had chosen instead to uphold it—even though that sometimes meant doing boring chores like brewing coffee and sweeping out the office. Grinning faintly, he turned and went back inside.

Marshal Luke Travis arrived at the office ten minutes later. He hung his hat on one of the pegs just inside the doorway, then took the cup of steaming black liquid that Cody handed to him and sipped it gratefully. As he strolled behind his scarred old desk that was piled with papers, he asked, "Anybody been around looking for me this morning?"

"No," Cody replied. "It's been quiet. Not too many folks up and about just yet."

"One fewer than yesterday," Travis grunted.

Cody frowned. "What do you mean, Marshal?"

"Abner Peavey died last night."

Cody's frown deepened. As deputy marshal, Cody had hauled in a drunken Abner Peavey many times and locked him in one of the cells. "What happened?"

"I found his body lying in the street when I was making my final rounds," Travis said. "Had to roust Cyrus Worden out of bed. We took Peavey to Cyrus's place and looked him over. There were no signs of foul play, but he had been drinking as usual. It's the coroner's opinion, and mine, too, that Peavey finally died from guzzling too much rotgut."

Cody shook his head. "That's a shame. Abner wasn't a bad sort. He never gave me any trouble when I had to arrest him and toss him in jail."

"Cyrus will be burying him today. I told him to send the bill to the county. Abner didn't have any folks around here, did he?"

"None that I know of."

The two lawmen said nothing further about Abner

Peavey's death. It was unfortunate, but both men knew that such unhappy endings were all too common in the West, even in so-called civilized places like Abilene. In fact, Cody thought as he went about his work, people seemed to take to drink more quickly as civilization approached from the east.

When the deputy walked to the Sunrise Café for breakfast a little later, he noticed that the temperature was rising as he had predicted. The fine film of frost that had blanketed everything earlier in the morning was gone. The air was still nippy, but it was a pleasant change after the hot summer that Abilene had just had.

Once inside the cheerful, clean café Cody ordered a big platter of bacon and flapjacks. He grinned when he saw the extra flapjacks on the plate. The larger portion was not unusual when the vivacious, redheaded young woman who brought him his breakfast was working. A green-eyed beauty, Agnes Hirsch worked part-time at the café and was a few years younger than Cody. He had known almost from the day she arrived in Abilene that she had a crush on him. He was genuinely fond of her, too, but not romantically so. At least that was what he told himself. Give Agnes a few more years and that might change, he mused. He smiled at her and watched her pale cheeks flush with pleasure as she hurried to refill his coffee cup.

When he had finished eating, Cody said good-bye to Agnes and strolled out onto the boardwalk. Judging from the amount of traffic now moving on Texas Street, Abilene's main thoroughfare, he figured it was about eight o'clock. Men on horseback threaded their way among wagons and buggies that maneuvered for space on the broad street. Cries of greeting, the clatter of wheels, the jingle of harnesses, and the clopping of horses' hooves filled the air. The raised plank board-walks that lined the street and connected the various businesses were crowded with chattering pedestrians.

Abilene was a thriving, growing city. For years it had been the center for shipping cattle by rail to the big markets in the East, but it was no longer the wild cattle town it had once been. The Kansas Pacific had pushed west, along with the frontier, and Abilene was becoming civilized. General mercantiles, hardware stores, and even a pharmacy now stood shoulder to shoulder with rowdy saloons. It was the good, solid citizens of this city that thronged the street this morning. In a couple of months winter would move in good and proper, and folks had plenty to do to prepare for it.

Travis had said that he had already eaten breakfast, which meant that Cody was at loose ends for the moment. He would return to the office later to relieve the marshal, but for now he could wander where he wanted.

Cody headed for the Kansas Pacific depot on Rail-road Street; he knew a westbound train was due this morning. Luke Travis had made it a practice to have one of the town's two lawmen meet the trains when they came in. Trouble might decide to get off at any time, and being careful was what kept them alive.

Cody stepped into the lobby of the big redbrick building and waved at Harvey Bastrop, the gray-haired, cheerful stationmaster, who was standing be-hind the ticket window. Under his green eyeshade, Bastrop smiled and nodded a greeting. Cody scanned the large room, scrutinizing the people sitting on the benches. Some had valises with them, clearly planning to depart on the westbound; the others were probably

waiting to greet passengers who would be disembarking.

Cody strolled over to the ticket window. "Morning,
Harve," he said. "The westbound on schedule?"

"Right on time, as far as I know," Bastrop answered. He pulled a fat engineer's watch from his vest
pocket and checked it, rather than looking at the big
clock on the lobby wall. "Ought to be here in another
five minutes."

Nodding, Cody turned away, ambled to the doors
that led to the platform, and pushed through them.
Cold air struck his cheeks. The platform was on the
south side of the tracks, blocked from the warm
morning sun by the massive depot and the awning that
shielded it from rain and snow. Because of the chilly
shade he had it to himself for the moment, but that
would change in a hurry when the train rolled in.

Leaning against one of the awning posts, he gazed
up the tracks, his eyes tracing their path past the
sprawling stockyards on the eastern edge of town and
onward to the rolling prairie beyond. A moment later
the faint sound of a whistle drifted in. Cody grinned.
Bastrop had been right; the westbound was on time.

The train rolled into the station accompanied by
the hiss of steam and the squeal of brakes. The people
who had been waiting inside the depot crowded onto
the platform. Cody stayed where he was, out of the
way of the embarking and disembarking passengers.

The usual assortment of people got off the train,
Cody saw. Businessmen and families made up the
majority of the passengers, but a few cowhands were
among the group, looking as if they wished they were
back on their horses.

Then a petite young woman emerged from one of

the cars and stepped nimbly down to the platform. Cody glanced in her direction, then after a moment took a more careful look.

He had always had an eye for a pretty girl, and this youthful newcomer certainly fit that description. She was so small that at first glance she might have been taken for a child, but her curvaceous form quickly dispelled that notion.

Cody guessed that she was in her early twenties. Dark brown curls surrounded her delicate, heart-shaped face; the rest of her long hair had been twisted into a bun, which was nestled at the nape of her neck. Evidently her journey had been long and rigorous, because several wisps had strayed appealingly from the disciplined coiffure. A straw hat was perched atop her head, and she wore a dark blue dress and close-fitting woolen jacket.

Something beyond her attractive appearance, however, held Cody's eye. She paused on the station platform and peered around as if she were looking for someone or something. When it was apparent that she could not locate the object of her search, Cody made his decision. He would go over to her, introduce himself, and offer his assistance. After all, it was his duty as a public servant, he told himself. The fact that she was a pretty young woman had nothing to do with it.

He started toward her, but before he had taken more than a couple of steps, she noticed him and her eyes lit up. Slipping into the crowd, she moved toward him.

When Cody reached her, he nodded and touched the brim of his flat-crowned black hat. "Morning, ma'am," he said.

"Oh, Sheriff, I'm so *glad* to see you," the young woman said effusively. "I would have asked directions to your office if you hadn't been here, but the fact that you are here must be some sort of omen. I believe I'll take it to mean that my mission here is preordained to be a success."

Cody blinked at the flurry of words that tumbled from her lips, and the half smile on his face slowly faded into a bewildered frown. "I'm afraid you've got the wrong fella, ma'am," he said. "I'm the deputy marshal, not the sheriff. But if somebody was supposed to meet you here, I'd be glad to help you look for him. My name's Cody Fisher."

The young woman thrust out a tiny, gloved hand. "I'm so glad to meet you, Deputy Fisher. I'm Bethany Hale. I'm afraid I haven't made myself clear. I merely meant that I was seeking to speak with the law enforcement officials here in Abilene, and that your being right here on hand as I got off the train was certainly fortuitous, don't you think?"

"It's something, all right," a puzzled Cody mumbled, taking her hand and shaking it absently. "If you've got business with the marshal, I can take you to the office. I'm sure Marshal Travis would be glad to help you."

Bethany Hale smiled, and Cody saw that a dimple appeared in her right cheek when she did. "Oh, I don't necessarily need to talk to the marshal," she went on. "I've just found that it's usually a good idea to apprise the local authorities of my presence in their town."

That made Cody frown even more. "Why? You don't look like a bounty hunter or hired gun."

Bethany gave a little laugh. "I suppose you could call me a hired gun of sorts, Deputy," she replied. "A hired gun on the side of everything that is good and decent and right in this world."

This was going too fast for Cody, and the way this young woman talked, he had a feeling it would be too fast for most folks. He said, "Why don't you come with me, and we'll get it all sorted out. Have you got a bag we need to get from the baggage car?"

"Several valises, in fact," Bethany admitted. "Thank you for offering to help me."

A few minutes later, Cody found himself staring at three large carpetbags and one smaller case. Forcing a smile, he hefted the bulky bags and shuffled awkwardly down the platform. Bethany, carrying the little case, walked beside him toward the depot.

"The marshal's office is over on Texas Street," Cody told her. "It won't take but a few minutes to get there."

"Well, I don't actually need to see the marshal now that I've met you, Deputy Fisher."

"Why don't you call me Cody?"

Bethany had been talking ever since she left the train, but Cody's simple request silenced her for so long that he turned to look at her. To his surprise, he saw she was blushing, a rosy glow that only enhanced her beauty. Finally she murmured, "I don't think that would be proper, Deputy. After all, we've just met. I hardly know you. I might venture to call you Mr. Fisher, if you insist."

"Uh, no, ma'am, not if it makes you uncomfortable. Deputy is just fine."

This Bethany Hale is a strange one, Cody thought. He was unaccustomed to ladies who required things to be so formal.

Now that he had agreed to her code of decorum,

Bethany seemed to regain her composure. "What I really would like you to do," she continued in her former high-spirited manner, "is direct me to the town's religious leaders."

Once more Cody was surprised, but he replied amiably, "Sure, I can do that. It just so happens that you're lucky again. My brother, Judah, is the pastor of the Calvary Methodist Church. Maybe your running into me was a double omen."

"That may well be true, Deputy. It is said that the Lord works in mysterious ways."

"Yes, ma'am. I reckon He does." As Cody guided her through the bustling traffic on Railroad Street, he shifted the heavy bags he was carrying to get a better grip on them. "But I don't think it would be a good idea to try to walk to the church. It's quite a distance." Glancing around, he spotted a man he knew sitting in a wagon parked across the street from the depot. "Hey, Dave, you busy right now?" he called.

The townsman looked around and saw Cody, loaded down with bags, approaching him. He grinned and quipped, "Not as busy as you are, Cody, leastways from the looks of it. I'm supposed to pick up a shipment of goods for Karatofsky once it's unloaded from the train."

"Is he in a hurry for it?"

Dave shook his head. "Naw. It's just some yard goods. The boxes can sit in the station for a while. You want to borrow the wagon?"

"I'd be obliged."

Dave swung down from the wagon and came over to relieve Cody of one of the bags. "Let me give you a hand with them," he said, carrying it to the vehicle.

Cody loaded the other two bags into the wagon bed,

then helped Bethany Hale climb onto the seat. "Thanks, Dave," he said. "I'll bring the wagon back in just a bit."

The man shook his head. "No hurry. I'll go over and shoot the breeze with Harvey Bastrop while I keep an eye on that shipment."

Cody climbed lithely up to the wagon seat and settled down next to Bethany. He noticed that she shifted ever so slightly to the far end of the plank bench, making certain several inches separated them. Evidently she was the soul of friendliness—as long as nobody tried to get too close or too familiar with her.

"Is that man a friend of yours?" she asked as he picked up the reins and got the team moving.

"Sure. He works for one of the biggest mercantile stores in town. He picks up freight and makes deliveries to the ranches for them."

"He won't get into trouble for letting you borrow his wagon, will he?"

Cody shook his head. "Dave's boss won't mind him doing a favor for me or the marshal or just about anybody who needed one. Folks are that way around here. We're friendly; we like to help anybody who needs it."

"I'm glad to hear that," Bethany said fervently.

Cody frowned again. Something in her tone bothered him. She sounded as if she was expecting nothing but trouble in Abilene. And why did she want to see the town's religious leaders?

"Once we get to the church, I can introduce you to Judah," Cody said. "He's not the only one out there that you'll want to meet, either. There's an orphanage associated with the church, and it's run by a nun named Sister Laurel. There're some other meetinghouses in town, but I reckon between Judah and Sister Laurel, they'd know just about everything going on in Abilene that's of a religious nature."

"Oh, but it's not the things of a religious nature I'm interested in, Deputy. Quite the contrary."

More puzzled than ever, Cody peered at her. "Ma'am?"

Bethany Hale favored him with a dazzling smile. "You see, I want to know all about the *sin* in Abilene."

Aware that he was gaping at her, Cody looked away. Finally he shrugged his shoulders and managed to mumble, "I reckon there's plenty of *that* around town, all right."

They had followed Railroad Street to where it merged with Texas Street. Cody planned to take Abilene's main thoroughfare to Elm Street, where he would turn north toward the church. The railroad crossing would not be quite so rough by this route. As the wagon rolled down Texas Street, Bethany looked at the businesses they were passing and said, "Yes, indeed. I would think there was an abundance of iniquity here. I've heard a great deal about these trail towns."

Cody saw that she was grimacing at Orion's Tavern as they passed it. Orion's was one of the most respectable drinking establishments in town, but Bethany apparently disapproved of it.

"Abilene hasn't really been what you'd call a trail town for a couple of years now," Cody pointed out. "I've been told it was pretty wild and woolly in its day, but the folks here have hired some good marshals to clean it up. Bear River Tom Smith was the first, then Wild Bill Hickok, and now my boss Luke Travis. That kind of man doesn't let things get too far out of hand."

After a few seconds Bethany said quietly, "I'm sorry, Deputy. I didn't mean to imply there was anything wrong with your law enforcement."

"No offense taken," Cody replied with a grin. "We still get our share of Texas cowboys here, and things do get a mite rowdy from time to time."

As they continued toward the church, Cody spun several anecdotes about some of the wild times Abilene had seen, toning down the roughest parts so as not to offend Bethany. She listened with polite interest.

Because the Calvary Methodist Church sat on a slight rise on the northwestern edge of town, the church steeple was visible for a good distance. Bethany seemed to perk up once she spotted it. As the wagon moved up the little hill toward the simple, whitewashed frame building, she exclaimed, "What a lovely church! Is that the orphanage next to it?"

"That's right. It used to be the parsonage, but it was too big for Judah to live in alone."

"Your brother isn't married?"

Cody shook his head. "No, ma'am, he's not. I suppose the right girl hasn't come along." He glanced at Bethany out of the corner of his eye and saw a tiny smile on her rosy-cheeked face.

"How did he come to establish an orphanage?"

"That was mostly Sister Laurel's doing," answered Cody as he swung the wagon into the circular drive that led up to the church. "She and the children were on their way to Wichita to establish an orphanage there. They ran into trouble on the trail, were sidetracked, and stopped here. Judah had the room they needed in the parsonage, so Sister Laurel decided there wasn't any point in going on. It's worked out real well so far."

As he brought the wagon to a stop in front of the church, he saw three small children playing in the yard between the church and the stable on the other side of the orphanage. Most of the orphans were of school age and, at this time of day, would be at the school that was run by Thurman Simpson and Leslie Gibson, Abilene's two teachers. As Cody climbed out of the wagon and went to assist Bethany, he heard the front door of the church open behind him.

A tall, slender man with brown hair and intense, penetrating eyes behind rimless spectacles stepped up to the wagon. He was dressed in a sober dark suit, white shirt, and string tie.

"Hello, Cody," he said. "Nice to see you out here for a change. And who might this charming young lady be?"

Cody turned and looked at his older brother. Although Judah was vastly different from Cody, he at times expressed some of the same reckless charm, especially when he smiled. This was one of those times, Cody saw as he introduced Bethany.

"Miss Bethany Hale," he said, "this is Reverend Judah Fisher, the pastor of this church. Judah, this is Miss Hale. She's just come to Abilene."

Bethany eagerly thrust out her gloved hand, just as she had when she met Cody. "Reverend Fisher, it's *such* a pleasure to meet you!" she said enthusiastically. "Your brother has been telling me wonderful stories about the way you took in the poor homeless waifs who came to you for succor."

She had her back to Cody, so he was able to raise his eyebrows and shake his head slightly as Judah glanced quizzically at him. Cody did not know what to make of Miss Bethany Hale, and he wished Judah better luck in figuring her out than he had had.

"Miss Hale wanted to meet the town's religious leaders, so I figured you and Sister Laurel would be the best place to start," Cody told Judah. "Is the sister around?"

"I believe so," Judah replied and, turning toward the children playing in the nearby yard, called to one of them. "Would you go tell Sister Laurel that I'd like to see her out here, please?" The little boy nodded eagerly and scurried off.

Bethany still held Judah's hand, a fact that did not escape Cody's notice. She said to the minister, "You must tell me sometime what it's like running an orphanage. I would imagine it can be a very fulfilling task."

"Sometimes," Judah agreed. "Sometimes it's just sad. What brings *you* to Abilene, Miss Hale?"

"I'd prefer to wait until Sister Laurel is here, so that I can tell both of you at the same time. Would that be all right?"

Judah assured her it would. A few moments later, the child Judah had sent to look for the nun appeared at the orphanage door. Behind him came a stern-faced figure dressed in the flowing black and white habit of a member of the Dominican order. As Sister Laurel drew closer, she looked less forbidding. Her compassion, as well as her strength and determination, radiated from her sympathetic blue eyes. "Hello," she said to Bethany, and then she smiled warmly at Cody. "How are you, Cody?"

"I'm fine, Sister," he replied. "This is Miss Bethany Hale, and she wants to talk to you and Judah about something."

Sister Laurel turned toward the newcomer. "How can we be of service to you, my dear?"

Bethany returned her smile. "I've come to Abilene

on a mission, Sister," she declared. "A mission from the highest possible authority. I'm sure you know what I mean."

"Indeed I do," Sister Laurel agreed.

Judah asked, "I don't doubt your sincerity, Miss Hale, but why are you telling us this?"

"Because I want to enlist you as allies in my cause," Bethany replied. "I can assure you that it is just and that you will want to join my crusade."

For such a little slip of a girl, she sure can string words together, Cody thought. And she sounded absolutely convinced of everything she said.

"You see," Bethany went on, "I've been sent here by the Christian Ladies Temperance Society. I'm bringing their message to Abilene."

Judah and Sister Laurel stared in surprise. "Temperance Society?" Cody muttered slowly.

"Of course, Deputy," Bethany said, smiling serenely at him. "Simply put, I've come to wipe out the scourge of demon rum in Abilene. And this is only the first stop." Her voice rang with conviction. "Before I'm through, I'll see liquor and all of its evil driven completely out of Kansas!"

Chapter Two

———◆———

Cody, Judah, and Sister Laurel were speechless for a long moment, so unexpected was Bethany's proclamation. Finally the deputy exploded, "That's the craziest thing I've ever heard!"

Bethany spun toward him, her eyes flashing. "Perhaps you think so, Deputy, but I assure you I'm completely sane! Sane enough to realize how imperative it is that all the saloons and taverns in Abilene be closed down."

Judah, lifting a hand, stepped between Cody and Bethany. "Ah . . . Miss Hale, I believe my brother means that such a goal, while it is certainly admirable, will be very difficult to achieve."

Bethany lifted her pert, determined chin. "That doesn't matter, Reverend," she declared. "No matter how long the struggle takes, we shall win in the end, especially with the help of fine, upstanding citizens like yourself and Sister Laurel."

"No one is questioning your sincerity, Miss Hale," the nun assured her. "We're just trying to make sure that you know how much opposition you'll face if you try to do away with drinking here in Abilene."

"I shall be fighting the good fight, Sister. I know I will prevail."

Ever since Cody had met her at the train station he sensed something was strange about Bethany Hale. Now he was sure of it. He glanced at Judah and saw that his brother looked equally perplexed.

"Uh . . . Abilene has always had a certain, uh, reputation," Judah began. "During the summers, the Texas cowboys would come in with the trail herds—"

"Deputy Fisher told me that Abilene was no longer a trail town," Bethany remarked, cutting him off.

"Not as much as it used to be," Cody put in quickly. "I also said that there were still quite a few cowboys around and that things could get a little wild sometimes. There're more saloons in Abilene than anything else!"

"I don't know about that," Judah said, "but there are still a great many saloons. People around here are accustomed to drinking, Miss Hale. You can't change habits like that overnight."

Cody noticed how Judah had paled the moment Bethany began talking about alcohol. Sister Laurel also cast concerned glances at the minister. Both of them knew something that Bethany Hale did not.

Reverend Judah Fisher had been a drinking man. In fact, when Sister Laurel first saw him, he was lying unconscious in the parsonage, drunk—a disgrace to his calling.

The corruption Judah had seen around him and the murder of his and Cody's father, Judge Lawrence Fisher, by that lawless element drove him to a state of mental degradation. As the corrupt organization solidified its control over Abilene he turned more heavily to drink in his rage and frustration.

Then Sister Laurel arrived, bringing the wagon train filled with orphaned children with her. Luke Travis, who had intervened when an outlaw band attacked them on the plains, accompanied her into Abilene, and his arrival marked the beginning of a turnabout in the town. The former marshal of Wichita could not walk away from the troubles he found in Abilene, and Cody joined him. When they were done, Abilene had been cleaned up—for the time being.

During that time Judah Fisher fought his own battle, one that saw him defeating the demons that ravaged him. Since then, he had not taken a drink.

But Cody and Sister Laurel, the two people closest to Judah, knew how he had struggled. They also knew it was an ongoing battle that would continue for as long as Judah lived.

Bethany Hale, however, was aware of none of this. She smiled at Judah and said with a confidence that bordered on smugness, "You'll see, Reverend. I won't allow myself or my cause to be defeated. Now, can I count on your support, yours and Sister Laurel's?"

Noticing Judah's hesitation, Sister Laurel replied smoothly, "I agree with the principles that guide you, Miss Hale. You are indeed fighting the good fight. But I fear that it will be a losing battle in this part of the country."

"I agree," Judah said at last, nervously licking his lips. "We have a small temperance society in Abilene, but the group has not been able to accomplish very much."

"Surely they try to educate the townspeople about the evils of drink?" Bethany demanded.

"Yes, of course. But lectures don't mean much to thirsty cowhands."

"Well then, the members will simply have to work harder to spread their message, as I shall do," Bethany declared.

"You're not intending to visit the saloons, are you?" Cody asked sharply.

She turned her charming smile on him. "What better place to reach the very people who need so desperately to hear what I have to say?"

Cody shook his head. "If a gal like you sashays into some of those places, there'll be trouble for sure—both for you *and* for the customers. Some of those men are liable to start shooting."

Bethany's eyes widened. "You mean they would shoot at me just because I implore them to turn away from alcohol?"

"No, they'd probably swap lead trying to see who'd get to dance with you first," Cody told her in all seriousness. "Most cowboys don't get to see a lady as pretty as you very often. They can get rambunctious when one shows up."

Bethany huffed and lifted her chin in determination. "If you're trying to sway me from my destined role, Deputy, you're going to be disappointed. I won't allow fear or personal danger to outweigh my commitment to an ideal."

"Those are lofty sentiments," Judah said. He had recovered from the initial shock, and some of the color was returning to his face. "I can almost believe that you'll be capable of doing what you say you're going to, Miss Hale. After all, a good deal of Kansas is dry already. If you can get rid of the liquor in the cattle towns, you will have accomplished a great deal."

"I will, Reverend. I promise you that."

Judah smiled slightly. "In that case, Miss Hale, given your attitude, I'm sure you'll be quite an inspiration to Abilene's temperance group. I've recently become a member, and it just so happens that we're having a meeting tonight. Would you be willing to come and let me introduce you to the other members?"

Bethany gave him a brilliant smile in return. "Would I be willing? Why, Reverend, I'd *love* to attend!"

Cody saw the dubious look on Sister Laurel's face, but Judah seemed to have been won over completely by Bethany's charm and conviction. The idea of getting rid of booze in Abilene was about the most unlikely thing Cody had ever heard, but obviously Bethany was not going to be steered from her chosen path.

Then Luke Travis and I will have to clean up any mess she leaves, Cody thought.

"Well, since you're determined to see this through," he said to Bethany, "we'd better take you back downtown and see about finding you a place to stay while you're here."

Before she could reply Judah said, "I'd be happy to accompany you to the hotel and make sure that you're able to find a room, Miss Hale."

She moved closer to him and slipped her arm through his. "Why, that's so thoughtful of you, Reverend," she purred. "I know my stay in Abilene will be productive with you looking after me and lending your assistance to my crusade."

Flushing slightly, Judah cleared his throat somewhat sheepishly. "Ah, of course. Shall we go?"

Bethany smiled at him again. Judah helped her onto the wagon seat and then swung up beside her. Cody noticed that she did not edge away from Judah, just as he had noticed the casual way she had linked arms with him. With Judah she was not at all reticent the way she had been with *him*. For the first time in his life, Cody was jealous of his older brother.

Judah picked up the lines and flicked them to urge the team into motion. As the wagon lurched and rolled away, Cody stared after it.

"Well, don't that beat all!" he exclaimed. "She had Judah eating out of her hand like he was a little speckled pup!"

Sister Laurel smiled. "Does that bother you, Cody?"

"Why shouldn't it?" he demanded. "They drove off and left me out here to walk back to town!"

Trying not to laugh, Sister Laurel watched as Cody stalked angrily away. Her expression became more serious as she thought about what Bethany Hale's arrival might mean, not just to the town but to the Fisher brothers as well. She suspected that there was more to Cody's anger than having to walk back to town.

During the conversation with Bethany, Judah had shaken off his initial nervousness about alcohol. She appeared to have won him over with her fervor. But if she intended to carry her crusade into the town's saloons, Sister Laurel foresaw nothing but trouble, just as Cody had. If Judah tried to accompany her—

Sister Laurel shook her head. She did not know

what would happen in that case. She would hate to see what effect being around liquor might have on Judah. He had struggled so mightily to throw off its grip the first time. If he was to succumb to its temptation again . . .

The nun sighed and turned to go back into the orphanage. At the moment she could do nothing about the situation—nothing but worry that Miss Bethany Hale would have as disruptive an influence on the whole town as she had already had on Cody and Judah Fisher.

Judah peered at his reflection in the mirror that hung on the wall of his room in the parsonage. He ran his fingers over his freshly shaven jaw and nodded, satisfied that he had not missed any spots. Then he lifted his chin and reached for the button at his throat to close the collar of his fresh white shirt. Picking up the string tie that lay on the dresser in front of him, he slipped it around his neck and tied it with practiced ease. He stepped back and slid a hand over his brown hair. Sometimes it stuck up in the most unlikely places, making him look like the gawky adolescent he had once been.

Even then, Cody had been the handsome, athletic one—the one with the quick, easy grin and the multitude of friends. The girls always liked Cody, and he returned their admiration.

Judah knew he was taking more care with his appearance than he normally did. He wondered if that was because he would soon be seeing Bethany Hale again.

There had been no trouble securing a room for her at the Grand Palace Hotel. Bethany had cast a disapproving glance at Orion's Tavern, located two doors

away, as she and Judah entered the hotel, but she had
not commented on the proximity of the tavern. She
seemed satisfied with Judah's choice. The Grand
Palace had seen better days and was not a fancy place,
but that was exactly what she had wanted, she told
him.

"We have to stop being concerned with surface
appearances," she proclaimed as he carried her bags
up to the small, tidy room on the second floor. "That's
one of the main things wrong with the world as far as
I'm concerned."

"I couldn't agree more," he told her.

And yet here he was, a few hours later, slicking
himself up just because he was going to take her to the
temperance meeting. His wide, mobile mouth twisted
in a wry grin at that thought.

Judah would not deny, even to himself, that he felt
his heart begin to pound faster when Bethany smiled
at him. He had been disturbed at first by all her talk
about liquor, but somehow she knew how to put him
at ease. He could still feel her warmth as she linked
her arm with his. He was a preacher, a messenger of
God's Word, but he was also a man.

A woman like Bethany would make a fine minister's
wife, he found himself thinking as he shrugged into
his coat and went down the stairs.

Sister Laurel came out of the dining room as Judah
entered the foyer. She smiled at him and said, "My,
don't you look handsome this evening, Judah!"

"Thank you," he said, blushing slightly. "I'll be
going now, if everything is under control here."

Sister Laurel nodded. "The older children are
studying, and Agnes has already put the younger ones
to bed. Don't worry about anything, just enjoy your
meeting."

"I'm not going for enjoyment, Sister. The Temperance Society hopes to make some great changes in Abilene."

"And so does Miss Bethany Hale," Sister Laurel commented. "She's a very charming young lady."

"Yes. She certainly is." Judah suppressed an impulse to tug nervously at his collar. The knowing smile on Sister Laurel's face, the scrutiny in her intelligent gaze, made him uneasy. Was he so transparent that she could read his every thought?

"Well, good night," the nun said, turning to leave the foyer. Judah tried not to heave a sigh of relief as he bid her good night.

In only a few minutes Judah had saddled his horse and was riding out of the carriage house next to the parsonage. He turned the animal toward downtown Abilene. The sun had set a couple of hours earlier, taking the warmth of the day with it, and a chilly breeze blew in his face. Judah buttoned his coat and pulled his hat down tighter.

As he walked his horse down the well-trodden drive, he thought about the local temperance society. He had only been a member for a short time, had in fact attended only a single meeting before this one tonight. The group had been founded almost a year earlier by Mrs. Eula Grafton, the well-to-do widow of one of Abilene's leading merchants and a very influential figure in the town's social doings. From the first, Mrs. Grafton tried to enlist him, but Judah resisted. He knew quite well that he had been a drunkard; being around members of the society and listening to lectures on the evils of drink would only be painful.

Finally he grew tired of Mrs. Grafton's persistence and joined the group. The first meeting went surprisingly well. Now he was ready for the second, and he would have a lovely visitor with him this time.

Judah felt his pulse quicken as the hotel came into view and he thought about Bethany. The night did not seem nearly as cold when he conjured up the image of her lovely face.

He tied his horse at the hitchrack in front of the shabby building and stepped onto the boardwalk. A nervous lump rose in his throat as he reached for the doorknob. He was behaving like a naive schoolboy courting a girl for the first time, and he told himself sternly to stop it. He had no reason to feel this way. Bethany and he were merely allies in a good cause—friends already perhaps, but certainly nothing more.

Judah walked into the hotel, saw Bethany sitting in the lobby, and suddenly had trouble breathing. She had changed her clothes and was wearing a full-skirted green dress with a short woolen jacket of a darker green over it. She was beautiful, absolutely beautiful.

She rose and came to greet him, a smile on her face. "Good evening, Reverend Fisher," she said, her voice tinkling like a cool, clear stream.

Judah nodded jerkily and quickly offered up a silent prayer that he would not make a fool of himself. "Good evening, Miss Hale," he replied a bit hoarsely. "You . . . you certainly look lovely."

A blush colored Bethany's cheeks, making her even more attractive as far as Judah was concerned. "Thank you, Reverend Fisher," she said, sounding genuinely embarrassed.

Judah heard the tone and berated himself for making her uncomfortable. He had no right to make such personal remarks to her, not when he'd only just met her. Neither one of them needed such distractions, considering the serious problem that had brought them together.

"Are you ready for the meeting?" he asked.

Bethany nodded. "I'm looking forward to it. Shall we go?"

Judah opened the lobby door for her. "Right this way." He made no move to take her arm this time, and she did not offer it to him.

Side by side, they strolled down the plank boardwalk toward the courthouse a couple of blocks away. The lanterns affixed to the boardwalk posts had been lit and brightened their passage through the chilly autumn night. After a moment, Bethany asked, "How large is Abilene's temperance group?"

"Oh, we're still fairly small," Judah replied. "Surely nothing like what you're accustomed to at the meetings of the Christian Ladies. We have perhaps forty members, but they are the leading ladies of the town."

"All the membership is female except for yourself, Reverend?"

Judah smiled. "Myself and the local schoolmaster, Thurman Simpson. So far we're the only men, but I'm sure that more men will join once they realize that liquor is a problem that affects everyone, not just the ladies."

"Indeed. Although it does seem to be the poor mothers and children who pay the highest price when a man takes to the devil's brew."

"That's true," Judah agreed. As they approached the brightly lit courthouse, he noticed several buggies and carriages parked in front of it. He led Bethany up the path across the wide lawn that surrounded the stately building, opened the heavy wooden door, and murmured, "Ah, here we are."

They stepped into a large, high-ceilinged room that was warmed by a pair of pot-bellied iron stoves. Quite a few people were gathered there as the vehicles parked outside had already indicated, and Judah wondered for a moment if Bethany and he were late. Then he saw that the meeting had not yet been called to order; the ladies in the room were busy talking among themselves. Most of the seats on the rows of benches were taken, but Judah saw some empty places toward the front of the room. He indicated them to Bethany and then started toward them with the attractive young woman at his side.

Thurman Simpson was turned around in his seat, talking to one of the ladies in the row behind him. The schoolmaster glanced up and saw Judah and Bethany, and a rare look of interest appeared on his usually pinched, disapproving face. He rose and hurried into the aisle. "Well, well, Reverend," observed the little man unctuously. "Whom have we here?"

Judah paused and drew a deep breath. He did not particularly like Simpson, who had a nasty reputation for using a switch on his students, but he did not want to go out of his way to insult the man. "Mr. Simpson," he said. "This is Miss Bethany Hale. Miss Hale, Thurman Simpson, the master of our local school."

"Indeed a pleasure, Miss Hale," Simpson said as he took Bethany's hand and pumped it. He was a short, slender man with lank, dishwater blond hair and a pasty complexion. Most of the time his features were set in a sour scowl, but they twisted into a smile as he greeted Bethany. "What brings you to our fair city?"

"I've been sent here to help your group in its mission, Mr. Simpson," Bethany replied. "I'm a representative of the Christian Ladies Temperance Society."

Simpson's eyebrows lifted in surprise. "Well! This is quite an honor that such a well-known organization as yours would take note of our humble efforts here in Abilene." He turned and, waving an arm in the air, called, "Mrs. Grafton! There's someone here you simply must meet."

A tall, formidable woman hurried toward Simpson from the front of the room. Mrs. Eula Grafton might have been handsome had it not been for the stern expression on her face. Her dark hair was only lightly touched with gray, despite the fact that she was in her fifties. She wore an expensive dress from Abilene's finest ladies' shop, and the scent of her toilet water was strong in the warm, closed room.

Judah would have preferred to wait until the meeting was under way to introduce Bethany, but he had no choice now. He could see curiosity shining in Mrs. Grafton's eyes and knew that she would have to be told the identity of the visitor.

"Good evening, Reverend," she said to him in her booming voice. Then she turned to Bethany. "Who is this?" she demanded bluntly.

Bethany extended her hand to Mrs. Grafton and saved Judah the trouble of making the introduction. "I'm Bethany Hale, ma'am. And you must be Mrs. Grafton. I've heard so much about you and the good work you're doing with the temperance society."

Mrs. Grafton beamed, her rouged and powdered cheeks creasing in a deep smile as she shook Bethany's hand. "How *nice* of you to say so, my dear. But where would you hear about our little group?"

"Why, at the headquarters of the Christian Ladies Temperance Society, we try to keep up with all of our allies in the struggle against Satan and his brew."

That was stretching the truth a bit, Judah thought.

Bethany had never heard of Mrs. Grafton and her group until Judah told her about them. But he supposed a little white lie was allowable under the circumstances. Mrs. Grafton was positively glowing, which was quite a change from her usual forbidding expression.

"You're from the Christian Ladies Temperance?" Mrs. Grafton asked, swelling with pride as she did so. "Oh my goodness, we're so proud that you've come to pay us a visit, Miss Hale." She raised her voice. "Ladies! Ladies! Gather around. I want to introduce a very special visitor to you."

Judah caught Bethany's eye and was rewarded by an enthusiastic smile as the members of the society began to flock around them. Relief surged through him once he realized she was not upset with him. She did look a bit uncomfortable when Mrs. Grafton introduced her to the other ladies. Obviously Bethany was not used to being the center of attention in large groups.

Greeting her warmly, the ladies bombarded her with questions about the society she represented. Bethany answered them as best she could. Nevertheless, Judah could tell that she was grateful when Mrs. Grafton finally said, "I suppose we should officially start our meeting. You will consent to address us, won't you, Miss Hale?"

"Of course," Bethany replied. "That's why I've come tonight, Mrs. Grafton. I thought you might do me the honor of allowing me to say a few words."

"The honor is all ours, my dear."

While Judah, Bethany, and the others took their seats Mrs. Grafton swept to the front of the room. Placing herself behind the lectern that stood facing the benches, she imperiously drew herself up to her full height and banged a gavel on the wooden surface.

After calling the meeting to order, she quickly disposed of the group's parliamentary matters.

Judah knew what was coming next. He glanced at Bethany and saw that she was equally aware. She looked a bit apprehensive, but at the same time he could see the eagerness and fervor glowing in her eyes.

"I know you're all anxious to hear what our distinguished visitor has to say to us," Mrs. Grafton was saying. "So without further ado, ladies—and gentlemen—allow me to present Miss Bethany Hale of the Christian Ladies Temperance Society."

There was polite applause as Bethany rose gracefully and walked quickly to the lectern. She turned to face the audience, and Judah could see a slight blush coloring her cheeks. But that was the only hint of self-consciousness in her demeanor.

"Good evening again, ladies . . . and gentlemen," Bethany began, nodding toward Judah and Thurman Simpson specifically. "I'm very glad to be here with you tonight. As you know, I've been sent to Abilene by the Christian Ladies Temperance Society. The message I bring to you is a simple one." She paused, then leaned forward and said fervently, "Liquor must be destroyed!"

The members applauded Bethany's proclamation vigorously. Judah joined in.

"We must fight side by side, shoulder to shoulder, in the battle to rid our fair land of the devil's potion!" Bethany continued. She was not shouting; she had raised her voice only enough to be heard throughout the room. But the words carried as much impact as those of any hellfire-shouting preacher Judah had ever heard. His sermons were not like that; he preferred to appeal to people's hearts and minds rather than their emotions. But he admired any speaker who could reach out and touch his listeners' souls, who could bend and shape them into something finer. Bethany Hale had that ability.

"Together we can drive the liquor peddlers out of our cities and towns and close down for all time the dens of iniquity that poison so many innocent lives." More hearty applause interrupted Bethany's speech. When it died down, she went on, "I have been sent by my organization to join you in this struggle—not to lead you. You have a fine leader in Mrs. Eula Grafton. But I am here to offer myself to you in whatever fashion you can make use of me. I give you my heart, my courage, my faith in the Lord. I ask you to devote yourselves equally to our sacred cause!"

Despite himself, Judah found he was caught up in her impassioned plea. She made it seem as though they could accomplish anything as long as they worked together. Her speech continued for another ten minutes as she recounted the evils brought on by drinking and spoke in ringing tones of the need to combat them. By the time she finished and stepped away from the lectern to the accompaniment of thunderous applause, even Judah believed she actually might make a difference in Abilene's moral climate.

Mrs. Grafton had enough sense to realize that she could not effectively follow such a stirring address. She thanked Bethany warmly for her words, then adjourned the meeting.

Even though the gathering was officially over, nearly everyone remained to exchange a few words with the visitor. Bethany was breathless after her fiery speech, but she graciously spoke to everyone who approached her. Judah stood nearby, ready to escort her back to the hotel once all questions had been answered.

As he listened with one ear to the chatter around him, he thought about what Bethany had said and realized that no actual plans to accomplish anything had been advanced during the meeting. An abundance of stirring rhetoric had been uttered but nothing else.

Bethany changed that as she said to Mrs. Grafton and the women gathered around her, "I have an idea for something I'd like to do, but we would need the support of the community for my plan to be successful."

"Then you shall have it, my dear," Mrs. Grafton assured her. "Just tell us what you need."

"Well . . . I was hoping to recruit some members of the community to stage a morality play that would vividly demonstrate the evils of drinking."

Judah frowned slightly, paying more attention now.

"I've seen such plays performed back East," Bethany went on. "The Christian Ladies have sponsored many of them. They are very popular with the common people, and they seem to be quite effective. We can draw the citizens in with the promise of entertainment and educate them at the same time."

"What an excellent idea!" Thurman Simpson exclaimed enthusiastically. "I've heard of these morality plays before, Mrs. Grafton. They're a means of getting down to the level of the unwashed masses and showing them their shortcomings."

Judah thought that was a rather arrogant way of putting it, but he, too, had heard of the morality plays and knew that they were popular. Mrs. Grafton was sold on the idea immediately. "We'll do it!" she told Bethany. "I'm sure we can get all the support and assistance we need from the town. Don't you think so, Reverend?"

Judah nodded. "I imagine so. Most of the towns out here in the West are hungry for entertainment of any sort."

Bethany gently touched his arm. "You'll help us, won't you, Reverend?" she asked.

"Of course," Judah heard himself saying. "I'll be glad to do anything I can to help."

Clearly delighted, Bethany smiled warmly at him. Looking into her warm, bright eyes, Judah suddenly knew he had made the right decision.

Shortly after that the group's members began to drift out of the hall, most of them buzzing with the plans they were making. There would be no shortage of volunteers to help with the production of the play, Judah thought.

When Bethany was ready to go, he opened the door and escorted her into the chilly night. They waved good-bye to Mrs. Grafton as the older woman got into her buggy, then turned to walk back toward the Grand Palace Hotel.

Bethany took a deep breath. "Well, how do you think the meeting went, Reverend?" she asked.

"It seemed to go very well," Judah replied. "I thought the ladies were quite responsive to your talk, and they were certainly enthusiastic about your suggestion of a morality play."

"What do *you* think about the play?"

Judah hesitated for a moment before saying, "I told you that you would be facing a great deal of opposition here in Abilene, Miss Hale, but I think you've hit on the best way to get around some of that. Everyone loves a play, even the cowboys. It should be a wonderful vehicle for your message."

"I'm so glad you think so, Reverend. I . . . I didn't want to be too bold and seem as if I was trying to take over your group."

Judah laughed. "Don't worry about that. Mrs. Grafton isn't about to give up the reins. But I think she'll be willing to work with you on anything you propose."

Bethany sighed, a satisfied, contented sound. "I think my visit to Abilene is going to be the best thing I've ever done, Reverend," she murmured.

Judah glanced at her and saw that her eyes were shining radiantly in the lantern light. She was hugging herself tightly, and he suddenly wondered if she was cold. The night air was quite chilly. It would be the most natural thing in the world if he were to slip his arm around her shoulders.

Judah told his arm to do just that, but it stayed at his side as if it had a mind of its own. He could feel his heart pounding with the desire to touch her. But the moment passed all too quickly. He looked up and saw they were already in front of the hotel. Judah grimaced, knowing he had missed his chance. He opened the hotel door and stepped back to let her precede him into the lobby.

"Thank you for taking me to the meeting," Bethany said, turning toward him just inside the doorway. "I'm really looking forward to working with you, Reverend."

"And I'm looking forward to our association as well," he replied.

"After my trip and the excitement of the meeting, I'm certainly tired. Good night, Reverend."

Judah swallowed. "Good night, Miss Hale," he mumbled, wishing he could say—and do—more. He stood with his hat in his hand, watching as she crossed the lobby and started up the stairs.

"You're letting in a draft, Reverend," called the clerk from behind the desk across the lobby.

"Oh. I'm sorry, Claude," Judah told the man. He clapped his hat back on his head. "Good night."

The clerk just grunted as Judah stepped out onto the boardwalk and closed the door behind him.

He took a deep breath and stood looking up at the stars in the clear night sky for a moment. A great deal had happened today, and he was going to have to ponder long and hard on all of it.

Judah untied his horse and swung up into the saddle, then rode at a quick trot toward the church and his home.

Across the street from the hotel, a dark figure lounged in the shadows of a doorway. Cody Fisher watched his brother mount up and ride away, just as he had watched him stroll down the street with Bethany. Cody had been able to see into the lobby of the hotel as the couple said good night to each other. There was a disgusted look on the young deputy's face as he straightened and shook his head.

Judah had wanted to put his arm around the girl. Cody could see that from across the street and a block away. But of course good old straitlaced Judah had done no such thing. He had not even shaken Bethany's hand before she went upstairs.

Cody grinned suddenly. If he had been the one walking with Bethany Hale, she never would have gotten into the hotel without a good-night kiss.

Chapter Three

---◆---

ABNER PEAVEY'S FUNERAL HAD BEEN HELD THAT AFTER-
noon. It was a grim affair with only Luke Travis, Cyrus
Worden, and Worden's two assistants in attendance.
The undertaker offered up a quick prayer for Peavey's
soul, and then the four men lowered the plain wooden
coffin into the ground at the rear of Boot Hill. A
county burial did not amount to much.

Still, it was more attention than Peavey had ever
gotten in life, Travis thought as he rode back to his
office. Nobody paid much attention to the man while
he was around; it was not surprising that so few took
notice of his passing.

Somehow, it bothered Travis anyway.

It was obvious that Peavey had drunk himself to
death, but something else nagged at Travis during the
rest of the day. He listened to Cody complaining

about having to walk back to the office after Judah had swiped not only the new girl in town but the borrowed wagon as well. Normally Cody's grousing would have provoked a chuckle from the marshal, but today Travis had other things on his mind.

If Abner Peavey's body had simply given out on him, why did the man have such an agonized look on his face? If he had died from too much drinking, it seemed more likely that he would have fallen down and gone to sleep peacefully.

Cyrus Worden had examined the body and determined that there were no signs of foul play—nothing to warrant an inquest. As the county coroner, Worden declared that Peavey's death was due to natural causes. That should have been the end of the matter.

But that evening Luke Travis found himself heading for the west end of town where Peavey had done his drinking. More than a half dozen dingy saloons were in this area, most of them without names. They were housed in ramshackle frame structures that had seen better days and served cheap, home-brewed whiskey rather than the top-quality liquor available in the better taverns like Orion's. Over their doors were signs that read simply SALOON or WHISKEY. Occasionally, one of them might boast a scarred, out-of-tune piano, but none of these places offered anything in the way of entertainment. A few prostitutes worked this neighborhood, drifting from dive to dive.

Travis would have liked to close most of the bars down, but they stayed within the law these days. When he first came to Abilene, this part of town had been rife with thievery and murder. But its denizens quickly learned that the new marshal would not put up with that. Travis had had to kill a couple of men in one of the saloons when he tried to arrest the pair for robbery and assault and they resisted. After that, the word spread rapidly.

Now, the saloonkeepers tried their best to keep lawlessness out of their establishments, and the patrons usually minded their own business.

Travis had no idea which saloons Abner Peavey had frequented, so he decided to check each one. Silence fell as he stepped into the first one, and the men who were standing at the bar watched him out of the corners of their eyes. When he went straight to the bar and motioned to the bartender, they returned to their drinking and quiet conversation.

"Evenin', Marshal," the dirty-aproned barman said with an insincere smile. "What brings you down here?"

Travis placed his hands on the bar. "Have you heard about Abner Peavey, Chet?" he asked.

The bartender nodded, a wary yet solemn expression coming over his face. "Sure did, Marshal. It's a damned shame, Peavey dyin' like that."

"Did he do much drinking in here?"

"Not much," the bartender replied with a shrug. "Enough so I knew who he was, but that's about all."

"Was he in here last night?" Travis asked.

The bartender shook his head. "I hadn't seen him in a little over a week, Marshal. He got mad the last time he was in here because I wouldn't give him any credit. Man's got to fork over before he gets a drink."

Travis watched the man as he answered, and as far as he could tell, the bartender was being truthful. "Where's he been doing his drinking since then?"

Again the bartender shrugged. "I wouldn't know. There's plenty of places around here. Doubt if Peavey could've gotten credit in any of them. He probably did some odd jobs and scraped a few coins together, but he didn't come back in here because he was still mad at me."

Travis mulled that over. The fact that Peavey had had a run-in with this man was interesting, but it did not really add anything important to what Travis already knew. Even if he suspected foul play, the bartender certainly had no motive for wanting Peavey dead.

Maybe Peavey had quarreled with somebody else, though, somebody who had decided to get rid of him—

Travis had to come back to the fact that the body had no marks, no wounds of any kind. Was he seeing a crime where one did not exist? Lifting a hand in farewell, he drifted out of the saloon and headed toward the next one.

He could not have said what he hoped to find. All he knew was that he wanted to talk to someone who had seen Peavey last night before he died.

His next two stops yielded the same lack of results. The bartenders knew Peavey, all right, but claimed that he had not been in their places recently. Travis had no choice but to believe the men. They had no reason to lie, as far as he could see.

The fourth saloon he dropped in on was probably the worst of the lot. It was a soddy—an earthen structure similar to those poor farmers built out on the prairie. The cabin had been there for twenty years or so, dating from the time when Abilene had been a tiny village of squalid huts.

Travis pushed aside the canvas covering the soddy's entrance and grimaced. The dimly lit room was dismal. The bar consisted of planks laid across empty barrels. A few rickety tables and chairs were scattered around the room on the hard-packed earthen floor.

The marshal noticed four farmers standing at the bar tossing back shots of whiskey from dirty glasses. One of the tables was occupied by a shaggy, shapeless lump that Travis recognized as Nestor Gilworth, a former buffalo hunter. Nestor always wore a heavy buffalo-hide coat, rain or shine, hot or cold, and now his equally shaggy head was lying on the rough surface of the table. *Passed out from too much rotgut,* Travis decided as he glanced bleakly toward the drunken man. Nestor was a regular in the jail, and that was a shame. From the stories Travis had heard about his buffalo-hunting exploits, Nestor had been quite a man in his time.

The bartender was a burly man with a fringe of red hair circling his balding, freckled scalp. He was called Earl; Travis had never heard his last name. He glared at Travis as the lawman walked toward the makeshift bar.

"Hello, Earl," Travis said with a nod.

"Marshal," the bartender rasped, his voice flat and unfriendly.

"You mind if I ask you a couple of questions?"

"I might," Earl snapped. "I thought you generally kept your nose out of our business in this part of town. We been keepin' things pretty law-abidin'."

"I realize that, Earl. I just wanted to know if you were acquainted with a man named Peavey."

"Peavey?" Earl jerked his blunt chin up and down. "I know the son of a bitch. What did he do now?"

Travis saw that the other men at the bar were watching him while trying to appear not to. For their benefit as well as Earl's, he raised his voice and said, "He died."

That got a frown from Earl. "Peavey's dead? He was just in here last night. What the hell happened? He pass out in front of somebody's wagon and get trampled?"

Travis shook his head. "According to the coroner, he just up and died." His voice got colder as he went on, "Too much of that rotgut of yours, I'd say that was the cause."

Earl's florid face tightened. "You got no call to say that, Marshal! It ain't my fault the bastard's dead."

"You admitted that he was drinking in here last night," Travis pointed out.

Earl gave a harsh laugh. "Peavey was drinkin' somewhere every night for the last ten years, Marshal. Just because the last time happened to be here don't make it my fault."

"How much did he have to drink?"

"Hell, I don't know," Earl growled. "I poured a few shots for him, don't remember just how many. Then he bought a bottle and sat down at a table to kill it."

"He finished off a whole bottle by himself?"

The bartender nodded. "Yeah, he was alone, and when he was done with that one, he bought another to take with him. That cleaned him out. He'd gotten a few dollars from old man Sheldon to fix some rain gutters, and he spent the whole wad in here last night."

"So he took a bottle with him." Travis remembered the whiskey bottle he had found near Peavey's body the night before. That agreed with what Earl just told him.

"No law says I can't sell him a bottle like that," Earl

objected. He squinted angrily at the marshal. "By God, if you're tryin' to railroad me into somethin', Travis—"

"Take it easy," Travis cut in. "Nobody's trying to blame you for anything, mister."

"Damn well better not. I just sell the booze. Man's got to take responsibility for his own drinkin', I say."

Travis pointed a finger at him. "Maybe so, but it wouldn't hurt for you to keep an eye on your customers in the future, Earl. If you see a man's had too much, send him on his way without a bottle next time. I don't want anybody else dying on the street like Abner Peavey did."

Behind Travis, a chair scraped suddenly, and then a deep voice rumbled, "Abner? Abner's dead?"

Travis turned to see Nestor Gilworth looming up out of his chair. The former buffalo hunter's long hair and bushy beard were tangled and matted, and in the coat he almost looked like one of the massive beasts that had once roamed these plains in huge herds.

Blinking his red-rimmed eyes, Nestor cocked his head to one side and gave it a little shake. "Abner's dead?" he repeated.

"I'm afraid so, Nestor," Travis said. "Did you know him?"

"He . . . he was my bes' friend," Nestor stammered in a choked voice. Then he roared, "Who done it?"

Nestor was still drunk, Travis knew. He had come out of his stupor long enough to hear Peavey's death mentioned, and that had jolted him awake. But the big man's brain was obviously besotted with whiskey.

"Take it easy, Nestor," Travis said, his voice steady and calm. "Nobody killed your friend, as far as we can tell. He just died from drinking too much for too long."

Nestor shook his nead. "Naw, not Abner. He wouldn't'a done that. Somebody must'a killed him, Marshal." Nestor stumbled as he tried to move from behind the table. "Marshal . . . killed him . . . killed Abner." His eyes widened, and he glared at Travis. "You killed him, Marshal! You killed my friend!" he cried.

"Now hold on, Nestor," Travis grated. "You're getting all confused. I found Peavey's body, all right—"

"I knew you done it!" Nestor howled. His huge hands clenched into fists, and he staggered toward the bar. "I'll kill you for doin' that, Marshal!"

Suddenly the other customers stampeded toward the soddy's door. All of them had seen a boozed-up Nestor Gilworth on the rampage before, and none of them wanted to be around if it was about to happen again.

Travis stood his ground as Nestor lurched toward him. A few months earlier, Cody and he had arrested Nestor after the big man shot up Texas Street with his Sharps rifle and his old Dragoon Colt in a drunken spree. Travis confiscated Nestor's weapons and did not return them, so there was a good chance Nestor did not have any firearms now. But he might have a Bowie knife under that buffalo coat. He could have anything short of a cannon under there, Travis thought grimly as Nestor advanced.

Travis's back was to the bar. Behind him, he heard Earl mutter, "Stand aside, Marshal. I've got a shotgun back here. I'll teach that monster a lesson."

"No," Travis roared. "I don't want him hurt."

Nestor steadied himself and then lurched at Travis with a guttural yell.

Travis darted aside, hoping that Earl would follow

his order and not start blasting with that shotgun. Nestor thundered past him and crashed into the bar, overturning the whiskey barrels and sending the planks flying. Earl, still clutching the shotgun, dove for cover.

Nestor somehow kept his balance and turned to charge at Travis again. The marshal slipped his Colt Peacemaker out of its holster. "Stop it, Nestor!" he barked.

Nestor ignored the warning and lunged. Once more, Travis was able to get out of his way, and the big man trampled one of the tables instead, reducing it to kindling. With surprising speed, he twisted around and lashed a long arm at Travis. Blunt, filthy fingers grabbed the lawman's coat.

Travis grimaced as Nestor jerked him forward. He would have to smash Nestor's head with the gun barrel and hope he did not hit him hard enough to do any permanent damage. He was just lifting his arm when he saw a flicker of movement out of the corner of his eye.

Behind the wrecked bar, Earl had regained his feet and was lifting the scattergun. Travis read the deadly intent on the bartender's face. Instantly he knew the story that Earl would tell. Nestor Gilworth had been on one of his rampages, Earl would say, and he had only been trying to stop the big buffalo hunter from killing the marshal. It was just bad luck that Travis had gotten in the way of the shotgun blast. With Travis gone, the saloonkeepers in this part of town could return to their old lawless ways.

Those thoughts flashed through Travis's mind in the instant it took him to shift his gun barrel and squeeze the trigger. The Colt cracked. The slug whined past

Earl's ear and thudded into the sod wall behind him. He paled and dropped the shotgun as Travis eared back the Peacemaker's hammer for another shot. Earl's hands flew into the air, and he staggered back against the wall. With that threat removed, Travis still had to deal with Nestor Gilworth. As Nestor engulfed him in a bear hug, Travis gulped down a deep breath. Once the big man's arms folded around him, he might need all the air he could get in his lungs before this was over. He raised the Colt to strike at Nestor's head.

Before the weapon could fall, Nestor suddenly stopped squeezing Travis's midsection. Instead, he stood still, and Travis saw his eyes beginning to glaze. The marshal pushed against Nestor's broad chest, but even though the big man was no longer trying to crush the life out of him, his arms seemed locked in place. Then Nestor started to sway.

Travis knew what was about to happen. Nestor, the liquor catching up to him again, had passed out on his feet. But if he collapsed on top of Travis, that would be just as dangerous as any bear hug.

Travis kicked out behind him, driving his foot against one of the tables. That motion was enough to throw Nestor off balance; the big man fell backward, taking Travis with him. Sunk in his stupor, he crashed to the earthen floor, but the impact loosened his grip. Travis jerked free, rolled away, and came up still holding his gun.

"Goddamn!" Earl exclaimed. "I thought he was goin' to kill you for sure, Marshal!"

"He tried hard enough," Travis panted, trying to catch his breath. Looking meaningfully at Earl, he went on, "Sorry my gun went off like that. Somebody could have gotten hurt if they were careless."

Earl swallowed nervously. "Yeah," he ventured weakly. Then he pointed at Nestor and asked, "What are you goin' to do with him?"

"Haul him to jail, as usual," Travis replied. "If I can round up enough men to help me, that is."

"What about the damage he did to my place?"

Travis shrugged, bent over, and rummaged around in the odorous buffalo coat until he found several coins. He flipped them to Earl, who caught them deftly. "Reckon that'll be a start on what he owes you," Travis observed dryly. "You'll have to settle with him after he gets out of jail, though."

Earl, nodding grudgingly, said, "You know none of this would've happened if you hadn't come in here askin' a bunch of damn-fool questions, Marshal."

Travis's eyes narrowed. "Maybe so, but you remember what I told you about Peavey and folks who have had too much to drink."

Earl just grunted.

Travis shook his head and went to look for somebody to help him drag Nestor Gilworth to jail.

Chapter Four

———◆———

THE NEXT EVENING IN THE BETTER PART OF ABILENE, Orion McCarthy, the burly, redheaded owner of Orion's Tavern, lifted a glass of his finest Scotch whisky and grinned. "To ye health, me dear."

Sitting across the table from him was an attractive blonde. She tapped her glass against his with a tiny clink, then returned his smile and said, "And to yours as well, Orion."

The brilliant green parrot perched behind the bar squawked and added in its raucous voice, "Drink hearty, me lads and lassies!"

Orion glanced at the bird and shook his head. "I dinna know how tha' creature always seems t'know wha' t'say."

"He probably had a good teacher," the blonde replied with a laugh. "After all, you're about the smoothest talker I've ever met, Mr. McCarthy."

Orion's face turned almost the same shade as his hair and shaggy beard. "Go on wi' ye, Joselyn. Ye be the smooth talker, not I."

Joselyn Paige laughed again, and Orion McCarthy thought, not for the first time, how glad he was that she had wandered into his bar one evening a week ago.

He had seen her around Abilene a few times before that, and she had caught his eye, as she would that of any healthy male. She was in her thirties and tall, and her full figure, which would have been considered lush on a smaller woman, was statuesque. Her honey blond hair fell in thick waves around a face that combined beauty and character. She dressed well and expensively, and it came as no surprise to Orion that Joselyn was one of the best gamblers he had ever seen. She handled a deck of cards with a deftness that spoke of years of practice. Her quick mind and unreadable features made her a deadly opponent across a poker table.

Not that Orion intended to waste any time playing poker with Joselyn. They shared too many other things in common, such as the fine whiskey they were sipping now.

"I'm glad I decided not to work tonight," Joselyn declared. "The Alamo and the Bull's Head are fine for gambling, but a girl has to relax every now and then. For that, I prefer a cozier place—like this one."

"Aye," Orion agreed. "'Tis not fancy, but 'tis mine."

The desire to find a quiet place to have a drink was what had brought Joselyn into Orion's Tavern in the first place. She had been frequenting the larger saloons; that was where the money was. Any games that went on in Orion's were likely to be penny-ante affairs.

The tavern was long and narrow, with a bar running

the length of the right side and tables scattered around the room on the sawdust-covered floor. The functional lanterns that lit it and the backbar with its well-stocked shelves could be found in hundreds of frontier saloons. The squawking comments of Old Bailey, the parrot, who paced back and forth on his perch behind the bar, were the only form of entertainment.

But that was exactly what Joselyn had been looking for. After long hours of high stakes and high pressure at the gaming tables in other saloons, she wanted a glass of smooth whiskey and a little quiet conversation, nothing more. Orion had been happy to provide both.

The two of them had hit it off from the start. Both had traveled widely. Orion had seen more of the eastern part of the country than Joselyn had, while Joselyn had traveled throughout the West. Joselyn did not mind talking about the places she had been, although Orion noticed that she was reticent about revealing any details of what she had done there. It was possible, given her looks and sensuous air, that she had been a prostitute at one time. Orion did not care about that; he had learned long ago that people did what they had to in order to survive. Besides, he felt no particular romantic interest in Joselyn. As far as he was concerned she was good company and had the makings of a splendid friend.

"Did I tell you what happened last night?" Joselyn asked now.

Orion shook his head. "I dinna think so."

"Some foolish young cowboy accused me of cheating." Joselyn laughed. "As if I'd need to cheat to take money away from some wet-behind-the-ears puncher who was too busy looking down my dress to concentrate on his cards."

Orion's eyes dropped for a second to the deep cleavage Joselyn's low-cut dress displayed. Her full breasts were impressive, as was the valley between them. Orion could see how such a view might distract a youngster who had not seen a woman in weeks. He shook his head and clucked his tongue. "The lad did'na know wha' he was saying."

"I set him straight pretty quick. Mike, the bouncer at the Alamo, was going to toss him out, and I thought for a minute that the kid was going to go for his gun. He didn't expect me to come up with a derringer."

Orion eyed the way Joselyn's dress hugged her figure and gave a mock-lecherous grin. "I reckon the young scut figgered there was no place ye could hide a gun."

Joselyn returned the grin. "You'd be surprised at the places I can hide things, Orion," she quipped in a throaty voice.

Orion threw back his head and laughed. But he suddenly stopped as he noticed the door of the tavern fly open and a small, slender young woman step inside, slamming the heavy door behind her.

Orion was dumbstruck. Abilene's ladies simply did not enter saloons. A gambling woman like Joselyn—part lady, part wench—was always welcome. Occasionally a prostitute would wander in.

But the proper, tiny woman who had slammed the door was a different story. As Orion watched her, he was reminded of an outraged society spitfire. She stood just inside the entrance glaring angrily around the room.

Silence fell over the tavern as the handful of customers and young Augie, who was tending the bar, stared at the newcomer. A frown appeared on Joselyn's face. A moment went by before the quiet was abruptly shattered.

"Come in outta the cold!" Old Bailey screeched. "Come in outta the cold, dearie!"

The young woman took a deep breath and stepped forward. Her face still tight with disapproval, she demanded, "I want to speak with the owner of this place."

Orion sensed this little mite of a woman meant trouble. He exchanged a quick glance with Joselyn and saw from her expression that she agreed with him. Pushing back his chair, he stood up and faced the young woman.

"Me name is Orion McCarthy," he rumbled, "and I be the owner o' this tavern."

The petite brunette peered at him, then strode purposefully toward him, her expression determined. But Orion thought he saw a hint of nervousness in her eyes. He knew his broad-shouldered, heavyset frame made him an imposing figure, and he probably appeared even more threatening to someone as tiny as this young woman.

"I'm Bethany Hale," she announced haughtily, stopping a few feet away from him.

Orion wondered if he was supposed to have heard of her. Judging by her attitude, he thought it was possible. But to the best of his recollection he had never seen her before in his life. "Good evening t'ye, Miss Hale," he said, keeping his voice pleasant. "Wha' kin I do f'ye?"

"You can close down this ungodly citadel of sin, that's what you can do!" Bethany Hale proclaimed.

Orion blinked and frowned. Behind him, he heard Joselyn gasp. The Scotsman said slowly, "I'm sorry, Miss Hale, but I dinna understand—"

"I'm from the Christian Ladies Temperance Society," Bethany cut in. "And I demand that you close this tavern and stop corrupting innocent people with your hellish liquor!"

Several customers gasped, but no one said a word, and a stunned silence fell over the room. Again the parrot broke it by squawking, "Devil be damned! Awk! Devil be damned!" Then Old Bailey let loose a streak of profanity that made even Orion pale.

"Shut ye beak!" he roared at the garishly colored bird. Then he swung around to face Bethany and went on hurriedly, "I'm apologizing t'ye, Miss Hale. I dinna know where yon bird learned such language."

"Probably from you and your customers, Mr. McCarthy," Bethany snapped. "Now, are you going to comply with my request or not?"

Orion spread his big hands helplessly. "I kinna. This tavern be me livelihood, miss."

"I'd be ashamed to admit I lived off the suffering of others," Bethany countered icily.

So far Joselyn Paige had been quiet, but now she stepped around the table and said angrily, "See here, you've got no right to talk like that! What do you mean, coming in here and insulting people and making ridiculous demands—"

Orion waved a hand to stop her. "I kin handle this, Joselyn, but ye have me thanks f'trying t'help. I'm sure the lass means no harm."

"That's where you're wrong, Mr. McCarthy," Bethany declared. "I do mean to harm you, or at least your unholy business. I intend to close it and all the other saloons in Abilene."

The tavern's customers muttered angry protests. They were not used to seeing righteous society women like Bethany in places such as this, and they certainly did not take kindly to being threatened. One of the cowboys at the bar called out, "What's the matter with you, little gal? You got a burr under your saddle or somethin'?"

Bethany swung to face him, her tiny hands clenching into fists. "I do indeed have a 'burr under my saddle,' sir," she raged. "It's the burr of evil drunkards like yourself!"

"Now hold on!" the puncher growled. "I ain't been drunk for nigh on to a month. You got no call to say such a thing."

"I have the highest call of all. I'm on a crusade to see that places like this are abolished."

Other customers began to protest more stridently, and soon the shouting in the tavern was deafening. Orion stepped to the center of the room, raising his brawny arms for quiet. "Tha' be enough from all o' ye!" he thundered. "I will not have a roo-kus in me tavern, and I will not have ye *gentlemen* speaking harshly to a lady."

"She's no lady," Joselyn roared. "She's one of those damned temperance fanatics."

Bethany gave her a disdainful look. "I'm not going to bother responding to comments from a . . . a woman of the streets."

"What?" Joselyn exploded. "What are you calling me, you . . . you little—"

Orion moved quickly between the two women, more quickly than a man of his bulk should have been able to. Facing Bethany, he said, "I think 'twould be best if ye left now, Miss Hale." He reached out to put a hand on her arm, intending to steer her gently toward the door. "I really must insist—"

"Get your hands off me, you whoremonger!" Bethany exclaimed. She lashed out with the purse she was carrying, smacking it into the side of Orion's head.

Under other circumstances this situation might have been comical, but Orion sensed it was about to deteriorate badly. He lifted his hands to ward off Bethany's blows. But before he could do anything else, an angry blond vision lunged past him. Joselyn clamped a hand on Bethany's shoulder, spun her around, and shoved her away from Orion. "Stop that!" she cried. "Stop it, you little bitch!"

"Oh!" Bethany's face paled, and her features twisted with pain or anger—or both. Something inside her seemed to snap, because her eyes narrowed peculiarly. She suddenly drove a fist toward Joselyn. The bigger woman made quite a target. Bethany's punch thudded into her midsection and made her stagger, as much from surprise as from the impact of the blow.

Joselyn glanced down at the spot where the punch had landed. When she looked up, she was grinning dangerously. "All right, lady," she declared. "If that's the way you want it."

Whoops of encouragement roared from the watching cowboys, while Orion shouted, "No!"

But his cry was too late. Joselyn threw a punch, hurling all her weight and strength behind it. Bethany's eyes widened in sudden fear, and she flung herself to the side just in time to avoid the main force of the blow. Still, it clipped her on the cheek and spun her halfway around. Clutching at a table, she caught her balance as Joselyn attacked again. Orion watched in horror.

Bethany was overmatched, and she seemed to know

it. Nevertheless, she met Joselyn's charge—grappling, clawing, and scratching. The two women staggered across the room. Bethany hung onto Joselyn with one arm and used the other to snap several punches into the older woman's breasts. Outraged, Joselyn howled and flailed at her opponent's head, but Bethany was too close. Joselyn did not have enough room to throw a proper punch.

But Orion knew it was only a matter of time before Joselyn's superior weight and experience would win out. If any of her punches connected fully, it would snap Bethany's head off. He moved forward, watching for an opening as the two women careened around the tavern. The cowhands at the bar kept hollering, anxious to see the young temperance advocate get what they thought was coming to her. Bets flew back and forth, most of the men wagering on Joselyn to win handily.

Suddenly Orion, thinking that he saw a chance to get between them and separate them, leapt at the battling females. At the same moment, Bethany ducked as Joselyn launched a punch. Orion arrived just in time for Joselyn's fist to crash powerfully into his nose. Orion yelped and stumbled backward, his hands flying to his injured nose as blood gushed from it.

"Orion! Oh, no! I'm so sorry!" Joselyn cried, cradling her throbbing hand.

She should not have turned her attention away from Bethany. The young woman lowered her head and charged, butting Joselyn in the stomach and grabbing her around the waist. Air heaved out of Joselyn's lungs. Bethany kept her feet moving, pushing her opponent toward the doorway.

Joselyn's back slammed into the door; the impact of the two bodies splintered the facing. The door burst open, spilling the women out into the autumn night.

Orion shook his head to clear it, and droplets of blood flew off his swollen nose. Then he charged after them. He had to stop this fight, or he would have a devil of a time explaining how two ladies had beaten each other to death in front of his tavern.

Cody Fisher, glad that he had thought to put on a jacket and hat before he stepped out in the cool night air, strolled down the boardwalk on the south side of Texas Street. It was early yet; Luke Travis would be making the official rounds later. Cody was heading toward Orion's. He was looking forward to having a drink and spending a few minutes conversing with the big Scotsman.

As he drew even with the entrance of the Grand Palace Hotel, Cody glanced through the glass panels in the double doors into the shabby lobby. He saw no sign of Bethany Hale inside, not that he really expected to see her. He had not spoken to her since she left him at the Methodist Church the day before to go off with Judah. Nor had he seen her since the previous night, when he watched the two of them coming back from the temperance meeting.

Miss Bethany Hale was none of his business, he told himself. She had made it clear that she preferred Judah's company to his, and it was all right with Cody if things stayed that way. Grinning, he shook his head and moved on. Maybe if he kept telling himself that, he would wind up believing it.

Whoops and yells coming from Orion's two doors away prompted Cody to increase his pace. Either the tavern's customers were having a mighty good time tonight, or something else was going on—like a fight. A mischievous grin tugged at Cody's mouth. It had been a while since he had seen a good saloon brawl. He might watch it for a little while before he broke it up.

He was in front of Aileen Bloom's office when Orion's door crashed open and two struggling figures half fell, half staggered onto the boardwalk. Cody yelled, "Hey!" The combatants, skirts swirling, stumbled to the edge of the planks, then lurched right off and landed in the dusty street.

Cody broke into a run, barreling toward the two women who were now rolling over and over in the dirt, clawing and punching each other for all they were worth. Orion burst out of the tavern, saw the deputy coming down the boardwalk, and shouted, "Help me stop 'em a'fore they kill each other!"

The battling women came up on their knees, their faces finally illuminated by the boardwalk lantern light and the glow that spilled through the tavern's open door. Cody was shocked when he recognized Bethany Hale. The big blonde fighting with her was Joselyn Paige, the gambling lady who had drifted into town a couple of weeks earlier, and it looked as though she definitely had the upper hand. She launched a blow that Bethany could not block in time, and with a sharp crack Joselyn's fist met the younger woman's jaw.

Cody reached Bethany in time to catch her as she fell backward. Orion swooped in, flung his arms around Joselyn, and picked her up, twisting away with her. She struggled for a moment longer, then realized who was holding her and sagged in Orion's arms.

Cody stood up, lifting Bethany; her head was lolling loosely on her shoulders. She was as light as he figured she would be. He easily carried her to the boardwalk and laid her gently on the planks. Then kneeling beside her, he cradled her head in his lap. In the lantern light he saw that her bruised jaw was already starting to swell and darken.

"I'm all right now, Orion," Joselyn said wearily. "Put me down." When he did, she hurried to the boardwalk and stared anxiously down at Bethany. "Oh, damn, I didn't kill her, did I?" she asked Cody.

"She's breathing," Cody replied. "I think she's just knocked out. That's quite a punch you've got, Miss Paige."

"Aye. I kin attest t'tha'," Orion put in and winced as he touched his nose. It had stopped bleeding, but the front of his shirt was spattered with crimson.

"What happened to you, Orion?" Cody asked. "You look like you ran into a wall." The deputy glanced at Joselyn. "You don't mean to tell me—"

"Aye, and certain I be ye will not tell Lucas about this little incident."

If he had not been worried about Bethany, Cody would have laughed out loud at the sheepish expression on Orion's face. As it was, he grinned for a second, then turned his attention back to the young woman lying on the boardwalk.

Bethany was slowly moving her head, moaning softly, and her eyelids were fluttering. A moment later she opened her eyes fully and stared up at him. "Wh-what happened?" she stammered weakly.

"You got knocked out," Cody told her. "Why don't you just lay still for a minute and rest?" He looked up at Orion and, without thinking, went on, "Bring us a shot of whiskey, will you? I reckon it might do Miss Bethany some good about now."

"No!" she cried before Orion could reply. "I . . . I don't want any of that . . . that evil liquor!" Bethany pushed herself to a sitting position and glared at Joselyn, who was standing nearby with a concerned look on her face. Pointing a wobbling finger at the older woman, Bethany said thickly, "I want that hussy arrested!"

"Wait just a minute," Joselyn countered. Now that it was obvious that Bethany was a little stunned but not seriously injured, Joselyn's anger returned. "*She's* the one who came into the tavern and started making a damned nuisance of herself."

"Oh!" Bethany cried, outraged at Joselyn's language.

"And she's the one who threw the first punch, isn't that right, Orion?" the gambling lady continued.

Orion shrugged his broad shoulders. "Aye, Cody," he rumbled. "Wha' Miss Paige says is true. 'Twas Miss Hale who struck the first blow."

Cody got to his feet and helped Bethany to hers. As she straightened her dress, the deputy asked, "What about that, Miss Hale? Is that the way it happened?"

"I was merely trying to convince a pack of drunken heathens that they had best change their ways," Bethany said righteously. "That . . . that woman assaulted me!"

"I just kept you from whaling the tar out of Orion!" Joselyn shot back.

Cody held up his hands. "Look, ladies, I reckon I understand that the two of you don't get along. You both took some punishment, so it looks to me like there's no need to arrest anybody. Why don't the two of you just shake hands and call off this fight?"

Both women stared at him as if that was the most

ludicrous idea they had ever heard. "Not likely," Joselyn said flatly. Bethany shook her head adamantly.

"This isn't over," she declared. "It was just the first battle in the war against alcohol." She turned to face Orion. "I'm warning you, Mr. McCarthy. Change your ways or suffer the consequences." With that, she turned and stalked down the boardwalk.

Cody glanced at the tavern keeper. "Are you going to be all right, Orion?"

"Aye, lad." Orion touched his bloody, puffed-up nose and grimaced. "I dinna think me nose be broken, just a wee bit tender at the moment."

"Oh, I'm so sorry, Orion," Joselyn murmured, slipping her arm around him. "I didn't mean to hit you. I was aiming at that little—"

"Ah, ah," Orion admonished her. " 'Twill do no good to call the lass unpleasant names. She has her way o' looking at things, and we have ours."

"Maybe so, but she doesn't have to be so damned snippy about it."

Cody looked at Bethany's stiff back disappearing into the darkness and thought he saw her stumble. "I reckon I'd best go after her and make sure she doesn't get into any more trouble tonight," he said. "I'll see you later, Orion."

The Scotsman lifted a big hand in farewell, and Cody hurried after Bethany. He caught up to her just as she reached the entrance to the Grand Palace Hotel, but to his surprise, she did not turn in. Instead she kept moving.

"Excuse me, Miss Hale," Cody said as he came up beside her. "Aren't you going back to your room?"

Bethany shook her head and answered without looking at him. "I'm too upset right now, Deputy. I think I need to walk a bit and cool off. Is there any law against that?"

"No, ma'am, none at all. But it might be a good idea if I walked with you. Like I told you—and like I reckon you've found out for yourself—Abilene can be a rough town sometimes."

Bethany still did not look at him. "Very well, if you want to accompany me, I suppose it would be all right."

As they continued to walk down Texas Street, Cody recalled the way she had drawn away from him when they were riding in the wagon and carefully avoided getting too close to her. He did not speak for a few minutes, unsure how Bethany would react if he tried to start a conversation. But a pretty girl had not yet been born whom Cody could not talk to, so he finally asked, "How's your jaw? It looked like you caught a pretty good wallop."

"It's sore," Bethany admitted grudgingly, "but I'm sure it will be all right."

"We could go to the doctor's office and have her take a look at it."

"I'm sure that's not necessary." Bethany paused, as if absorbing the meaning of his words. "*Her?* You mean the doctor in Abilene is a woman?"

"That's right," Cody assured her. "Dr. Aileen Bloom. You won't find a better sawbones anywhere on the frontier. It took folks a while to get used to it."

"It's highly commendable that the town has allowed a female doctor to practice here." Bethany sniffed. "I've often thought that the world would be a better place if there were more women in positions of authority, instead of—"

"Instead of us whiskey-guzzling men?" Cody finished her statement with a grin.

"Now that you've stated it so bluntly, yes. That's exactly what I meant to say."

He shrugged. "Could be you're right. Men have made plenty of mistakes. Most folks do, I reckon."

Bethany did not reply. After a few moments Cody went on, "Did Judah know what you were going to do tonight?"

Bethany shook her head. "He had nothing to do with this. I simply had to do something, after seeing that tavern so close to the hotel. It was like . . . like it was ordained that the first battle would be fought there."

"For such a little gal, you sure are big on talking about battles," Cody commented dryly.

She stopped walking and turned toward him. "And what would you have me do, Deputy?" she demanded. "Give up all of my principles, give up on the cause to which I've devoted my life? Perhaps I should just admit that the war to defeat liquor cannot be won and slink home like a dog? Is that what you want?"

As the words tumbled from her lips her eyes flashed, and Cody thought she was even prettier tonight than she had been the day before. Even disheveled from the brawl, even with her discolored jaw, Bethany Hale was a lovely young woman. And her voice had the same fiery sincerity that he had heard when she was talking to Judah and Sister Laurel at the church.

He held up his hands, palms out, in surrender. "Now just a minute," he chuckled. "I don't want anybody giving up on something that's important to them. I reckon we've all got to fight our own fights. But there might be better ways of going at it, instead of barging into a place and hoo-rawing the folks who are there."

"Perhaps you're right." Bethany sighed. "Sometimes I feel as though this whole business is just too much for me, Deputy."

That was the first sign she had given of opening up with him, and Cody wanted to keep her talking. As they started walking down the street again, more slowly this time, he asked, "You mentioned going home. Where is that?"

Bethany hesitated, then said, "I was born and raised in Philadelphia. That's where I lived until my . . . until I came to Kansas."

"What do your folks think of you coming out here like this?"

"My parents are dead, Deputy. There's just me and—" Bethany drew a quick breath and shook her head. "There's just me now."

Cody frowned. That was the second time she had started to say something about somebody else. Trying to draw her out, he asked, "You don't have any other family at all?"

"None," she declared, shaking her head vehemently. "I'm on my own. All I have are my allies in the fight against liquor. They're all I need."

"Like Judah." Cody's words were a statement, not a question.

"Your brother is an honorable man. He tried to tell me that I would face quite a difficult task here in Abilene, but he never tried to dissuade me."

"No, I don't reckon he would." Cody had not meant to steer the conversation around to Judah. Now he regretted giving Bethany the opportunity to tell him what a wonderful fellow Judah was. Cody admired his brother; he knew some of the things Judah had gone through. But that did not mean Cody wanted to hear about it from Bethany Hale. "What made you so opposed to liquor in the first place?" he asked, changing the subject.

Bethany did not reply for a long time, and he sensed she was mulling over her answer. Finally, she said, "It seems clear to me. Alcohol is a great danger. People can . . . can be hurt because of it."

Then her lips closed firmly, and she refused to answer any more questions about her background. Cody tried a couple of times, attempting to be subtle about it, then gave it up as a bad job. Whatever had happened to Bethany in the past—and he was sure there was *something*—she was keeping it to herself.

He looked up and saw that they had walked in a circle. They were approaching the Grand Palace Hotel again, and this time when they reached the door, Bethany started to go in. Placing a hand on her arm, Cody stopped her and was surprised that she did not pull away from him.

"Look, Miss Hale," he said sincerely, "I don't want to tell you your business, but I'd appreciate it if you'd be more careful about what you say when you go into the saloons around here. Orion's is a nice, peaceful place. You start a fight in the Bull's Head or another saloon, and it's liable to get out of hand in a hurry. Folks could be badly hurt, and you might be one of them."

"Thank you, Deputy," she replied. "I realize you're just worried about keeping the peace. That is your job, after all. But I'm afraid I have to follow a higher law than that set down by the State of Kansas. I . . . I hope you understand."

"I'm trying to," Cody admitted. Then, remembering Judah's timid behavior of the night before, he abruptly decided to see what Bethany would do if he tried to kiss her.

His lips had barely brushed hers when she sprang back and brought her palm across his face in a ringing slap. "How dare you!" she exclaimed. "I had thought you might have the makings of a gentleman, Deputy, but I see now that I was wrong!" Haughtily she turned and stalked into the hotel, slamming the door behind her.

Cody grinned despite the stinging imprint of her hand on his cheek. He had to find out, and now he supposed he knew. It was not the first time he had been slapped. And, he told himself ruefully, it probably would not be the last.

Chapter Five

———◆———

THE INCIDENT AT ORION'S WAS THE FIRST OF MANY clashes that occurred over the next few days. Each night Bethany Hale visited several of Abilene's saloons and demanded that they close. She was greeted with hoots and catcalls from the customers and polite refusals from the owners.

Word of her battle with Joselyn Paige had traveled around town quickly and caused a minor sensation. Eventually, dozens more people than could ever have been packed into Orion's would claim to have witnessed the short brawl. But the gossip alerted the town's saloonkeepers to keep an eye out for Bethany, and they issued strict orders to their employees not to be provoked into a fight or even an argument with the tiny temperance crusader.

Cody had visited a few taverns, letting the saloon

owners know that he would not like it if anything happened to Bethany. If they wanted to take that as an official warning from the marshal's office, he thought, that was their business.

Luke Travis was aware of the situation as well, having been told about Bethany not only by Cody, but also by Orion. Travis had stopped at the Scotsman's tavern for a beer and been surprised by the state of Orion's nose.

"Mule kick you?" Travis asked sardonically.

Orion frowned darkly. "Has Cody been talking t'ye?" he asked.

Travis shook his head. "He didn't say anything about you being in a fight, if that's what you mean."

"Ah. Well, in tha' case, I ran into a door."

"I see," Travis replied dryly. "Must have been a door with a pretty good punch to make a man's nose swell up like that."

"Aye, Lucas, tha' be the truth!" Orion jerked his head for emphasis.

Nevertheless, Travis quickly learned the truth about the battle at the tavern. After mulling it over, he decided not to get involved for the time being. Cody seemed to be keeping an eye on Bethany Hale, and Travis trusted his deputy's judgment—at least most of the time.

Where a pretty girl was concerned, however, it might be wise not to trust Cody too much, Travis told himself.

Luckily Bethany did not spend all her time harassing the patrons of the town's saloons. She was also busily preparing for the morality play.

Several days after the incident at Orion's, Judah Fisher was sitting at his desk working on a sermon in his study at the parsonage when someone knocked softly on the door. He put his pen in the inkwell and called, "Come in."

Bethany opened the door and stepped into the small, cozy study.

"Hello, Reverend Fisher," she said, smiling at him. There was a small, leather-bound book in her hands.

"Miss Hale." Judah nodded as he stood up. "How are you today?" Judah noticed immediately, since she wore no cosmetics, that the bruise on her jaw was fading. Like everyone else in town, Judah had heard about the brawl and briefly considered discussing her crusade with her, but now he decided not to raise the issue and embarrass her.

"I'm quite fine, thank you. I was wondering if I could consult with you on a certain matter."

"Of course." A thought occurred to Judah. "How did you get out here? Did someone bring you from town?"

Bethany shook her head. "I thought it would be good for me to have a means of getting around so I rented a buggy at the livery stable."

"That is a good idea," Judah agreed. Then he gestured to the two plush armchairs that stood facing the fireplace at the far end of the sunlit room. "Now, have a seat and tell me what you wanted to talk to me about."

When both of them were comfortable, Bethany handed the book to Judah. "This is a volume of morality plays such as we discussed at the temperance meeting the other night. I thought you might look at the one I've marked and see if you think it would be suitable for our performance here in Abilene."

Judah took the book and opened it to the place that was marked. The play that began there was entitled

Adrift and Astray; the author was someone named Florence Singleton Weems. He scanned the opening lines of the first act. He flipped through the rest of the play, pausing here and there to read a few lines. Apart from some overly dramatic passages and a tendency toward being redundant, the play seemed fine.

"It seems perfectly suitable to me," he said a few minutes later. Closing the book, he handed it back to Bethany. "Where did you happen to find a volume of such plays around here?"

"Well . . ." Bethany blushed. "I brought it with me. I thought even before I arrived that a morality play might be just the thing to wake Abilene up to the danger it faces."

"The danger of liquor, you mean."

"Of course. What else?"

Judah sighed inwardly; he sensed that now was definitely not the time to mention the uproar she had been causing. He was glad he had not raised it earlier. Instead he asked, "What else can I do to help you?"

Bethany's pretty face brightened with enthusiasm. "If you could see your way clear to allow it, Reverend, we should like to rehearse here at the church. The performance will be held in the courthouse, but the carpenters will be busy there, building sets and painting scenery and such."

"Carpenters?"

"Yes, Mrs. Grafton has persuaded several of the townsmen who are good builders to assist us. And some of the merchants are donating other things we will need, such as furniture and costumes. Mrs. Grafton has even persuaded some of the townspeople to take roles in the play. Isn't it wonderful? Everything is going so well!"

Judah smiled. He could imagine how Mrs. Grafton

was *persuading* the townspeople to go along with her. *Browbeating* was probably a better word. Mrs. Grafton had considerable influence, and she had never been shy about using it. Still Judah supposed it was all for a good cause.

"I don't see anything wrong with letting the actors rehearse here," he said, responding to Bethany's question. "The church isn't used much during the week. Have you set a date for the performance?"

Bethany shook her head. "We'd like to put it on as soon as possible, but there's just so much to do." She started to reach toward him, then hesitated. Finally, she placed her hand on his arm and looked at him intently. "I'm so grateful to you, Reverend. You've been so helpful and friendly. . . ."

The warm touch of her fingers made Judah's heart race. He had been surprised by her bold gesture, but he made no move to break the contact. "Your cause is certainly a good one, Miss Hale. I'm just glad I can be of some assistance." Then an idea occurred to him. "We could probably get the children here at the orphanage to help, too," he suggested. "I'm sure the older boys would be glad to help build the sets. We could have some posters printed to advertise the performance, and the younger children could take them around town and put them up."

"What a wonderful idea!" Bethany exclaimed. She squeezed Judah's arm and then lifted her hand. Instantly he missed the warmth of her touch. Bethany was saying, "I'm sure this play is going to make a tremendous difference."

Judah was not so certain of that; he doubted that anything would ever wipe out drinking in the town entirely. But they did have an opportunity to do some good.

Bethany stood up. "I'll talk to Sister Laurel about letting the children help," she said. She gazed at the minister for a moment, and then went on, "Thank you again . . . Judah."

"You . . . you're quite welcome, Bethany." Judah swallowed. Her name came so easily to his lips, the sound of it beautiful to his ears—just as beautiful as she was.

For several minutes after she left his study, Judah tried to work on the sermon. Finally he had to give up. Regardless of the words he tried to scratch onto the paper, all he could really see was the lovely face of Bethany Hale.

As Judah had predicted, the children from the orphanage were more than happy to pitch in. Each afternoon after school, the older boys went to the courthouse to work with the carpenters building the sets. Some of the younger children ran errands or helped Bethany gather the smaller props. Agnes Hirsch, the pretty redhead who was the oldest of the group, quickly made friends with Bethany and volunteered to help her make copies of the play so that all the actors could have scripts. Bethany was only a few years older than Agnes, and the two young women chatted happily as they sat with pen and paper and printed the lines.

The result of all this preparation was a pleasant frenzy. Bethany was at the church every day, sometimes for long hours, and not a day went by that Judah did not see her and talk to her.

On one of those days Judah was sitting in a pew at the back of the simple, white chapel watching Bethany and a few of the actors rehearse their lines, when he heard a rustling sound moving up the aisle next to him. Agnes Hirsch, followed by her younger brother, Michael, had slipped into the room. Judah could not help smiling at the pair. Michael's hair was as red as his sister's, and his impish face was sprinkled with a mass of freckles. His intelligent eyes usually danced with some mischief he was about to commit. Judah had never known a lad who could get into trouble as easily as Michael, but he also knew that the boy had a good heart.

Now, as Michael traipsed up the aisle after Agnes, he suddenly dropped to his knees, lifted his arms penitently, and cried, "No! Please don't hit me again!"

Agnes stopped in her tracks and spun around. "Michael . . . ! What are you doing, for goodness' sake?"

"Please don't beat me, Father!" Michael wailed. "I promise I'll never spill your rum again, if only you won't hurt me or . . . or Mother." The youngster doubled over, his shoulders hunched, and sobs seemed to wrack his body as his voice trailed off.

"Michael, get up!" Agnes hissed, casting a glance over her shoulder at Bethany and the others, who were watching with great interest. "I don't know what's gotten into you! Those are lines from the . . . Oh!"

Judah stood up and clapped, applauding the performance he had just witnessed. "Bravo, Michael!" he called. Then he glanced at Bethany as he went down the aisle toward the front of the church. "That is what the audience says at a play, isn't it, Miss Hale?"

"When it's good they do, Reverend," she agreed. Turning to Michael, she went on, "And that *was* a good performance, Michael. I see that you've been reading the play your sister and I copied."

Michael straightened and leapt to his feet, a broad

grin on his freckled face. Clearly the praise he was receiving for his acting talent—which he had never revealed until now—thrilled him.

Well, at least Michael had never acted in the usual sense of the word, Judah mused with a smile. He had known Michael to give some fine performances and spin some highly unlikely yarns when he had been caught doing things that he should not have been doing.

Now the youngster hurried up to Bethany and said, "I know there's a part in the play for a boy about my age, Miss Hale. Do you think I could play it?"

"I don't see why not, Michael," Bethany replied. "But to be fair, we really ought to see if anyone else here at the orphanage would like to try out for the role."

"There's nobody," Michael said confidently. "All the rest of the fellas think that this acting is sissy stuff." He shrugged. "I don't know, maybe they're right. But it seems like fun to me to get up on a stage and run around and yell and pretend you're somebody else. So do I get to be in the play?"

Bethany laughed. "I don't see why not—as long as it's all right with Sister Laurel."

"Oh, it is. You can ask her yourself."

"I intend to," Bethany assured him. "Are you sure you're up to memorizing all the lines that little Ferdinand has in the play?"

Michael pulled a copy of the play out of his back pocket. "I've already been studying it, Miss Hale. I wanted to be ready in case you said it was all right." Then he grimaced. "But can't we do something about the name of the fella I'm going to play? Ferdinand is so dumb! Can't we change it?"

Bethany put a hand on his shoulder and shook her

head. "The lady who wrote the play used that name for a reason, Michael," she told him firmly. "We can't presume to change things in the script just because we don't like them. Why don't you wait over there for a few minutes, and then you can do some more of your lines for me?" Bethany was nodding toward the front pew.

"Aw, I reckon you're right," Michael grumbled. He walked away muttering, "Seems to me we could change it. The lady probably just made up the whole thing as she went along anyway!"

Judah strode to the front of the church. He patted Michael on the shoulder as he passed the boy and then smiled at Bethany. "It all seems to be going well," he said.

"We're making progress," Bethany told him. "This production certainly won't be as polished as some of the ones I've seen back East, but we'll do our best."

"I'm sure it will go over just fine in Abilene. Now, I'd better get out of your way, so that you can get on with your rehearsing."

"Judah . . ." She spoke his name so sweetly that he stopped and turned toward her again. "Could I speak to you in your study in a short while?"

"Of course," he replied. "I'll go there now and wait for you. That's where I was headed; I've got some reading to do."

He nodded and left, but as he walked through the passage that connected the church to the parsonage, his mind was whirling. He wondered what Bethany wanted to speak with him about. Whatever it was, she could count on him for his support. She should know that by now, he thought.

Once again he could not concentrate on the task he had set for himself. He gave up, closed the book on his desk, and sat back to wait for Bethany. When she arrived some twenty minutes later, her eyes were sparkling with excitement.

"I take it the rest of the rehearsal went well?" Judah asked as she sat in the straight-backed wooden chair next to his desk.

"Very well. Of course, we've really just gotten started. There's so much left to do. You know, despite Mrs. Grafton's best efforts, some parts in the play still haven't been cast yet."

"I'm sure you'll find people to play them."

Bethany was holding one of the scripts. She leaned forward and handed it across the desk to him. "Believe it or not, we still don't have anyone to play the role of Charles Abernathy."

Judah took the script and flipped idly through the pages. "I'm not sure I remember which character he is."

"Why, his is the leading role! Charles Abernathy succumbs to the evil lure of alcohol and plunges his whole family to the brink of ruin by his weakness. It's the most important part in the play."

"And the most difficult, I'd think," Judah observed.

"Indeed. That's why we need someone special to perform the role. Judah, I want *you* to play Charles Abernathy."

Judah's head snapped up, and he stared across the desk at her, stunned. Bethany merely smiled at him. Finally, after a long moment, he stammered, "But . . . I can't . . . I simply couldn't. . . . I'm no actor!"

"You're the only man in town who has the necessary experience," she insisted, her lovely eyes imploring him.

Blanching, Judah caught his breath. Someone must

have told her about his shameful past. But surely she would not be so thoughtless as to be referring to that. "What do you mean by that?" he asked cautiously.

"You've spent years speaking in front of crowds when you deliver your sermons. You know how to make your voice fill a room. More importantly, you know how to communicate with people, to reach out and touch them with your message. You can do that with this play, if only you'll take the role of Charles Abernathy."

"I . . . I don't know what to say."

Bethany reached out, placed her hand over his, and squeezed. "Say yes!" she urged. "It would mean so much to me, Judah. I *want* this play to be successful, to really show Abilene the evils of drink!"

Judah looked into her eyes, felt the warmth of her fingers as she clutched his hand, and in that moment he knew he was lost. He would do anything she wanted him to do, and there was no point in fighting it. But he silently vowed she would never know the similarities between the fictional character she was asking him to portray and the reality of his life.

"All right," he said, a dubious smile on his face. "I suppose you've got yourself another actor."

Judah had been committing his sermons to memory for a long time, but he found that memorizing lines for a play was totally different. In a way it was easier, because there were all the cues from the dialogue with the other characters. But the emotions involved made acting more difficult. He found himself saying and doing things that he would never have said or done in real life. In the course of the play, Charles Abernathy went from a fine, upstanding citizen to a drunken lout who was quick to strike his wife and children. It was hard for Judah to even pretend to do that. The most trying scenes of all, however, were the ones in which Charles Abernathy became a hopeless drunkard.

Judah remembered all too well the dizzy euphoria that accompanied a drinking spree. He knew that the stimulation was followed by an inevitable crash. He recalled the splitting headache, the heaving stomach, the sharp pain with which the harsh daylight of countless mornings had struck his eyes. Memories of all the binges came back to him, filling his mouth with a bitter taste even as he spoke the words of the script.

"Marvelous!" Bethany had exclaimed after he played a long scene with the other cast members for the first time in rehearsal. "A superb performance, Reverend Fisher."

"Thank you, Miss Hale," Judah replied. The formality between them was for the benefit of the other performers and the people who were working behind the scenes. Any time they were alone now, they were always Judah and Bethany.

"I knew you were the perfect person to play the role," she went on. "And the rest of you were wonderful, too. I just *know* the play will be a smashing success."

Judah raised his handkerchief and mopped the perspiration from his forehead. *I should not be sweating,* he thought. It was cold outside; autumn was tightening its grip on Kansas, and while the church was warmer inside, it was not hot enough to justify such a reaction.

He knew what was causing him to sweat. He was remembering when crude, vulgar displays such as the ones put on by his character in the play had been a part of his everyday life.

He had to excuse himself then and walk quickly to

his study. As he left, he could feel Bethany's eyes following him curiously. He knew she was wondering what was wrong, and she was probably worrying that he would somehow ruin the production.

He uttered a silent prayer for strength. He *had* to get through this. After all, he had given her his word. He had to do his absolute best to carry out his promise.

As the rehearsals went on, Judah became more accustomed to his role. By the time a week had passed, he had memorized his lines and only occasionally had trouble remembering a speech. Bethany was always close by to prompt him and make helpful suggestions.

Michael Hirsch had proved to be a natural actor. In the role of Ferdinand Abernathy, Charles's son, the youngster performed well in rehearsal. The part of Heloise Abernathy, Charles's wife, was being played by a young woman named Ellen Miller. Bethany had approached Dr. Aileen Bloom about the role, but Aileen had politely declined, citing her work as being too time-consuming.

Judah knew little about drama, but he could tell that all the actors were doing their very best to make this play succeed. Mrs. Grafton came to watch the rehearsals several times, and she was as lavish in her praise as Bethany had been.

"This play will turn Abilene on its ear," she predicted boldly. "Mark my words. This town will never forget the message it will receive."

Early one morning Bethany, Judah, and Mrs. Grafton met at the church to decide upon the date of the play. After conferring for an hour they agreed to present it on the coming Saturday night. On Saturdays, the farmers, ranchers, and cowboys who lived in the outlying areas normally came into town to shop or enjoy themselves. A large crowd would be on hand to see the performance.

That gave them five days to promote the production, and Mrs. Grafton promised to have posters printed and ready by that afternoon. Judah assured the ladies that as soon as the children from the orphanage returned from school for the day, they could begin posting the handbills.

Bethany bustled out to tend to another errand. As she left, Judah thought he had never seen her look prettier. Of course, he thought that every time he saw her. He was staring after her when Mrs. Grafton said in a low voice, "Reverend, could I speak to you in private, please?"

A little surprised at the request, Judah nodded. "Certainly. Come with me."

They went to his study. As soon as Judah closed the door behind them, Mrs. Grafton began, "I hope you won't think I'm being an awful busybody, Reverend, but someone has to say something. Have you heard what Miss Hale has been doing in the evenings?"

"I know she visited a few of the saloons and caused a scene or two," Judah said as he sat down behind the desk and motioned Mrs. Grafton into a chair. "But I thought she had stopped all that to concentrate on the play."

"I only wish that were true," Mrs. Grafton said solemnly. "There haven't been any more, er . . . brawls like the one at Mr. McCarthy's tavern, but Miss Hale is still managing to stir up quite a tempest."

Judah laced his fingers together, placed his hands on the desktop, and leaned forward. "And what's wrong with that?" he wanted to know. "I thought the whole purpose of the temperance society was to let people know about the evils of drinking."

"That's true, that's true. But I'm afraid that if she continues to make trouble, the marshal may have no choice but to arrest her for disturbing the peace."

Judah sat back, shocked. "No!"

"Marshal Travis came to see me," Mrs. Grafton advised him. "He wanted to know if I was encouraging Miss Hale to disrupt the saloon trade. I told him that I certainly supported her efforts but that I was hardly ordering her to carry out any of her activities. The marshal told me that he has received numerous complaints."

"Complaints from saloonkeepers," he remarked, waving it off. "That's to be expected. They have no legal right to keep Bethany out of their places, nor can they tell her what she can say once she's there."

"But I understand that there have been several threats on her life."

That shocked Judah even more. Speechless, he stared across the desk at his visitor.

"You know I have never been one to sit back and let a wrong go unaddressed, Reverend," Mrs. Grafton went on. "I've always believed in speaking my mind and letting the chips fall where they may, as my late husband used to say. But I would hate to see anything happen to such a wonderful young woman as Miss Hale. I thought perhaps you could talk to her. . . ."

"And tell her what?" Judah asked. "Give up her crusade? I can't do that, Mrs. Grafton. It would break Bethany's heart."

He saw immediately that Mrs. Grafton had noticed his use of Bethany's first name, but she did not comment on it. Instead she said, "It will do more good in the long run to show people the error of their ways by means of this play. That's what Miss Hale should be doing. I just thought she might take it more kindly from you instead of me."

Slowly Judah nodded. "I'll have to think about this, Mrs. Grafton. I'd rather Miss Hale didn't expose herself to those sordid places, either, but she has a mind of her own, as you well know."

"Indeed." Mrs. Grafton stood up. "Well, Reverend, I just wanted you to know."

"And I appreciate it." He pushed his chair back. "Here, let me show you out."

"Never mind, I know the way. Good day, Reverend."

Judah said his farewells and sank down in his chair as Mrs. Grafton shut the door behind her. Closing his eyes, he lifted a hand and massaged his temples. More than once he too had thought that Bethany was doing the wrong thing in visiting the saloons, but it was difficult to change her mind once she started on something. But if there were as many hard feelings around town as Mrs. Grafton had hinted, it became even more important that Bethany use some common sense. Judah decided he would talk with her, but he was not convinced it would alter her plans.

He was still sitting there, mulling the matter over, when there was a knock at the door. Absently he called, "Come in," then straightened abruptly when he realized it might be Bethany.

Instead, the broad-shouldered form of Orion McCarthy stepped into the minister's study. With a grin, Orion said, "Good day t'ye, Rev'rend." The brawny tavern keeper was carrying a large crate, its contents clinking faintly as he entered the room.

"Why, hello, Orion," Judah replied, surprised to see

the Scotsman. "What are you doing here? I don't believe I've ever seen you at the church before."

"I ain't much of a church-going man, Rev'rend, ye know. But I like t'think the Good Lord and me are on pretty good terms." Orion hefted the box in his arms. "I brought ye something t'help out wi' tha' play ye be doing." He put the box on the desk and lifted the lid.

Judah peered in and saw that it contained two dozen empty whiskey bottles adorned with many different labels. From the way they glistened in the light from the window, they had apparently been washed and dried, and each bottle had a cork in its neck.

"I . . . I don't understand," Judah began.

"Ye kinna have a play 'bout drinking wi' no whiskey bottles," Orion said. "So I want t'give ye these empties."

In the rehearsals they had been using other kinds of empty bottles as props during the drinking scenes, but the real thing would give the performance an air of authenticity. Judah nodded. "Thank you, Orion. These will come in handy."

"I figgered ye could fill them wi' tea or some such, t'make it look real." Orion held up a blunt finger. "There is one condition t'this gift, Rev'rend."

"Oh? And that is?"

"Tha' ye dinna tell anyone where ye got these bottles. I got a reputation in this town t'consider, dinna ye know?"

Judah laughed. "All right, Orion. Agreed. No one will know where they came from." He extended his hand to the big tavern keeper. "Thank you."

"Ye be most welcome," Orion said as he returned the handshake. "Now I best be going, a'fore somebody sees me here."

When Orion had gone, Judah sat down at the desk and plucked one of the bottles from the box. He pulled the cork from its neck and lifted it to his nose. There was no scent of whiskey clinging to it, and the bottle smelled clean as well. It was just a plain glass vessel with a hint of amber in its color.

But as Judah's fingers slid over its cool smoothness and then traced the lettering on the label, he felt something clutching at his insides. His breathing quickened, and his pulse pounded in his head.

He had guzzled whiskey out of dozens, maybe hundreds, of bottles just like this one. And as he all but caressed the bottle, the realization burst clearly in his mind—the craving was still there. God, he wanted a drink!

He thrust the bottle back in the box and closed his eyes, feeling sweat pop out on his forehead. And once more he offered up a prayer for strength.

He was going to need all the help he could get.

Chapter Six

JUDAH FISHER HAD HEARD THE EXPRESSION *BUTTERFLIES in his stomach* before, but he had never really understood it until tonight. The performance of *Adrift and Astray,* by the immortal Florence Singleton Weems, was only an hour away, and he was so nervous he was pacing restlessly back and forth in his study.

He had delivered countless sermons, before audiences both large and small, but he had never felt this apprehensive about any of them. As he had learned over the last couple of weeks, acting was very different from preaching.

During the last few days, rehearsals had been held at the courthouse, where tonight's performance would take place. The sets were finished, all the props in place—including the mock barroom with its shelf full of whiskey bottles Orion McCarthy had anonymously provided.

Bethany had wanted to know where Judah had gotten the bottles, but he honored his promise to Orion and kept secret the donor's name. Judah thought bringing the bottles to the church had been a noble gesture on Orion's part, considering the fracas that Bethany had started at his tavern—not to mention the bloody nose he had suffered in the fight.

Judah thought last night's dress rehearsal had gone well. The cast seemed to know their lines, and the backstage crew did a good job of switching the scenery between acts. For a group of amateurs, they were going to put on a good show. Bethany had obviously studied stagecraft. Even if she had not admitted that doing this morality play was not a spur-of-the-moment idea, he would have suspected it anyway. He had a feeling that Miss Bethany Hale usually knew exactly what she was doing.

Judah felt so confident of the other members of the troupe that he knew he had no reason to be so nervous. He should be looking forward to the performance, to making Bethany proud of him as he helped to bring her message to the people of Abilene.

Instead, his hand was trembling as he lifted it to wipe the sweat from his brow. He knew what was wrong; he just did not want to admit it, even to himself.

Throughout the rehearsals, each time he raised a whiskey bottle to his lips to swallow some of the weak tea, he wished it were the real thing. Nor had the problem gotten better with time, as he hoped it would. In fact with each passing day the cravings got stronger.

He had been so distracted by these unsettling impulses that he forgot his promise to Mrs. Grafton and neglected to speak to Bethany about her saloon visits. But he knew that she had stopped them of her own accord, so that she could devote more time to getting ready for the play. She was usually at the church or the courthouse in the evenings, and Judah had escorted her back to the hotel every night when the rehearsals were over.

Once or twice when they parted company, he sensed that she would not mind if he kissed her or at least took her hand for a moment. But so far he had done neither. They were friendly, could laugh and talk about almost any subject, but Judah still held back, even though he later regretted the missed opportunities. Perhaps tonight, after the play was over and had been a rousing success . . . Yes, that would be the time to kiss her, especially if he had given a good performance.

Judah stopped pacing. He would not remember his lines if he did not calm down, he told himself sternly. He had to do something to settle his nerves.

Turning, he went to his desk and opened the bottom drawer. He held his breath as he reached inside and brought out a dark-brown glass pint bottle.

The blood pounded in Judah's head. Several months ago he had taken the bottle of whiskey away from a drunken cowboy who wandered into services one Sunday and started to disrupt the sermon. Judah took the puncher aside and had a few words with him. Shamed, the cowboy handed over the bottle and then sat contritely in one of the front pews during Judah's message. He never would have suspected that a preacher would threaten to thrash the living daylights out of him if he did not behave. The possibility quickly sobered him up.

Judah had intended to pour out the whiskey and throw the bottle away after the service, but instead he stuck it in his desk drawer for some reason. Now he could not even remember what that reason had been. Perhaps he had not wanted to handle the whiskey any more than he had to. In any case, he was glad that it was still there.

One little sip would not hurt, he decided. If anything, it would help. The liquor might settle his nerves, and it would also serve as a reminder of the days when he had been a slave to the stuff. He could draw on those memories in his portrayal of Charles Abernathy. He was only doing this for the good of the play. Judah pulled the cork, lifted the bottle to his lips, tilted back his head. He drank, long and deep.

We're going to have a large crowd, Bethany Hale thought as she edged the makeshift curtain aside and peeked out at the audience gathering in the courthouse. People were still coming in, and the chairs were filling up fast.

A rough, small stage had been erected at the front of the room and a curtain strung in front of it. The rest of the hall had been filled with chairs, as many as could be found. Bethany estimated that, with the space at the back for standing room, an audience of several hundred could pack the courthouse to see the performance.

Anticipation and anxiety vied within her, with anticipation triumphing. Tonight, she would reach more people with her message than ever before, and her crusade would win many converts. At least she prayed that it would.

But where was Judah?

All the cast members were there except the minister. All were ready to take their places, and the people working behind the scenes were also prepared. But Judah had not arrived, and the play could not begin without him. The first scene was one of domestic bliss and tranquillity in the Abernathy household, before it was torn apart forever by the specter of liquor. In fact, Judah spoke the opening lines.

Mrs. Grafton bustled up to Bethany. "Oh, my dear, I'm so excited," she gushed. "This is going to be the most important night in the history of our little society. Isn't it time to start?"

Bethany nodded. "Very soon. We're waiting for Judah."

"Well, he had best arrive soon. That audience will get impatient in a hurry. They came to see a show, and they expect it to start on time, even if they didn't have to pay an admission charge."

Bethany peeked through the curtain again and studied the audience. Quite a few townspeople were in attendance, as were a large number of cowhands from the surrounding ranches. She also noticed railroad workers, farmers, and other rugged types crowding into the large room. Most of them had postponed their Saturday night drinking for a couple of hours to see the play, and they would demand to be entertained. Bethany knew their sort quite well; that was why the advertising posters for the play had emphasized its drama, pathos, and scandal.

She let the tiny gap in the curtain sag shut as the murmuring from the crowd seemed to grow slightly louder. "You're right," Bethany said, turning to Mrs. Grafton once more. "Perhaps I'd better go look for Judah and make sure nothing's happened to him."

She started toward the rear door of the courthouse, but before she reached it, it suddenly opened. Judah Fisher stepped inside and let the cold wind slam the door behind him. He was wearing his own dark, conservative suit, which would serve as the costume for Charles Abernathy during the opening scenes, before he began his descent into the besotted state of the later acts. But he had no hat, and Bethany was surprised that he had ridden bareheaded from the church on such a cold night.

No matter, she told herself. He was here now, and that was all that counted. Quickly she came up to him and said, "Hello, Reverend Fisher. We were beginning to worry about you."

"Nothing to worry about," he said breezily, a smile appearing on his lips. "I'm here, aren't I?"

"Yes, but it's time to start the play—"

"Then let's get on with it, shall we?" He started to stride toward the armchair in the middle of the stage where he would be sitting when the curtain opened. But before he reached the chair, he turned and said to Bethany, "Aren't you going to wish me good luck?"

"Of course. Good luck, Judah."

She had called him Judah. It was out in the open for everyone to hear. Perhaps he would take that for what it was, a sign of how she felt about him. It might spur him to give his best performance.

Judah stumbled on his way to the chair. Bethany frowned slightly but did not have time to worry, because everyone else was in place and waiting for her command to begin. She nodded to the actors, then scurried off the stage, gesturing to two teenaged boys from the orphanage who were in charge of the curtain. They began pulling it open, and a round of applause came from the eager audience.

Judah sat in the chair, waiting for the clapping to stop. When it did, he looked to his left offstage and called, "Oh, Ferdinand, bring me my newspaper like a good lad, will you?"

Is there something wrong with his voice? Bethany

asked herself. The words came out plainly, but he was speaking a little slower and not as precisely as he had during the rehearsals. Not surprisingly, Judah had the best diction among any of the amateur actors. Speaking before a crowd *was* part of his job.

Michael Hirsch hurried onto the stage, bringing a folded newspaper with him. "Here you are, Father," he said as he handed it to Judah.

Ellen Miller, in the role of Heloise Abernathy, entered on Judah's right. She carried a pipe and gave it to him as she spoke her first line. "And how was your day, dear?"

Judah reached for the pipe but suddenly fumbled it, almost dropping it. He recovered quickly but then looked around for a second, blinking rapidly. Bethany realized he was flustered and had forgotten his line. She was about to hiss the first few words when his face brightened. "Just fine, my darling," he intoned. "How could it be anything else when I can look forward to coming home to you and dear little Ferdinand?"

Bethany heaved a sigh of relief. Judah still did not sound quite right, but at least he had remembered his line before she had to prompt him. During the next few minutes, she saw that he seemed to be in the flow of the script.

Then he stumbled again as he moved from one side of the stage to the other. That uncertainty was not like him, Bethany thought. Still, she had heard it was not uncommon for actors to get very nervous during a performance, no matter how good they were during rehearsals. That was probably all it was, she told herself, just a case of nerves.

During a brief pause between scenes, Bethany hurried over and asked, "Judah, are you all right?"

"Certainly I'm all right," he snapped. "You're not going to hold one or two mistakes against me, are you?" He pulled a handkerchief from his pocket and mopped the sweat from his face.

"Of course not. I'm just worried about you. You don't seem quite yourself."

Judah laughed harshly. "I'm not myself. I'm Charles Abernathy, remember?" Then he turned abruptly and stalked away to take his place for the next scene.

As this scene began, Bethany moved to the far edge of the curtain and peered at the audience again. Mrs. Grafton and the other members of Abilene's temperance society were in the front rows. Bethany spotted the distinctive habit of the Dominican nun, who was speaking with the young Dr. Aileen Bloom. To her surprise, Orion McCarthy was sitting with them. But Joselyn Paige was not with him. Nor did she see either of Abilene's lawmen. She had thought Cody Fisher might attend, since his brother was playing the lead.

But not playing it well, Bethany realized glumly as the performance went on. Judah was having trouble, tangling both his feet and his lines several times. But somehow he always recovered, sometimes remembering what he was supposed to say, occasionally departing from the script and ad-libbing his way out of trouble. Bethany watched, gnawing her lower lip and wondering what had happened to him. During the rehearsals he had been so determined to give a good performance.

As the first act progressed, he avoided her during the scene breaks, and Bethany's concern grew. Perhaps he was ill, she thought. She wished he would just tell her what was wrong.

The final scene of Act One took place inside a room where Abernathy and some new cronies he had met in the course of his business were playing cards. The script called for one of the men to bring out a bottle and pass it around, but as Bethany watched in amazement, Judah reached into his coat and drew out a small, dark-brown bottle. Bethany did not recognize it as one of the props they had been using. Judah pulled the cork from its neck with his teeth, spit it out dramatically, and lifted the bottle to his mouth. Liquid gurgled out of it. He took a long swallow, then thumped it down on the tabletop and glared at the other actors as if daring them to take it away from him.

Bewildered, the men looked at each other, then tried to play the scene as it was written, ignoring the bottle that Judah had brought out. However, when the prop bottle of tea was offered to him, he shook his head and took another sip from his own bottle. As the scene ended, he got to his feet, headed for the side of the stage, and stumbled again, almost falling.

Bethany, her face a mask of horror and anger, all but ran to him once the curtain was closed. When she reached his side, she clutched at his sleeve. "Wait, Judah!" she exclaimed.

He jerked around to face her. "Leave me alone!" he snapped. "I'll be fine. I'll get through the play. Just . . . leave me alone."

Bethany stepped back, recoiling from his sour, whiskey-laden breath. What she had suspected was true! Judah was drinking real liquor during the play. Worse than that, he had obviously been drinking even before the performance began. Now he was drunk.

If it had not been so awful, Bethany might have

laughed at the ironic situation. The leading actor in a temperance play—drunk!

"Oh, Judah," she wailed. "How could you?"

He smiled bitterly at her. "You wanted a morality play, didn't you, my dear? You wanted to teach all the frontier bumpkins about the evils of drink? Well, now you have what you wanted! Witness, my friends, the destruction of a man by Satan's potion!"

He had raised his voice, and everyone backstage was staring at him. Bethany prayed that the audience could not hear his drunken ravings through the closed curtain. If she was going to salvage this performance, she had to do something quickly.

Judah still held the liquor bottle. Moving too quickly for him to react, she reached out and plucked it from his grip, then in the same motion turned and flung it toward the rear wall of the building. It shattered, splashing what was left of its contents over the wall. As Bethany whirled to face him, she saw Judah gaping at her.

"You listen to me, Judah Fisher," she said in a low, urgent voice. "You are not going to ruin this play, do you hear me? I will not allow it! You're a fine, decent man, a minister, one of God's chosen servants. You are not going to do this, do you understand?"

For a moment, as his face twisted in a grimace, she thought he might strike her, but then a great shudder went through him and he took a deep, ragged breath. "You're right," he agreed slowly. "You're absolutely right, Miss Hale. And you have my apologies. I will . . . will persevere to the best of my abilities."

Bethany drew a deep breath, too. "Thank you, Judah," she murmured. "I know you won't let me down." She looked around, saw that everyone was waiting for them before resuming the performance. Bethany put a hand on Judah's arm and gently steered him back to his place for the opening of the next scene. Then she nodded grimly to the others and moved offstage.

She prayed they would get through it. That was all she wanted now, just to be done with this play. Once it was finished, she could give the short lecture she had prepared, and this evening would be over.

Bethany saw that Judah made a valiant effort to shake off the effects of the alcohol, but he was only partially successful. He still stumbled, still forgot his lines. But at least he did not seem to be getting any worse. The audience might not even be aware of what was going on, she thought. Judah's missteps and misstatements might be interpreted as part of the play. The audience seemed to be laughing and booing in the right places. As the play grew more and more poignant, several spectators began to cry.

Bethany began to hope that they would actually get through the performance without any catastrophes. That was a far cry from the thrilling success she had anticipated, but it was about the best she could wish for now. And when this was all over, she was going to have a long, angry talk with Reverend Judah Fisher.

Standing in the back of the room with his arms crossed as he leaned against the wall, Cody Fisher watched the performance and wondered what was wrong with his brother.

Cody had arrived just before the play started, slipping in and finding a spot where he could see the stage. Irked because Bethany seemed to prefer Judah's company to his, he had planned not to come, but at the last minute his curiosity had gotten the best of him.

Early in the performance he sensed that something was bothering Judah. At first he attributed it to the fact that Judah was playing a role; he was not supposed to sound like himself. But there were just too many slips, too many pauses when Judah was obviously trying to remember what he was supposed to say next. If Cody had not known better, he would have said that Judah was drunk.

During the break between Acts One and Two, Cody heard a loud voice backstage that sounded like Judah's. That was followed a moment later by the sound of breaking glass. He started toward the stage to see if there was any trouble, but then he hesitated. If Bethany needed help, she could come and ask for it, he decided. He was not going to poke his nose in where it was not wanted.

As the play went on, Judah looked more and more haggard, and Cody grew increasingly uneasy. It certainly looked as though Judah had started drinking again—or he was the best actor Abilene had ever seen, not that that would take much. But Cody did not think Judah was acting.

He was sure now that his brother had fallen off the wagon, gone back to the way he had been in the dark days after their father had been murdered. Cody watched grimly and shook his head. He would have to have a long talk with Judah and try to straighten him out. Chances were he would not take too kindly to that, but somebody had to do it.

The play ended with Charles Abernathy still a broken man, still a drunkard, but vowing to change with the help of his family. It was a conclusion full of hope, if not fulfillment. The audience applauded enthusiastically as the curtain was closed for the final time. They stayed in their seats, expecting the cast to come out for another round of applause, but instead Bethany Hale parted the curtain and stepped in front of it alone. She walked to the center of the stage, faced the audience, and began to speak.

"Thank you for coming to see tonight's performance of *Adrift and Astray*. As you know, this play was sponsored by the Abilene Temperance Society and put on with its support. For those of you who don't know me, my name is Bethany Hale. I am visiting your city on behalf of the Christian Ladies Temperance Society, a national organization dedicated to the eradication of liquor and its evil consequences."

Most of the audience listened attentively, but some of the cowhands began to laugh when she mentioned doing away with liquor. Bethany ignored the distraction and continued with her speech, launching into a condemnation of alcohol and everything associated with it. The cowhands' muttering and laughter grew louder.

Cody frowned. The cowboys had not minded sitting through the play, preachy though it had been, but they were not likely to sit there for long and let someone tell them how wrong they were to drink—even if the someone doing the telling was a pretty young woman like Bethany.

One of the punchers suddenly stood up and called out, "Honey, if I give up booze, will you go walkin' in the moonlight with me?" His companions laughed raucously.

Bethany flushed but said, "I can tell you this, sir. No

decent young lady would want to be your companion when you are in a besotted state."

"Shoot, I never said I was interested in decent young ladies, gal!"

Mrs. Grafton stood up and, turning around, glared at the cowboy. "Sit down, you lout!" she commanded. "Let Miss Hale speak."

"Who you callin' names, lady?" he shot back. His friends supported him with catcalls.

Now several other members of the local temperance society turned in their seats and began to rail at the cowhands. Two young men stood up to join their companion. The three of them ignored the scolding of the temperance ladies and called ribald questions to Bethany. She stood on the stage, silent and blushing furiously, obviously mortified.

"Why don't you ruffians just leave?" Mrs. Grafton demanded, shaking her purse at the three troublesome cowhands.

"Shut your trap, you old bat!" the leader shouted at her. "I'll tell you what you can do with your damned play!"

An offended uproar from some of the townsmen drowned out most of the cowboy's obscene suggestion. Several men who were seated around the cowhands surged to their feet, fists clenched. It was clear that within minutes there would be a brawl.

Cody had watched long enough—too long, really, he thought. He should have stepped in and broken this up when the first cowhand stood and taunted Bethany. But he had wanted to see how she would handle it. If she insisted on trying to wipe out liquor, she would encounter this kind of opposition everywhere she went.

So far, Bethany had not done anything but stand in the center of the stage, lips pressed tightly together, while the uproar grew louder and potentially more violent.

Finally she raised her voice and cried, "Please! Please stop arguing, everyone! There's no need for this!" It was hard to hear her over the angry din, but after a few moments the audience quieted down somewhat.

Bethany took a deep breath and went on, "You see, this is just the kind of thing I've been talking about. There wouldn't have been an argument in here tonight if those men had not been drinking." She leveled a finger at the three cowboys, who were still on their feet.

"That's a damned lie!" their spokesman protested. "We just don't want some little chippy comin' in here and tellin' us how to live!"

Cody shouldered his way forward. He would give the three cowboys a choice—settle down and get out, or go to jail. But before he could reach them, the curtain on the stage was suddenly pushed aside, and a tall figure bounded out. Judah leapt off the platform and headed toward the cowboys. In three quick strides he was standing in front of them. His fists were clenched, and he said between gritted teeth, "You can't say that about Miss Hale, you . . . you . . ."

Judah had had little experience in cursing. Unable to find the word he wanted, he did the next best thing.

Cody saw his brother's shoulder drop and knew what was about to happen. He yelled, "Hold it!" but he was too late. Judah's fist was already smashing into the cowhand's face. The young man fell back against his friends, who caught him before he could drop to

114

the floor. The cowboy staggered to his feet, shaking his head, then howled furiously and flung a punch at Judah.

Judah tried to get out of the way, but the liquor had slowed his reflexes. The blow clipped his chin and jerked his head around. As he lurched backward, several townsmen leapt to his aid, throwing themselves at the cowboys with fists doubled.

A hard hand clamped down on Cody's arm. Spinning around, the deputy looked into the grim face of Luke Travis. "You intend to let them beat each other to a pulp before you do anything about this?" the marshal asked sharply.

Cody shook his head. He slipped his Colt from its holster and said, "Nope, I reckon I'll stop it right now."

He aimed the barrel at the ceiling and triggered two shots. The gunfire boomed deafeningly in the close quarters. A stunned silence fell over the crowd, and fists froze in uplifted positions before punches could be thrown. Cody strode forward, his gun still in his hand. "All right, that'll be enough!" he cried.

Travis, his Peacemaker drawn, moved right behind him. "Break it up!" he called. "The show's over, so you folks might as well go on home."

From the stage, Bethany protested, "But, Marshal, I was just starting my discussion—"

Travis shook his head. "There won't be any discussion tonight, miss. I won't have a brawl in the courthouse. Everybody go home."

There was some muttering, but the audience seemed glad to be able to leave without having to listen to the rest of Bethany's talk. Within moments, most of them had filed out of the room. The three cowhands who had harassed Bethany tried to leave with the others, but Travis stopped them with a gesture of his Peacemaker.

"I've had trouble with you and your friends before, Stoddard," he said to the leader. "I'm not sure how this started, but I'll bet you had something to do with it. Stay out of trouble for the rest of the night, or you'll have to explain to your boss why you missed a few days' work while you were sitting in jail. Understand?"

"Sure," Stoddard muttered in surly tones. "Is that all, Marshal?"

"That's all."

The cowboys went out, still looking angry.

Cody turned to Travis. "I didn't think you were coming tonight."

"I didn't come to see the play," the marshal replied. "I was just taking a turn along the street when I heard the yelling. You should have made sure things didn't get this far out of hand, Cody."

"I know. Sorry, Marshal," Cody agreed with a curt nod.

Travis shook his head and started toward the stage, where Bethany still stood, her shoulders sagging. As Cody followed Travis, he felt sorry for her. The evening had gone badly; she had seen her grandiose plans go up in smoke.

"Miss Hale," Travis greeted her, touching the brim of his hat. "I'm sorry I had to call off the rest of your meeting, but some folks were liable to get hurt. Those cowboys can be pretty hotheaded."

"They were drunk," Bethany said contemptuously.

"No, ma'am, I don't think so. They might've had a drink or two earlier this evening, but I imagine they were putting off their serious drinking until after the play."

"They had been guzzling whiskey. You could tell from the way they acted." Bethany sounded completely sure of herself.

"I won't argue that with you, ma'am." Travis's voice was flat and hard. "But I will ask you not to stir up any more trouble while you're in Abilene."

"Me stir up trouble?" Bethany exclaimed, incredulous. "Why, Marshal, anyone can see that liquor was to blame for all of this evening's problems, not anything I did."

"Just remember what I said." Travis turned away with a weary shake of his head. He moved past Cody and headed for the door. Orion, Sister Laurel, and Dr. Aileen Bloom joined him.

Cody watched them leave the building, and then he faced Bethany. "I'm sorry things turned out this way, Miss Hale," he began. "I reckon we all told you it'd be hard convincing folks around here that drinking is bad."

"Perhaps you did, Deputy," Bethany replied tightly. "Nevertheless, I have to continue with my mission. As long as I have men like your brother to help me—" She broke off abruptly, and Cody remembered the way Judah had helped her tonight. From the anxious look on her face, Bethany was recalling the same thing.

Cody glanced around. "Where is Judah, anyway?" he asked. "He was here just a few minutes ago; he launched that punch at Stoddard."

Bethany looked around the hall and began to frown. "I—I don't see him," she stammered. "I thought he was right here."

But it quickly became obvious that Judah was not in the building. He had vanished in the uproar of the near-brawl.

Cody remembered the state his brother had been in and began to worry even more. "I'll find him," he grimly told Bethany, and then he turned and stalked out.

Chapter Seven

———◆———

CODY FISHER STEPPED OUT OF THE COURTHOUSE AND was stung by the night's bitter wind. Buttoning his jacket tightly, he pulled up his collar, jammed his hat firmly on his head, and strode down the long courthouse path and onto Texas Street. He spent the next hour combing the saloons and streets of Abilene searching for his brother. Finding no sign of him, he grew increasingly anxious and decided to ride out to the Calvary Methodist Church to see if Judah had slipped past him and gone back to the parsonage.

During the performance Agnes Hirsch had stayed at the orphanage to take care of the children who were too young to attend. When she told Cody that she had not seen Judah since he left for the courthouse several hours earlier, he became even more concerned. As unlikely as it seemed, his brother had vanished.

Thanking Agnes but keeping his worry to himself, he rode back downtown.

As he approached the marshal's office, he saw Travis standing in the glow of lantern light talking to two people. Cody made out the figures of Orion McCarthy and the lady gambler, Joselyn Paige. Orion was nodding and rumbled, "Aye, Lucas," as Cody reined in and dismounted. But before Cody could join them, Orion took Joselyn's arm and started down the boardwalk toward his tavern.

Cody stepped onto the boardwalk and nodded toward the retreating couple. "What was that about?"

Travis did not answer; instead he asked, "Have any luck?"

"I can't find Judah anywhere," Cody replied anxiously. "I'm worried, Marshal. I think he's been drinking, and you know what that means."

"It's not good, not for him," Travis agreed. "But I imagine he'll turn up. He's probably either too sick or too ashamed to show his face."

"I hope you're right."

Travis inclined his head toward the office door. "Come on inside and have some coffee," he offered soothingly. "That was probably a cold ride back from the church."

Cody admitted that it had been and followed Travis into the office. The sound of stentorian snoring rumbled from the open cellblock door, and Cody, forgetting his concern, began to grin. "Sounds like we've got a guest," he quipped.

"Nestor," Travis remarked with a snort. "He was down at the Bull's Head getting drunk and telling his stories about the old days when he trapped beaver with Kit Carson and hunted buffalo with Bill Cody. Some young puncher told him he was just an old windbag, and Nestor took exception—to the tune of a couple of busted ribs."

Cody let out a low whistle. "Is the cowboy going to press charges?"

"No, I don't think so. Aileen patched him up. He was drunk, too, and when he sobered up some, he said it was his own fault. He knew better than to argue with Nestor. But I thought it might be a good idea for the old boy to sleep it off in a cell tonight. Keep him from getting into any more trouble."

Cody nodded solemnly. Travis's recounting of Nestor Gilworth's latest antics had distracted him briefly, but now his worry about Judah returned to gnaw at him. He knew Travis was right, however; they could do nothing but wait for Judah to show up.

Telling himself to relax, Cody poured a cup of coffee. Then he sat in one of the straight-backed chairs and tilted it against the wall as he sipped the strong, steaming brew. Travis settled down at the desk to do some paperwork. In another hour or so, Cody realized, it would be time to make the final rounds for the night. Travis often handled that chore alone and did not mind doing it, but if Cody did not do something to distract himself, he would only get more and more agitated about Judah.

Luke Travis, breaking the uneasy silence that had reigned over the office for several long minutes, asked abruptly, "Has that temperance gal told you how long she intends to stay in Abilene?"

Cody shook his head. "Judah's the one she talks to, Marshal, not me."

"Well, she's been stirring up trouble ever since she got here. I reckon Judah likes her, but I won't be sorry to see her go."

"Judah likes her, all right," Cody agreed. "But I don't know how she'll feel about him after tonight."

The two lawmen passed more time in silence; only the scratching of Travis's pen and an occasional crackle from one of the logs burning in the stove intruded on the quiet.

In the soothing warmth of the still office, Cody began to doze. Shaking himself awake, he stood up to get more coffee, hoping it would ward off the weariness. He was reaching for the pot when he heard running footsteps pounding on the boardwalk outside. Just as he turned toward the door, it burst open.

A cowhand, a long bloody scratch vividly marking his cheek, stumbled into the office. "Marshal!" he exclaimed. "They're bustin' the place up good! You'd better go stop 'em 'fore somebody gets hurt bad!"

Travis, his face an unreadable mask, rose from his chair in a single smooth motion. "Slow down, mister!" he rapped. "Now tell me what's going on. Who's busting things up, and where?"

As the cowboy took a deep breath, Cody realized that he was one of the three men who had been harassing Bethany during her talk. "It's Stoddard and Dowling," the man panted. "We all went down to Earl's place, and I reckon they got too likkered up. Stoddard wanted to fight ever'body in the place. He give me this when I tried to stop him." He gestured at the wound on his face.

"All right," Travis snapped. Moving from behind the desk, he strode toward the line of pegs next to the door and grabbed his hat and coat. "Come on, Cody. Looks like Nestor's going to have some company." To the cowboy, he said, "How come you didn't jump in there with your pards?"

The puncher shook his head. "I like a drink as much

as anybody, Marshal, but Stoddard and Dowling really tied one on. And they're downright crazy when they get too much whiskey. I just hope Stoddard don't shoot 'fore you get there! They ain't bad fellas, really. I'd hate to see 'em hang."

Cody had slipped on his hat and jacket, and he was right behind Travis when the marshal stepped onto the boardwalk. Travis's horse was tethered to the hitchrack next to Cody's. Jerking the reins loose, both men mounted quickly and kicked their horses into a brisk trot, leaving the cowboy standing on the boardwalk.

Within minutes, they were reining in in front of Earl's disreputable saloon. As they dismounted, they could hear the crash of men fighting and furniture breaking inside the place. It sounded as though a battle was going on. Both lawmen had their hands on their guns as they pushed aside the canvas that covered the entrance.

Cody saw a flicker of movement out of the corner of his eye and ducked to avoid a flying chair. The chair hit the wall, inches from where his head had been, and splintered into kindling. Travis gestured with his Peacemaker. With a nod Cody followed his orders and moved around the left side of the room. The marshal went to the right, and the two lawmen flanked the knot of men struggling in the center. A nervous Earl was crouching behind the bar, his head bobbing up and down as debris flew at him, while an aging bar girl stood screaming in one corner.

Suddenly the lantern light flickered on steel in the middle of the fight. Travis darted toward the flash, raising his Colt as he lunged. The barrel thudded against the skull of the cowboy called Stoddard just as he tried to bring his own gun to bear on one of his opponents. Stoddard stiffened, gave a groan, and slumped to the sawdust-covered floor.

Cody, seeing the other man, Dowling, reaching for his gun, flung out his left hand and grasped his wrist before the draw could be completed. As the deputy moved in, the five other men who had been brawling fell back. Dowling tried to jerk free, but Cody managed to spin him around.

The deputy had not pulled his Colt, so his right hand was free. He clenched it and hammered Dowling's beard-stubbled face. The powerful blow—a short right cross—snapped Dowling's head around. Cody hooked a boot around the man's ankle and gave him a shove, grabbing the butt of Dowling's holstered gun at the same time. The weapon slid out of the holster as Dowling toppled heavily. He lay on the floor and shook his head groggily as Cody covered him with his own gun.

"All right," Travis announced in a hard voice. "It's all over."

Earl poked his head up over the bar and shouted, "I want those bastards arrested, Marshal! Look what they did to my place!"

Glancing around, Cody surveyed the wreckage and saw a couple of broken tables. Travis nodded. "They'll have to pay the damages, all right, and a fine, too." He looked at Dowling and went on, "Get up, mister. You're going to have to haul your friend down to the jail."

Dowling opened his mouth as if to protest, but when he looked at Travis's stern face, he swallowed hard and was silent. He staggered to his feet, then grabbed Stoddard under the arms and pulled him up. Stoddard moaned and sagged against him.

Travis scooped Stoddard's fallen gun from the floor,

then gestured with it toward the doorway. "Get moving," he ordered Dowling.

"What about those damages, Marshal?" Earl called out.

"You'll have to wait until the hearing," Travis told him over his shoulder.

The saloonkeeper was grumbling as Travis and Cody, prodding Dowling and Stoddard in front of them, left the ramshackle tavern. The lawmen mounted up and walked their horses slowly behind the prisoners as they went back to Texas Street. Stoddard was barely conscious, and Dowling wound up half carrying him most of the way.

By the time they reached the office, the cowboy who had brought word of the fight was gone. Cody figured he had headed back to the ranch where Stoddard, Dowling, and he worked.

Nestor Gilworth was still snoring when they took the prisoners inside. Stoddard's senses were returning, and he protested loudly as they ushered him into the cellblock. "You can't put us in there with Nestor! That buffalo coat of his stinks worse'n anything I ever smelled."

"Reckon you'll just have to get used to it, Stoddard," Travis snapped. "I warned you about causing more trouble tonight. You didn't have to get drunk and start a fight."

"Hell, it weren't much of a fight. You had no call to break it up."

Travis slammed the cell door shut. "You were about to start shooting folks."

Dowling grinned from inside the enclosure. "Yeah, but ol' Stoddard here was too drunk to hit anybody, Marshal. It woulda been blind luck if anybody'd got hurt."

"Been known to happen," Travis said dryly. "You men sleep it off. In the morning we'll talk about damages and your fine with the judge."

Cody looked at the night's prisoners and smiled to himself. Stoddard and Dowling both sat down on the cell's single bunk and put their hands to their heads. They had consumed enough liquor to guarantee that they would have powerful headaches by morning. In the cell next to them, Nestor continued to snore.

Cody shut the cellblock door and followed Travis into the office. They hung up their hats and coats, and Cody went to the stove to pour a fresh cup of coffee. "You know, maybe Miss Hale's right," he said over his shoulder. "Maybe folks would be better off if they just gave up drinking."

"Might help," Travis grunted. "But it wouldn't get rid of all the trouble in the world, and you know it, Cody. High-spirited young cowboys like those two in there would find some way of raising hell, even if there was no such thing as whiskey."

"I suppose so," Cody said. He sat back down in the chair against the wall and propped his feet up on the desk.

Travis tried to return to his paperwork, but he seemed to have trouble concentrating. Finally he put his pen back in the inkwell and said, "Come on, Cody. We might as well make the last rounds for the night."

"Sure thing," Cody replied, getting up and reaching for his hat. He was closer to the door than Travis, so he was the one who grasped the knob and opened it. As the door swung back, he heard someone standing outside utter a startled gasp. Surprised himself, Cody stopped and peered at the pretty features of Bethany Hale.

"What are you doing here?" he asked abruptly, not caring that he did not sound very polite.

"I'm sorry, Deputy. I was just about to knock when you opened the door."

That explained her wide-eyed look, but not the reason she was standing in front of the marshal's office this late on a cold night. She had on a fur-lined jacket, and a small hat was perched on top of her brown curls.

Cody did not reply but simply stared at her until she went on nervously, "I wanted to know if you had found Judah. I . . . I thought he might come to the hotel to see me, but the clerk says he hasn't been there."

Cody shook his head, his concern for Judah returning. "He hasn't turned up," he said. "I reckon he's all right, though. Judah knows how to take care of himself."

At least he does when he hasn't been drinking, Cody added silently.

"I feel as if this is all my fault," Bethany said mournfully.

Cody did not admit that he agreed with her. Instead he stepped back and said, "Why don't you come on in for a minute, maybe have some coffee and warm up? Then I'll walk you back to the hotel."

Bethany hesitated, then nodded. "That sounds nice," she mumbled, stepping into the office. Cody closed the door behind her. She looked over at Travis and nodded nervously. "Marshal."

"Miss Hale," Travis greeted her noncommittally. He had his hat and coat on and was ready to make his rounds, so he moved past Cody and Bethany toward the door. To Cody, he said, "I'll go ahead and take a turn around town."

"All right, Marshal."

Before Travis had opened the door, a moan came from the cellblock. The pained sound was plainly audible over the rumble of Nestor's snoring. Travis glanced at Cody and said, "Stoddard or Dowling must be having trouble."

"I'll check on them," Cody offered, tossing his hat on a peg as he went to the cellblock door. He stepped inside and saw Stoddard reclining on the bunk, his head in his hands. Dowling sat on the cold stone floor, his head sagging between his knees. He looked up as Cody entered the cellblock, and Stoddard moaned again.

"He drank too much cheap rotgut," Dowling drawled. "Says his head's like to bust. You got any coffee out there, Deputy?"

"Sure," Cody replied. "I'll fetch some for both of you."

Travis appeared in the cellblock doorway. "Are they all right?" he asked.

"Too much booze, that's all," Cody answered. "I told them they could have some coffee."

Travis nodded. "Good idea. Both of them could still use sobering up."

As the lawmen stepped back into the office, Cody noticed that Bethany Hale was standing beside the stove. Two extra cups normally sat on the shelf above the stove, and she had taken them down and was pouring coffee into them. "I overheard," she called. "I'm pouring coffee for those two poor men."

"Those 'two poor men' caused the ruckus that broke up your meeting earlier," Cody told her. "They're cowpokes called Stoddard and Dowling."

"That's perfect," replied Bethany. "This will give me another chance to get my message across to them."

Travis and Cody exchanged a glance, and the marshal said, "I've got rounds to make. You can handle this, Cody." Despite his serious tone, his eyes were twinkling humorously.

"Sure, Marshal," Cody replied, rolling his own eyes. He was not looking forward to another round with Bethany, but at least Stoddard and Dowling were behind bars and could not cause trouble if she started lecturing them.

Travis left the office. Bethany had picked up both cups of hot coffee and was walking carefully toward the cellblock. Cody stepped out of her way.

Dowling, who was still sitting on the floor, glanced up as she stepped into the cellblock. An expression of amazement came over his face when he saw the pretty young woman. "You're that temperance gal!" he exclaimed. "What are you doing here?"

"I thought you might like some coffee," Bethany said, her voice pleasant and cheerful.

"Yes, ma'am, we surely would," Dowling agreed. He scrambled up from the floor and came to the cell door to take the cup she handed to him through the bars. "Hey, Stoddard, look at this!"

Stoddard, glaring angrily, swung his feet off the bunk and sat up. When he saw Bethany, his expression shifted from anger to shock. But he stood up and came to the bars, reaching for the other cup. "Thanks," he grunted.

"I want you men to know that I bear you no ill will," Bethany told them. "Even though you were rude and abusive to me earlier, I realize that you were simply under the influence of alcohol. No man can think straight when he has been imbibing."

"I told you, lady, we wasn't drunk," Stoddard growled. "We didn't do hardly any drinkin' until later, after your stupid meetin' was over. We appreciate the coffee, but if you aim to preach at us, you might as well leave—" He swayed as he broke off, and his face grew pale.

"Bucket's under the bunk if your stomach starts acting up," Cody called. "Come on, Miss Hale. We'd best let them drink their coffee in peace."

"But . . . I want to talk to these men . . ."

Stoddard snarled, "There ain't nothin' you can say that'll mean a damn thing, lady. Now leave us be."

Cody took Bethany's arm and steered her gently toward the door. She protested again, but the deputy was adamant. "I promised you a cup of coffee, too," he insisted. "Come on and I'll get it for you."

With a sigh, Bethany gave up her struggle and let Cody guide her out of the cellblock. But as they moved into the office, she cast an angry glance over her shoulder at Stoddard and Dowling, who were drinking the coffee she had brought them. "I suppose some people just won't allow anyone to help them," she muttered.

Cody shut the cellblock door and led Bethany to a chair. He went to the stove and lifted the pot, then frowned. "Shoot, the prisoners must've gotten the last two cups. I can put some more on, though."

Bethany waved off the offer. "Please, don't bother, Deputy. I'm not really in the mood anymore. I'd rather just sit here for a few minutes and rest. This evening has been . . . rather tiring."

Cody could understand that. First, there had been the play and the problems that Judah had caused, then the fracas afterward, and now Judah's puzzling and worrying disappearance. Cody was getting pretty tired himself. He sat down and waited for Bethany to say something else, but instead she was silent—a silence that stretched out and became awkward. And Cody could not think of anything to say to her; she seemed to take offense at so many things.

Travis came in a few minutes later and looked a bit surprised to find Bethany still there. He glanced at Cody and asked, "Any trouble?"

Cody shook his head. "Stoddard jawed a bit, but Miss Hale listened to reason and decided to leave them alone. I haven't heard a sound for the last ten minutes, except for Nestor, so the other two may have gone to sleep."

Travis nodded and hung up his hat and coat. As he turned he inclined his head toward Bethany's back and arched an eyebrow quizzically. Cody lifted one shoulder in a tiny shrug to indicate he was not sure what was going on, either.

Someone in the cellblock screamed.

Bethany jumped out of her chair, wide-eyed, a hand pressed to her mouth. Travis exclaimed, "What the devil!" and started toward the cellblock door. Cody bounded up and reached it at the same instant.

They hurried into the big room and stopped short as they surveyed the scene. On the floor, Dowling was clutching at his stomach and writhing as he shrieked again, a long agonized scream that seemed to be wrenched from his very core. Stoddard was lying on the bunk. Sweat covered his face, which was twisted with pain. He was shaking and clawing at his belly.

"Damn," Travis grated. "I'll get Aileen!" He turned and ran from the cellblock.

Cody felt a hand grasp his arm and looked down to see that Bethany had followed them into the cellblock. "My God," she whispered, her face pale. "What's wrong with them?"

"Something bad," Cody mumbled. He looked back

at Stoddard and Dowling. Stoddard howled again, but the cry seemed to be weaker.

In the next cell, Nestor Gilworth snorted, rolled over on the bunk, and almost fell out. He slowly sat up and thumped his big booted feet on the floor. "Wha' in blue blazes . . . ?" he growled. "Wha's all the ruckus about?" Then his bleary eyes focused on the two groaning, sick men in the next cell. He stood up too quickly and had to slap a callused palm against the wall to catch his balance. Blinking at Cody, he went on, "Wha' the hell's wrong with them two, Deppity?"

"Don't know, Nestor," Cody replied, his voice tight. "But the doctor's on the way."

Dowling was whimpering now. Stoddard's feet suddenly beat a rapid tattoo against the wall. His head jerked back, his torso arched up off the thin mattress. An awful rattle came from his throat, and then he slumped on the bunk. Dowling screamed once more, and then he, too, lay still and quiet.

Cody was turning to get the cell door keys when Bethany's fingers dug into his arm. "Are they . . . are they dead?"

Cody nodded slowly. "I reckon so."

Bethany sobbed and pressed her face against Cody's shoulder. Under other circumstances, her closeness would have been a pleasure, but at the moment Cody could only feel cold and sick. He was accustomed to the sight of violent death, but he had never seen men howl and writhe like this. He stared at the bodies while Bethany sobbed and Nestor wrenched his battered felt hat off his shaggy head in a gesture of drunken respect.

Cody heard the front door of the office slam and then Luke Travis was saying, "Looks like we're too late." The deputy turned and saw the marshal just inside the cellblock doorway with Aileen Bloom at his side.

Abilene's physician hurried forward. "Unlock that door for me, Cody," she ordered. "There may still be a chance—"

Gently pushing Bethany away, Cody grabbed the key ring from the wall and unlocked the cell door. Aileen stepped inside and went to Dowling first, kneeling beside him and feeling for a pulse at his throat. After a moment, she shook her head and straightened, then went to the bunk and checked Stoddard's body, with the same result. Both men were dead.

As Aileen turned away from the two bodies, her expression was grim. She was tall for a woman, with thick brunette hair and a beauty that only enhanced her intelligence and strength of character. She asked quietly, "What happened here?"

"We arrested those two for being drunk and causing a fight," Travis told her. "They seemed all right when we brought them in."

"When did they get sick?"

"Well, they were feeling the whiskey they had put away," Cody replied, "but they didn't really seem to be in bad shape until just a few minutes ago."

Aileen nodded and picked up her medical bag, which she had placed on the floor next to Dowling's body. "I want to do a more thorough examination," she said. "Cody, why don't you take Miss Hale outside?"

"That's a good idea. Come on, Miss Hale." Cody steered the young woman out of the cellblock. A silent Bethany did not protest, evidently relieved to get away from the place where two men had died so hideously.

"What a terrible thing to happen," Bethany murmured once Cody had led her out of the office and they were standing on the boardwalk.

"It was pretty bad, all right, even for a couple of no-accounts like Stoddard and Dowling." He took her arm again. "I'd better see you back to your hotel."

Bethany nodded. "That would be fine," she said softly and then was silent for most of the walk to the Grand Palace Hotel. But when they neared the place, she asked, "You're going to keep looking for Judah, aren't you?"

"Of course I am. He's my brother. I want to make sure nothing has happened to him."

She hesitated a moment, then said softly, "He was drinking during the play, you know."

Cody sighed heavily. "I figured as much. I could see he was having a lot of trouble."

"Why would he do such a thing?" Bethany asked plaintively. "Of all the people to . . . to give in to temptation! I never would have thought that he could be like that."

"You don't know all there is to know about Judah, Miss Hale," Cody said quietly. "He went through a rough time a couple of years ago with whiskey."

"Judah? You can't be serious! He's such a fine man."

"He *is* a fine man. But he's got weaknesses just like anybody else. He beat the liquor craving once before, though, so I reckon he can do it again."

Bethany shook her head. "I just never would have believed it if you hadn't told me, Deputy."

"It's true. But maybe we can find him before he has a chance to hurt himself too badly."

"I hope so. If there's anything I can do to help . . ." Bethany offered, stopping at the front door of the hotel and turning toward him.

"I'll let you know," Cody replied. He touched the brim of his hat and wished her good night, leaving unsaid the thought that had come to him when she offered to help. The way he saw it, Bethany had already done more than enough.

Aileen Bloom snapped her medical bag shut and wearily ran a hand over her eyes. Travis watched grimly as she straightened from her work and came out of the cell. In the next cell, Nestor had retreated to his bunk and gone back to sleep.

"What do you think?" Travis asked, following her into the office.

"They were poisoned, both of them," she declared. "I'm sure of it, given the condition of the bodies and what you and Cody have told me of their symptoms."

"How the devil did that happen?"

"You said they were drunk. The most obvious explanation is that they got hold of some bad whiskey."

Travis nodded thoughtfully, then looked at her sharply as something occurred to him. "You remember Abner Peavey?" he asked.

"The man who died a couple of weeks ago? I remember your telling me about him. I don't think I ever treated him or even met him."

"When I found him he had the same look on his face that Stoddard and Dowling have, and he had been drinking in the same saloon these boys were in tonight." Travis rubbed his chin and stared at Aileen intently. "What are the chances that he was poisoned, too?"

The doctor shook her head. "I have no way of knowing, Luke. What did Cyrus Worden say?"

"He listed the death as natural causes. We just

figured that Peavey finally drank himself to death after years of heavy drinking." Travis gestured toward the cellblock. "But neither of those boys was twenty-five. They haven't had time for liquor to wear out their bodies. We know they were poisoned, and now it seems to me Peavey might've been, too."

"That sounds like a logical conclusion," Aileen agreed.

Travis's face was bleak. "I think we've got some bad whiskey floating around," he declared.

"What are you going to do?"

The marshal reached for his hat. "I'm going to try to track it down and find out where it's coming from." He took a deep breath. "If I can't, we're liable to have a lot more folks dying."

Chapter Eight

───◆───

THE NEXT DAY WAS SUNDAY, AND SINCE JUDAH FISHER was still missing, one of the elders of the Calvary Methodist Church was pressed into service to deliver the morning sermon. As usual, Luke Travis attended church and, after the service was over, assured the worried members of the congregation that he was making every effort to locate the minister.

Then Travis turned his attention to the question of the bad whiskey. He had returned to Earl's saloon the night before after walking Aileen to the boarding-house where she rented a room, intending to ask the saloonkeeper where his supply of whiskey had come from. But when he arrived the dingy saloon was dark and empty, the canvas over the door fastened shut. Travis supposed that Earl had shut down until he had a chance to clean the place up; it was only eleven o'clock, much too early for an Abilene tavern to close on a Saturday night. Not knowing where Earl lived, the marshal decided to wait until morning to question him and went in search of Cyrus Worden to have him remove Stoddard's and Dowling's bodies from the jail.

On this bright autumn Sunday as he rode from the church toward downtown, he swung into the old west end to go by Earl's saloon. As he approached the soddy he heard noises inside and noticed the canvas flap over the doorway had been pushed back. Reining in, Travis dismounted and stood at the entrance, peering into the seedy tavern.

Earl was sweeping debris from the earthen floor in front of the bar. Across the room another man, a stranger to Travis, was picking up pieces of splintered wood that had been a table. As the lawman's big frame blocked the daylight at the doorway, Earl glanced up and, when he saw who was entering, glared at him. "Come to give me the money for the damages, Marshal?" he snarled.

"I told you that would have to wait until those prisoners had had a hearing," Travis replied. "Now it looks like there won't be one."

"What?" Earl exclaimed, so startled he dropped his broom. He took a step toward Travis, his face flushing angrily. "You didn't let those damn cowhands go, did you? They were supposed to pay for what they done here!"

Travis had anticipated the man's reaction. He took several bills from his pocket and held them out. "That's what they had on them," he said flatly. "I figure you're lucky to get that much."

Earl snatched the money and quickly counted it.

"This won't pay for hardly half what they done! What'll I do about the rest of the damage?"

"Like I said, be glad you got that much," Travis said with a shrug. "The county could have taken that for the burial expenses."

The saloonkeeper opened his mouth to protest, then as the meaning of Travis's words sunk in gaped at the marshal. Finally he recovered his wits and muttered, "Burial expenses?"

Travis's eyes narrowed, and he looked coldly at Earl. "Both of them got sick and died after we took them to jail last night. You wouldn't know anything about that, would you, Earl?"

"What are you tryin' to blame me for, Marshal?" demanded Earl defensively. "I didn't see those boys after you hauled 'em out of here."

"I didn't say you did," Travis pointed out calmly. "But under the circumstances, I reckon it'd be the wise thing for you to answer a few questions."

Ever since Travis had entered the dive, he had been aware that the other man was watching him. The stranger pretended to be going about his work, but Travis could tell that he was listening to the conversation with great interest. When the marshal finished speaking, he came over and said, "Howdy, Marshal. I may be sticking my nose in where it's not wanted, but don't you think you're being a little rough on Earl?"

Travis swung to face the stranger. He was thick-bodied, a little below medium height, with a balding head, blunt features, and a nose that showed he had a considerable interest in drinking. He wore a white shirt that was open at the neck and the trousers of a rather flashy suit. When Travis glanced around he spotted the suit jacket hanging on the back of a chair with a gaudy tie draped over it. A derby lay on the table next to the chair. Obviously the man had come into the saloon, taken off his hat, coat, and tie, rolled up his sleeves, and pitched in to help Earl.

"If you don't mind my asking, mister," Travis said, ignoring the man's question, "who are you?"

The man brushed his right hand on his pants and stuck it out. "Peter J. Wallace, representative of the Wagon Wheel Distillery in Kansas City, Missouri, Marshal. I'm very pleased to meet you."

"Drummer, eh?" Travis shook his hand, even though he disliked traveling salesmen instinctively.

"A whiskey drummer to be precise, sir," Wallace replied with a grin. "I don't mind admitting it, because I represent the finest liquor distillery east of the Rockies, and probably west of it, too!"

Travis stared at the pushy little man. Evidently Wallace had come to try to sell something to Earl, and he was just helping him clean up to worm his way into the saloonkeeper's good graces. Turning back to Earl, Travis asked, "What about those questions?"

Earl scratched his freckled scalp. "I don't know, Marshal. I don't like the sound of this. A man'd think you was accusing him of something."

"All I really want to know is where you've been getting your liquor." Travis looked at the drummer. "He hasn't been buying it from you, has he, Mr. Wallace?"

Wallace shook his head. "Nope, that's why I'm here. I'm trying to talk this fine gentleman into placing an order. And make it Pete, Marshal."

Travis grunted. "What about it, Earl?"

"I don't have to tell you nothin', Marshal. Where I buy my stock is none of your business."

"It is when it looks like you've got some bad whiskey, bad enough to kill three men," Travis said coldly.

"Three men? I thought you said—"

"Abner Peavey may have been poisoned, too. You know anything about that, Earl?"

The saloonkeeper flushed again. "I wouldn't poison anybody—" he began hotly.

Wallace stepped in, smoothly moving between Travis and Earl. To the saloonkeeper, he said quickly, "I don't think that's what the marshal meant, Earl. I figure it must have been an accident. Isn't that right, Marshal?"

"Could have been. And the doctor agrees with me that it's a possibility."

Bad whiskey was fairly common on the frontier. Travis knew only too well that people who brewed moonshine habitually tossed all sorts of things into the mix. Chewing tobacco, gunpowder, red peppers, some even claimed that rattlesnake heads could be used, all those things and more went into the barrels with the cheapest alcohol. The product that came from the distilleries back East was the real thing, but it was expensive and there was not always enough of it to go around. Anybody with some kettles and enough imagination could come up with ungodly concoctions that would satisfy the thirsty cowboys and drunkards who frequented Earl's place and other saloons like it. It was unusual for someone to die from the stuff, but not unheard of.

"Look, Marshal, if I got hold of some bad booze, it's not my fault. Hell, I drink the same whiskey I serve to my customers! You reckon I'd do that if I knew it was bad?"

Earl sounded sincere, Travis thought, but he knew better than to trust the man's word. He remembered all too well how Earl had almost blasted him with a shotgun while he was trying to subdue Nestor Gilworth a couple of weeks ago.

"If it was an accident, then you won't be held accountable, Earl," Travis assured him. "But I've got to know where you've been getting your stuff. And if I were you, I'd dump what I had on hand, just to be safe."

Earl closed his eyes, moaned, and lifted a hand to his head. "Don't it ever stop?" he wailed. "I'm just a hardworkin' man tryin' to make an honest livin'—"

"The whiskey, Earl," Travis cut in, a sharp edge to his voice.

"Oh, hell, I might as well tell you. I been buyin' it from the Barlows for the last month. If there's somethin' wrong with the booze, it's the fault of them damn pig farmers!"

"Barlow . . ." Travis murmured, turning the name over in his mind as he tried to place it. "They've got a farm north of here, don't they?"

"Yeah, eight or ten miles. I don't know exactly where it is. I never been there. They deliver the stuff to me."

"Make it themselves, do they?"

Earl nodded. "I reckon they do. They sell to several of the smaller saloons in town, and I've heard they supply some of the roadhouses around here, too. All I know for sure is that their whiskey is cheaper than I could buy it anywhere else."

"Which just goes to prove the old saying about getting what you pay for, Earl," Pete Wallace chimed in. "If you had been doing business with Wagon

Wheel, this never would have happened, because we take care to see that only the finest whiskey goes into a bottle with our name on it."

Earl shook his head gloomily. "May have to do that, Mr. Wallace," he muttered, "once I get over these hard times. Shoot, if I have to pour out my stock, I'll have to replace it with somethin', or I might as well close up for good."

"We can't have that," Wallace said heartily, slapping Earl on the back. "I'm certain we can work out something where you won't have to come up with too much cash right away. We'll work together to keep you in business, Earl. And call me Pete, please."

Watching the oily way Wallace moved in to close the deal with Earl made Travis shudder inside. He felt sure most drummers would say anything, do anything, just to push a sale. Ignoring his dislike for the stocky man, he said, "I suppose I'd better ride out and have a talk with the Barlow family. How many of them are there, Earl?"

"Four that I know of," the saloonkeeper answered. "Couple of brothers named Kermit and Denton, and then there're their cousins, Amos and Jed." Then he grimaced. "You really intend to go out to their place, Marshal?"

Travis nodded. "I want to find out what they've been putting in their whiskey, and then I'm going to warn them to stick to raising pigs."

"Best be careful if you go out there," Earl warned. "They're not the friendliest bunch. I've heard they sometimes shoot first and then try to find out who was visitin' after the dust settles."

Travis was a little surprised that Earl would give him such a warning; he figured it would be all right with the saloonkeeper if someone shot him. But it could be that Earl did not want anyone to suspect later that he had sent Travis into a trap.

"I'll watch my step," the marshal said. "And you get rid of that whiskey."

Earl nodded sadly. As Travis left the saloon, Pete Wallace started talking again about setting up an order, and Earl said, "Reckon I'll have to. I'm sure as hell not buying any more of that Barlow moonshine!"

Travis stopped to have Sunday dinner at the Sunrise Café and found Cody sitting at one of tables eating a piece of apple pie. "Any sign of Judah?" he asked the deputy.

Cody, his dark eyes hollow with worry, frowned and shook his head. "I've looked all over this damned town," he said, frustration plain in his voice. "It's like he just vanished off the face of the earth!"

"Maybe he left town," Travis suggested. "A man with his troubles might do something like that."

"His horse is still at the parsonage," Cody replied. "And drunk or not, I can't see Judah stealing somebody else's horse. There haven't been any reports of anybody losing a mount, have there?"

This time it was Travis's turn to shake his head. "Judah will get through this all right, Cody," he said quietly. "He's a good man, a strong man."

"When he's not drinking . . ." Cody murmured.

Travis shrugged. "All we can do is wait and see. In the meantime, I'm going to ride out to the Barlow place and see if they've been selling bad whiskey to some of the saloons around town."

"Barlow . . . name's familiar, but I don't reckon I know them."

"They sold Earl the whiskey he's been serving for

the last month or so. They've got a place north of town."

Cody nodded. "Sure, I recollect now. They raise pigs." Relaxing visibly, the deputy grinned for the first time since the marshal had entered the café. "I've seen them a few times in town buying supplies. You can tell they spend most of their time around hogs, all right."

Travis returned the smile. "Want to ride out there with me?"

"Somebody really should stay and keep an eye on the town, Marshal. You know how wild some of these Sunday afternoons can get," Cody joked lightly. "But I don't reckon I'll mind doing that."

"All right." Travis laughed. "But I want some dinner before I start out there."

"Good idea," Cody agreed.

The sun was warm on Travis's back as he swung his brown gelding north out of town at an easy trot. Kansas was in its familiar autumn pattern, cold nights and sunny, warmer days. In just a few weeks the "northers" would start rolling in, bringing frigid temperatures and hints of blizzards, but for now the weather was crisp and pleasant. A gentle breeze blew in Travis's face as he rode.

While he knew the approximate location of the Barlow farm, after about an hour in the saddle that breeze told him he was getting close. Travis wrinkled his nose. Even if he had not known that the Barlows raised pigs in addition to making whiskey, the odor would have told him. He rode up a swell in the rolling prairie and paused to study the farm that lay below him.

On his left, a ramshackle cabin was nestled in a clump of leafless, stunted brush. A large barn, its doors hanging askew on their hinges, stood in a muddy open area with pole corrals spread behind it. But instead of the cattle or horses that were usually kept in such corrals, these pens were full of hogs. Even at a distance of a quarter mile, Travis could hear them grunting as they rooted in the mud.

He looked more closely at the barn and noticed a thin thread of smoke rising from it. *That's probably where the still is,* he thought. He wondered what the Barlows could have put in their moonshine to make it so lethal, if that was indeed the cause of the three deaths.

If he discovered that it was not, Travis thought, then he would have an even deeper mystery on his hands— because he was convinced that someone had killed Peavey, Stoddard, and Dowling, accidentally or not.

Then he spotted a puff of smoke coming from the chimney of the cabin; evidently someone was home. Travis heeled his horse into an easy walk and rode slowly down the slope.

The grunting of the hogs grew louder as he approached. Some fifty yards beyond the house he spotted a small creek, and Travis supposed that was where the Barlows got the water for the hogs as well as for their homemade liquor. The pigs would eat the mash left over from the distilling process, too. It seemed to be a good setup, Travis thought as he reined in beside a rough-hewn water trough in front of the cabin.

Someone was bound to have seen him riding toward the farm. Remembering Earl's warning, he decided to stay in the saddle until he knew how the Barlows would welcome him. "Hello!" he called loudly. "I'm Marshal Luke Travis from Abilene! I've come to talk to the Barlows!"

Suddenly the front door of the house creaked open, and a rifle barrel was thrust out. Travis saw it and threw himself out of the saddle just as smoke and lead belched from its muzzle. The slug whined past his head as he fell, and he landed heavily behind the water trough. His horse danced nervously away toward a clump of brush on the far side of the cabin.

"Dammit!" he grated, grabbing for his own gun.

The rifle cracked again, and this time the bullet thumped into the trough. As he hugged the dirt, he heard running footsteps. He looked up and glimpsed a man with a rifle darting toward the barn. The marshal knew that if the man reached it, he would be caught in a crossfire. He twisted around and triggered two quick shots.

His bullets kicked up dust a few yards in front of the running figure. The man yelped and reversed his course, ducking back into some brush where Travis could no longer see him. But that meant the man did not have an angle from which to shoot at him, either. Again the rifle in the cabin cracked, and once more Travis felt the bullet slam into the water trough. Dust and splinters flew in his face.

"Hold your fire!" he shouted. "I'm a lawman!"

To his surprise, a voice called back from the cabin. "You're one of them no-good, whiskey-thievin' sons of bitches!" it shouted angrily. "You can't fool us, mister!"

Travis stayed low, blinking against the dust. "I'm Marshal Luke Travis!" he repeated. "I'm looking for Kermit Barlow, his brother, and his cousins!"

For a long moment no reply came from the cabin, but no one fired a gun, either. Finally the voice said, "I'm Kermit Barlow. If you got business with me and mine, state your piece, mister."

"Put those guns up first," Travis told him.

"No, sir. Even if you're who you say you are, we still might want to shoot you."

Travis took a deep breath. He would not argue with Kermit Barlow's logic. "I just want to talk to you about your whiskey!"

"Sure you do," Barlow scoffed. "Reckon you want to buy a few pints, is that it, Marshal?"

Well, at least the man's willing to admit I'm a marshal, Travis thought. *That's progress.* He called, "Look, I'm going to holster my gun and stand up. All I want to do is talk to you boys, but if you feel you have to shoot me, just go ahead. My deputy knows I rode out here, and when I don't come back, he'll be paying you a visit with a posse and probably a lynch rope. Just want you to know that before I stand up."

It was a calculated risk, but despite the close call when he first rode up, Travis figured they would hold their fire. The Barlows had not lived in the area for long, and they might not know that there was no chance of a lynching in Abilene, not as long as either Travis or Cody was alive.

He slipped his Colt back in its holster and then climbed slowly to his feet, keeping his hands in plain sight. Facing the cabin, he saw the rifle barrel still glinting in the sunlight that hit the open doorway. The oilcloth over one of the windows had been pulled back, and the double barrels of a shotgun poked through that opening. Crouched at the corner of the house was the young man who had tried to flank him and reach the barn. This man had his rifle trained on Travis, too. That accounted for three of the four Barlows, and Travis guessed the other one might be in the barn with the still.

A couple of minutes that seemed like hours dragged

by. Finally, Kermit Barlow's voice came from the cabin. "All right, boys, I reckon we won't shoot the feller after all. I'll go out and talk to him. But if'n he tries anythin' funny, you blast the hell outta him!"

The door creaked open, and a lean man of medium height stepped out of the shadowy opening into the sunlight. Kermit Barlow had several days' growth of beard on his sharp-featured face and shaggy brown hair that hung to his shoulders. He wore a battered black felt hat, a threadbare jacket, a woolen shirt, denim overalls, and mud-covered work shoes. The mud on his boots had dried, and several clumps fell off as he stepped into the yard. Keeping his rifle leveled at Travis, he asked, "Now what the hell was it you wanted, Marshal?"

"I'm told that you and your family make whiskey and sell it to some of the places around here," Travis said evenly. "Is that right?"

Barlow shrugged, and the muzzle of his rifle bobbed up and down. "Folks got to make a livin'," he replied. "What business is it of your'n?"

"You know a man named Earl who has a saloon in Abilene?"

"Maybe we do, maybe we don't." Barlow squinted at Travis. "How come you want to know?"

"Some of his customers died after drinking the whiskey you sold him," Travis told him.

"That's a goddamn lie!" a new voice protested from inside the house. "Ain't nothin' wrong with our whiskey!"

Barlow jerked his head around and snapped sharply, "Shut up, Amos! I'm the head of the family, and I'm handlin' this!" His eyes flicked back to Travis. "You're sayin' that our whiskey was the cause of them folks dyin'?"

"Not necessarily. But they're still dead, and it's my job to find out why. Men have died from bad whiskey before."

Barlow shook his head. "Not ours. There ain't nothin' wrong with our home brew, Marshal, not one damn thing. Hell, we test ever' batch. If anybody was goin' to die, looks like it'd be one of us!"

That was the same argument Earl had used, and Travis had to admit it made some sense. But having met the Barlows—or at least one of them; he still had not gotten a good look at the others—he could easily believe they would toss anything into their brew to liven it up, even something dangerous.

"How about letting me take a look at your still?" he asked.

"The hell you say! Us Barlows ain't in the habit of rollin' over and playin' dead for ever' lawman who comes along, mister. We didn't do it back in Tennessee, and we sure as hell ain't doin' it here in Kansas!"

So they're hill people, Travis thought. That was not surprising. He said, "I could get a posse and come back out here, force you to show me your operation."

"Yeah, and we could plug you right now," Kermit Barlow sneered. "Amos, Jed, get out here!"

The young man crouching at the corner of the house stepped out into the open. The other man inside withdrew his shotgun from the window and emerged from the door a moment later. Travis glanced from one to the other and blinked. The two men, who were barely out of their teens, had the same stocky build, lank brown hair, and stained buckteeth. Earl had not mentioned that Amos and Jedediah were twins.

Their cousin Kermit nodded toward Travis. "Keep an eye on him," he ordered. "I'll go get Denton. He ought to be in on this, too."

Travis wondered just what Kermit had in mind. As he watched Barlow hurry toward the barn, his mind was spinning. He knew he could draw his gun and drop both twins before they could get a shot off. They were watching him, but the dullness in their eyes told him their reactions would be very slow.

He decided not try anything; a shootout with the Barlows would not solve the problem. It would be better to wait and see what Kermit had in mind.

Kermit returned from the barn a few minutes later with another man, this one blond and pudgy. Denton Barlow, Travis decided. He looked younger than Kermit but older than Amos and Jed. Kermit was hurrying him along, clearly the man in charge in this family.

"This here's all of us, Marshal," Kermit said when Denton and he had reached the water trough. "Now, I'm goin' to ask these boys a question, and I want you to listen right smart to their answer."

"All right," Travis replied with a nod.

"Fellers," Kermit said, facing his brother and cousins, "have any of you put anythin' in that booze that'd hurt anybody?"

The twins shook their heads, and Denton Barlow said, "Lordy, Kermit, you know we wouldn't do that. We drink it ourselves!"

Kermit turned to glare at Travis. "There's your answer, Marshal. Now, unless you want to call any of us liars, you'd best get on your hoss and ride out of here. We ain't particular who comes to see us, but I reckon we'll draw the line at you."

Travis kept a tight rein on his temper and tried to ignore the man's goading. "You won't let me take a look at your still?"

"You're on our property, Mister Lawman. You got

no right to do anythin' we don't want you to." Kermit gestured sharply with the rifle in his hands. "Now git!"

Travis sighed and walked over to his horse, which was munching on the brush now that the shooting had stopped. As he caught the reins and swung into the saddle, he said, "You boys would be better off if you gave up moonshining and stuck to raising hogs. Earl's not going to be buying any more booze from you, and I figure word will get around pretty quickly about what's happened."

"Told you, it ain't our fault those fellers died. We didn't have nothin' to do with it." Kermit laughed harshly. "Don't reckon all of our customers will desert us."

Travis had the sinking feeling that Kermit was right. Most of the men who operated the area's roadhouses and dives would not care that they might be taking a chance with their customers' lives. As long as the Barlows sold their whiskey cheaper than anyone else, they would have buyers.

"You'd better be real careful with that brew," Travis warned. "If anybody else dies, I'll come out here with a posse."

Kermit dropped the barrel of his rifle slightly and pressed the trigger. The weapon blasted, and the bullet slammed into the ground in front of Travis's horse, making the animal dance nervously backward. "Told you to git," Kermit said with a gap-toothed grin.

Travis stared at him for a moment longer, then wheeled his horse and urged it to a trot. The muscles in his back felt tight; he knew the Barlows were watching him ride away. But none of them tried to put a bullet in him, and he breathed a little easier when he topped the rise and rode out of sight of the farm.

He was furious. The Barlows had taken several shots at him, and he could have arrested them for that. But they would not have gone peacefully, and Travis felt certain that someone would have died if he had pressed the issue. Three men had died already. He wanted to avoid any more deaths.

But all the way back to Abilene, he felt by turns angry and puzzled.

Kermit Barlow had sounded sincere when he claimed that they had not produced any bad whiskey, and so had the others. Of course, they might not know that something was wrong with their brew. They might have just been lucky that it had not killed them, too.

But if the whiskey had not killed Peavey, Stoddard, and Dowling, what had?

Travis was still mulling that over as he rode back into Abilene later that afternoon. When he arrived at the marshal's office he found no one there, so he strolled down Texas Street to Orion's, looking for Cody.

"Aye, Lucas, the lad was here earlier," Orion told him as he drew a mug of cold beer for Travis. "He was still looking f' his brother."

Travis nodded, not surprised. He took a grateful sip of the beer and then said, "I've got something else on my mind right now, Orion. Do you know some people named Barlow?"

The Scotsman's face reddened. "Aye, and a filthy lot they be!" he grumbled. "The scuts come in here a while back and tried t'sell me some o' their foul brew. I took one taste and told 'em t'peddle their poison elsewhere. I serve only the finest whiskey, as ye well know."

"Poison, eh?" Travis said, his interest quickening.

Orion waved a big hand. "'Twas only a figure o' speech, Lucas. I dinna know wha' was in the stuff, but 'twould give even an Indian the blind staggers, I'm telling ye."

"They manage to sell some of it, though."

"Oh, aye," he grunted disgustedly. "Some saloonkeepers only care f' the money they can make by stocking such cheap whiskey. But Orion McCarthy is not one o' tha' breed!"

Travis laughed. "And your customers appreciate that, Orion." He drained his beer mug and placed it on the bar. "I suppose I'd better go find Cody and make sure everything was quiet while I was gone." He dropped a coin on the hardwood next to the mug. "Is everything all right here?"

Orion winked slowly and nodded. "Aye, 'tis coming along just fine, Lucas."

With a wave, Travis left the tavern and strolled out into the late afternoon sunlight. He groaned inwardly when he noticed a figure striding jauntily up the boardwalk toward him. Peter J. Wallace of the Wagon Wheel Distillery cut quite a flashy figure.

When Wallace recognized Travis, he grinned broadly. "Good afternoon, Marshal," he called heartily. "You've been in Orion's, I see. That's just where I was headed. If you'd care to return, I'd be glad to buy you a drink."

"No, thanks, Wallace," Travis said shortly, struggling to keep his dislike for the drummer from surfacing. "I've got work to do."

"As do I, Marshal, as do I." Wallace's grin widened.

"Lawmen and salesmen don't get the Sabbath off, do they?"

"Lawbreaking goes on seven days a week."

"And so does opportunity." Wallace gave Travis a friendly nod and moved past him to the door of Orion's.

Travis wondered if Orion would buy some whiskey from the persistent drummer just to get rid of him. The marshal shook his head and, smiling faintly, walked away to look for Cody.

Chapter Nine

───────◆───────

THE WAGON BOUNCED OVER THE RUTTED TRAIL, JARRING the four men who rode in it. Kermit Barlow and his brother Denton were on the seat, Kermit handling the reins, while their cousins Amos and Jed rode in the wagon bed. Luke Travis had visited their farm the day before. Nevertheless, they were headed south, toward Abilene.

"I still ain't sure about this, Kermit," Denton said worriedly to his older brother. "That marshal's liable to be mad at us. He might try to make trouble if'n he sees us in town."

Kermit snorted derisively. "I ain't a-scared of no marshal, and I sure as hell ain't goin' to let him buffalo us. We need some supplies, and we'll go into town and get 'em, by God!"

Amos leaned toward the wagon seat and yelled over

the rattling of the wheels, "But what if he decides to put us in jail for shootin' at him?"

"He was trespassin' on our property!" Kermit growled. "We was just protectin' our place when we shot at him. We didn't know he was a marshal—"

"But he sang out and told us who he was," Jed cut in.

"Will you shut up?" Kermit said angrily. "I'm tellin' you the way it was, so just keep your yap shut and listen!"

"Awright, awright," Jed mumbled, glaring down at the wagon bed.

"The marshal was trespassin'. That's our story if we need one. All of you understand?"

"Sure, Kermit," Denton whined. "We ain't stupid, you know."

Kermit snorted disgustedly but did not reply.

Maybe he was pushing things by going into Abilene so soon after the run-in with Travis. In the time they had lived on the farm, they had avoided dealing with the law, and that was the way Kermit liked it. But he was not going to let any man back him down, not even a star-packer like Luke Travis.

They reached Abilene about midmorning and pulled the wagon to a halt at Karatofsky's Great Western Store to stock up on supplies. Kermit collected the flour, sugar, coffee, beans, and salt they needed, while Denton, Amos, and Jed paid more attention to the jars of candy sitting on top of the main counter. Kermit had to smile a little as he listened to them arguing about which was better, licorice or peppermint. *They're good fellows,* he thought, *not long on brains, but a man has to stand by his kin.*

It was nearly noon by the time the supplies had been bought and loaded onto the wagon. Kermit had given in to the pleas for a treat, and each of the other three had a string of licorice to take home with him. As they stood on the boardwalk in front of the store preparing to climb into the wagon, Denton looked down the street and said, "Kermit, you think we could get somethin' to eat? I'm powerful hungry."

"You got licorice," Kermit pointed out.

"No, I'm talkin' about a real meal, somethin' at a café. We ain't et in a café in a long time."

"I reckon that's true enough," Kermit mused. So far they had not encountered the marshal during this trip to town, but if they stayed around longer, that would increase the odds of a meeting that might turn out to be troublesome. The smart thing would be to get into the wagon and head out of Abilene while they could.

"Can't we do what Denton says, Kermit?" Amos wailed plaintively. "We might even find us a place that's got a purty little servin' gal."

Kermit nodded abruptly. "All right. Let's go find us a place to eat." The others had obviously forgotten about Luke Travis, and Kermit was damned if *he* was going to worry about him.

The Barlows strolled down Texas Street, looking for a café that struck their fancy. They passed the marshal's office on the other side of the street, and Kermit found himself glancing nervously toward it.

"How about here?" Denton asked a moment later. He pointed to a tidy building with bright gingham curtains in its clean windows and gilt letters on the glass that read SUNRISE CAFÉ.

"Looks fine," Kermit agreed. "Come on, boys."

As he opened the door, a little bell above his head

tinkled. Surprised, Kermit glanced up, then stepped inside, the others following closely behind him. The café was doing a brisk business at this time of day, but Kermit spotted a vacant table in the center of the room and led the Barlows toward it.

He noticed the disapproving looks that some of the customers cast their way, and he glared right back at them. He knew very well that he and his relatives smelled of hogs and were not as clean as most folks, but that was their business. If somebody did not like it, they could just leave as far as Kermit was concerned.

One man gave them a particularly hostile look. Kermit returned the scowl and growled, "Somethin' botherin' you, mister?" As he spoke he rested his hand on the hilt of the knife sheathed on his hip.

The man hurriedly shook his head when he saw the look in Kermit's eyes. "Nothing bothering me," he mumbled, then turned back to his food.

"Didn't think so," Kermit rasped. He led the way to the empty table and sat down.

When all of them were seated, Kermit looked toward the counter where some of the diners sat and noticed a pretty, redheaded young woman standing behind it and looking apprehensively at them. She was wearing an apron and had to be the serving girl. Putting a leering grin on his face, Kermit raised a hand. "Oh, miss," he called in a deceptively mild voice.

The redhead took a deep breath and came over to the table. "Hello," she said in a quavering voice. "What can I do for you?"

"We want to eat!" replied Amos excitedly.

Jed nodded. "Can you bring us some food?"

"Well . . . I guess so. But I have to know what you want."

Denton, Amos, and Jed exchanged surprised glances. "You mean we get to pick what we want?" Denton exclaimed.

The young woman pointed to a menu board that was hanging on the wall behind the counter. "That's what we're serving today. You just look it over, tell me what you want, and I'll bring it to you." She blushed nervously and hesitated, then went on, "You . . . you do have some money, don't you?"

"We can pay, gal," Kermit said. "But we don't read so good. Reckon you've got steaks, don't you?"

"Yes, sir, we surely do."

"Bring us the biggest four you got with plenty of taters and beans and cornbread. That be all right?"

"Yes, sir, that will be fine." The waitress started to turn away.

"One more thing, gal," Kermit called after her. "What's your name?"

She hesitated, then finally said, "It's Agnes, Agnes Hirsch."

"Well, we're right pleased to meet you, Agnes. I'm Kermit Barlow, and these here are my brother, Denton, and my cousins, Amos and Jed. Say howdy to the lady, boys."

The others jerked their hats off and nodded to Agnes. Amos started to say something, got his tongue tangled, and stopped in embarrassment. Agnes said quickly, "Ah, I'll get your food," and hurried off.

Jed turned to his brother and swatted Amos with his hat. "You scared her off, ya damned fool! What was you tryin' to do?"

"Kermit told us to say howdy," Amos protested.

"That's all I wanted to do. Lordy, did you ever see a gal quite so purty?"

"I never did, not in all my born days," Jed agreed. "Ain't nothin' purtier'n a redhaired gal."

Kermit sat back and listened to his cousins talk about Agnes. Both of them were obviously quite taken with her. She was pretty enough, Kermit supposed, but he had other things on his mind these days besides females. But getting all worked up over a gal was to be expected with young fellows like Amos and Jed.

"I think I'm goin' to court her," Amos said, leaning forward excitedly and casting glances toward the kitchen door where Agnes had disappeared.

"Hell, you can't court her!" Jed exclaimed.

Amos frowned darkly. "Why not?" he asked.

"Because I'm courtin' her, that's why!"

"The hell you are!"

"That's right, I am, and there ain't nothin' you can do about it, Amos Barlow."

Amos scraped his chair back and started to stand up. "That's what you think, you polecat! Get up and we'll just see who's goin' to—"

Kermit reached out, grasped the sleeve of his cousin's coat, and yanked him back into his seat. "Both of you boys settle down," he snapped. "You go to fightin' in here, you'll just get all the other folks upset."

"Yeah, and somebody's liable to call that marshal!" Denton added.

Amos and Jed quieted down, but they kept glaring at each other. They had always been friends, the way twin brothers should be, but Kermit could tell that their mutual interest in Agnes Hirsch might drive a wedge between them.

"Just take it easy," he advised them. "You boys got

more important things to worry about than some gal, even a redhaired one." He lowered his voice so that he could not be overheard as he went on, "We got that load to take over to Shumate's place this afternoon."

The twins nodded grudgingly, remembering the barrels of whiskey that had to be picked up at the farm and then delivered to a roadhouse a few miles east. "All right," Amos muttered. "But I'm goin' to tell that gal how purty she is."

"Not if I tell her first!" Jed shot back.

Kermit scowled at both of them to keep the argument from starting all over again, and the Barlows were fairly quiet then as they waited for their food. A few minutes later Agnes bustled through the kitchen doorway, carrying several huge platters. With practiced ease, she brought them to the table and placed a platter in front of each of the four men.

"Now don't that look downright dee-licious," Kermit said, sniffing the air and gazing down at the thick steak and the heaping mounds of vegetables on his dish. The others were equally impressed.

Agnes started to step away from the table, but Amos stopped her by saying, "Miss Agnes, there's somethin' I got to tell you—"

"You're the purtiest gal we ever seen!" Jed interrupted, grinning up at her.

"Dammit, Jed, I was goin' to tell her!" Amos exploded. He snatched up a piece of cornbread and drew back his arm. "I oughtta chunk this at you!"

"Amos!" Kermit said sharply. "We don't fight with food when we ain't at home, you know that. Now put that down."

Amos sighed. "Awright." He looked up at Agnes and went on, "But I'm tellin' you right now, Miss

Agnes, I intend to come courtin' you. Whereabouts do you live?"

Before the astonished Agnes could answer, Jed said, "I'm courtin' you, too, ma'am. So you're goin' to have to make up your mind which one of us you want."

"I . . . I . . ." Agnes stammered. She glanced around wildly.

Kermit nodded solemnly and said, "I can see where it'd be a right hard choice, ma'am, seein' as how both of my cousins are such handsome, upstandin' fellers. You just take your time and think it over."

"No," Jed protested. "I want her to make her mind up right now."

"So do I," Amos insisted. "Choose me, Miss Agnes. I'm a heap smarter than Jed."

"The devil you say! Come on! Come on, boy, let's have this out! Winner gets the gal."

Amos doubled his fists and started to stand up. "Fine by me!" he declared.

A flustered Agnes finally found her voice. "You . . . you're letting your food get cold. Don't you think you ought to sit down and eat and settle this later?"

"Naw, it's too important," Amos told her. "We got to decide right now. We sure as hell can't divvy you up."

With the tinkling of the little bell, the café door opened, and Agnes threw a frantic look over her shoulder. A huge sigh of relief escaped from her lips as Deputy Cody Fisher strode into the room.

"I'm sorry, boys," she said hurriedly. "But I don't think either of you can come to court me. You see, I've already got a steady beau." She turned around and practically ran to Cody, who had started to greet her but stood with a puzzled expression on his face as she clutched his arm. Agnes tilted her head back, smiled dazzlingly up at him, and said in a loud voice, "Hello, darling!"

Then she rose up on her toes and planted a kiss on his lips.

Kermit thought the deputy looked a little surprised, but then Cody's arms slipped around Agnes and tightened, pulling her into an embrace just the way a beau would. The kiss certainly looked genuine. "All right, boys," Kermit said flatly. "You can see for yourself that the gal's got herself a man already, so I don't want no more arguin' about this."

"Aw, hell!" Jed said disgustedly. Amos echoed that heartfelt sentiment.

"Enough romance." Kermit pointed toward the steaks. "Eat your food 'fore it gets cold."

"We could shoot that fella," Amos suggested in a low voice, nodding toward Cody.

Kermit shook his head. "Women ain't worth shootin' folks over. They ain't like hogs."

"That's true," Denton added sagely.

The twins sighed again, picked up their knives and forks, and started to take out their frustration on the thick steaks. Kermit was just glad they had decided to listen to reason before he had to whip some sense into them.

Cody slowly disengaged himself from Agnes, even though he hated to break the contact with her soft, sweet lips. He looked down at her, his arms still around her, and grinned. "Shoot, I'm going to have to stop thinking of you as a little orphan girl, Agnes. How'd you learn to kiss like that?"

"I was desperate," she hissed. "I had to kiss *somebody.*"

Cody chuckled. "Thanks," he said dryly. "And here I thought it was my charm."

"Oh . . ." Agnes made a face. "Come over here where we can talk, and I'll tell you about it."

Cody followed her to an empty stool at the end of the counter, then glanced over his shoulder at the odorous farmers seated in the center of the room. He had spotted them as soon as he came in. Now he recognized them as the Barlows and was aware that they were looking at him from time to time with great interest. As he sat down, he asked, "All right, what's this all about?"

"You see those four farmers over there?" Agnes replied, inclining her head toward the table where the four men sat.

"Sure. I've seen them in town before; I know who they are. Have they been bothering you?"

"The twins think they're in love with me. They wanted to come courting."

Cody's eyes narrowed. "Did they insult you?"

"Oh, no, they were actually fairly polite to me. They wanted to kill each other, but . . . Anyway, I'm glad you came in when you did. I hope you don't mind, but I told them that you and I are . . . well, that you're my steady beau."

"Reckon I understand now." Cody grinned. "That was the reason for the kiss, huh?"

"Well, I had to make it look real."

Cody's grin broadened. "You did that, all right," he replied. "It was mighty nice, Agnes."

"Yes. It was, wasn't it?" A pretty red flush appeared on her fair skin, and her green eyes sparkled.

"Still, you shouldn't have lied to them like that. It could get you in trouble someday."

"You're not angry with me, are you?"

Cody shook his head. "No, I'm not mad. Reckon I ought to feel honored. You think you could get a cup of coffee for your steady beau?"

Agnes smiled brightly. "I sure can."

She returned with the coffee a minute later, placing the steaming mug on the counter in front of Cody. Then she went about her business, waiting on the customers who had come to sample the Sunrise Café's food.

Cody paid no attention to the Barlows, but he sensed they were still watching him. When he finally glanced in their direction, he saw that the twins were both glaring at him as if they wanted to skin him alive. He looked at them coolly for a moment, then returned his attention to his coffee. Agnes paused next to him several times to chat, and he knew she was trying to maintain the image of the relationship she had claimed. He also knew she would not mind turning the phony courtship into a real one.

When the Barlows finished their meal, they got up and went to the door. Kermit Barlow paused to leave several wadded-up greenbacks on the counter near Cody. He pointed them out to Agnes, then turned to follow his brother and cousins. He hesitated again, this time to trade cool stares with Cody. Then he walked quickly to the door and led the others out.

They were a strange bunch, Cody thought. Travis had told him about the hostile reception he had gotten on his visit to their farm. They certainly looked capable of brewing up something that would kill the people who drank it. But that was hardly enough to convict them of murder.

Sliding off the stool, Cody dropped a coin on the counter for the coffee, waved to Agnes, and left the café. He thought briefly about stealing another kiss but decided not to lead her on. Now that the Barlows were gone, so was the reason for the charade.

He stepped out onto the boardwalk and gazed up and down Texas Street, looking for any sign of the family. A moment later, he spotted them on a wagon that was pulling away from one of the general stores. They appeared to be on their way out of town, and Cody breathed a little easier once he realized that. While the Barlows were in Abilene, the potential for problems loomed. Cody had never shied away from trouble, but he liked to face it on his own terms when he could. That meant that innocent people like Agnes or passersby on the street had to be safely out of the way.

The deputy had a feeling he would be seeing the Barlows again.

On the way back to the farm, Kermit doubled over and clutched at his stomach with one hand. Denton peered at his brother, saw the lines of strain on Kermit's face, and asked anxiously, "What's wrong?"

"That damn steak must've been bad," Kermit answered. "My gut's kickin' up a hell of a fuss!"

"You need me to take the reins?"

Kermit shook his head. "I'll be all right. Let's just get back home."

But as the wagon rolled north toward their farm, he continued to complain of stomach pains and let out a low moan from time to time. By the time they arrived, Kermit was trembling and saying he felt faint.

"You'd better go inside and lay down," a concerned Amos told him. "We'll haul that booze over to Shumate's by our lonesome."

"You sure you boys can handle that?" Kermit asked dubiously.

"Hell, yes!" Denton replied. "You go on and take it easy, Kermit. Shoot, you work too hard anyway."

"Well . . . maybe I will stretch out for a mite."

"Don't you worry 'bout a thing, Cousin Kermit," Jed assured him. "We'll take care of ever'thin'."

Still looking doubtful, Kermit went into the cabin while the other three unloaded the supplies and then drove the wagon over to the barn. The Barlows stored their whiskey in barrels inside the barn, and it took only a few minutes for Denton, Amos, and Jed to lift three barrels into the wagon bed.

After they had finished, Denton went into the cabin and found Kermit lying on one of the bunks. "You sure you'll be all right here by yourself?" he asked.

Kermit nodded. "I feel bad 'bout this, Denton, leavin' this chore up to you boys."

"Hellfire, Kermit, we ain't little kids no more. It's time we was takin' some responsibility for runnin' the business. It's ours, too, you know."

"Sure it is. You go ahead. Just make sure Shumate pays you. That ol' bastard's liable to try to swindle you when he sees I ain't along."

Denton grinned. "Ain't nobody goin' to swindle us, brother. Sure as hell Shumate ain't."

Kermit nodded his agreement, put his head back, and closed his eyes. Denton went out to the wagon, climbed onto the seat, and took the reins.

Gray clouds began moving in from the north as the wagon rolled over the prairie toward the roadhouse. "Looks like it's goin' to storm, Denton," Jed said, looking anxiously at the sky.

Denton shook his head and tried to sound wise as he declared, "Naw. Them clouds ain't got no rain in 'em. They'll just cool things off a mite."

"Hope you're right," Amos replied. "I'd hate to have to come back from Shumate's in the rain."

The roadhouse was around five miles from the farm, and they had covered about half the distance when Jed sat up straighter in the back of the wagon. He raised an arm and pointed, calling, "Riders comin', Denton."

Denton's eyes followed his cousin's outstretched arm and saw a small group of men coming toward them. He was able to count half a dozen of them, and they were riding fast, kicking up a cloud of dust with their passage.

"Get your rifles ready," Denton ordered, feeling panic flutter inside. He was used to Kermit handling situations like this, and knowing that Amos and Jed were looking to him for leadership made him nervous.

"You reckon they mean trouble?" Amos asked.

"That many men in a hurry out here on the plains don't hardly ever mean anythin' but," Denton snapped. He slapped the reins, trying to hurry the team along, and the wagon jounced recklessly as they picked up speed.

Suddenly Denton saw puffs of smoke rising from the group of riders and then heard a series of faint cracks. As cold fear ran up his spine, he exclaimed, "Dammit, they're shootin' at us!"

"Goddamn whiskey thieves!" Amos yelled. He leaned over the back of the seat and lined his rifle on the strangers. The Winchester blasted, sending lead screaming toward the men.

Jed began firing at the riders as Denton shouted and hauled on the reins, making the team veer off the trail to the left. Amos and Jed bounced wildly as the wagon jolted over rugged ground, but they kept shooting.

The riders were close enough now for the Barlows to make out their features—or at least they would have been if the men had not been wearing bandannas over the lower halves of their faces. They carried rifles and handguns, and they fired a barrage of bullets at the wagon. Denton heard slugs whining through the air close to his head. He yelled and tried to urge the team on to greater speed. Amos and Jed tried their best to return the gunfire.

"Hang on!" Denton shouted.

He jerked the reins, forcing the team to make an even sharper turn. Their rickety, cumbersome wagon could never outrun a group of men on horseback. But maybe he could zigzag the vehicle back and forth and stay out of the line of fire until his cousins could pick off a few of the raiders. Amos and Jed were firing as fast as they could, but so far they had not hit any of the men.

Then Amos pressed the trigger, and one of the attacking figures slumped and slid out of the saddle. "I got one of the bastards!" he whooped excitedly. The other ambushers paused for a moment, but then they renewed their attack, charging the wagon with their guns blazing.

"I got one, too!" Jed cried as another rider fell.

The would-be thieves began to veer away. They had lost two of their number, and they had to be wondering about the high price of capturing three barrels of whiskey. Evidently it was not worth it, because they turned and rode away, leaving their companions where they had fallen.

"Whooo-eee!" Denton shouted. "We run 'em off!"

"We sure did!" Amos joined in. "That was mighty slick drivin', Denton."

"Thanks," a grinning Denton replied as he hauled

the team to a stop to let the overheated, breathless animals rest. "You and Jed were the ones doin' the shootin', though. Those fellers probably wouldn't've turned tail and run if you hadn't dropped a couple of 'em."

"It *was* pretty damn good shootin', weren't it?" Jed crowed with a proud grin.

A few minutes later Denton started the team moving again, and it was not long before they were back on the trail. Within an hour, they pulled up to Shumate's dilapidated roadhouse, which was nothing more than a soddy like so many of the dives that dotted the plains, and were unloading the whiskey for the fat, unkempt owner.

Shumate stood next to the wagon as they worked, watching them. "Where's Kermit today?" he asked shrewdly.

"Feelin' a mite puny," Denton told him.

The stout tavern keeper nodded. "I reckon he'd want me to wait to pay for this load until he's along. I'll just catch up next time."

"No, sir," Denton snapped. "Kermit, he told me to be sure you paid today."

"He did, did he?"

"Yes, sir. Else I was to cut your ears off and bring 'em back to him, he said." Kermit had told him no such thing, of course, and Denton had to suppress the grin that tugged at the corners of his mouth. The threat sounded good.

Evidently it was enough to impress Shumate. The roadhouse owner grumbled as he reached into his grubby pants, pulled out a bag of coins, and tossed them to Denton. Denton would have counted them if he had been able to go beyond twenty, but he supposed he would have to trust Shumate until Kermit could check the amount. If the man had shorted them, Kermit would know it. Then they would come back and teach Shumate that it was not smart to try to cheat folks from the hills of Tennessee.

Denton tucked the bag inside his grimy shirt and nodded. "Thank you, Mr. Shumate. You just send word when you need some more whiskey."

Shumate grunted and went inside his roadhouse. Denton turned the wagon around and started it toward home. He grinned over his shoulder at his cousins. "Reckon we done a right good job, fellers," he said. "We fought off them jaspers who tried to steal our whiskey, and we got ol' Shumate to pay up. Yes, sir, Kermit's goin' to be mighty proud of us."

Sighing with satisfaction, Denton reached into his pocket and drew out the string of licorice Kermit had bought for him in town. He was still grinning as he took a bite of the candy and tried to remember if he had ever been this happy before.

Chapter Ten

───────◆───────

CODY FISHER STEPPED OUT OF THE MARSHAL'S OFFICE that clear, cool evening and looked up and down Abilene's main thoroughfare. It was a quiet Monday night. A few men on horseback were riding by; a couple of wagons rolled along the hard-packed dirt street. Tinny music tinkled faintly from the saloons, all of which had their doors closed against the cool autumn air. In the summer, when the doors were open and only batwings barred the entrances, a dozen different melodies would float into the street, blending together to make one special sound.

Leaning against the boardwalk post, Cody tried to relax. Luke Travis was having dinner with Aileen Bloom. He would come back to the office afterward, and then he would no doubt be reticent, almost stiff-necked, about his evening. Cody smiled to himself. He wondered if Abilene's marshal and its doctor would ever get it through their heads that they felt more than friendship for each other.

He stretched and rolled his shoulders. He ought to be out looking for Judah, he told himself, his grin gradually fading as the troubling thought of his brother crossed his mind yet again. In the forty-eight hours since Judah's disappearance, he had scoured the whole town, talking to everyone who might have seen him. A couple of drunks who frequented the town's dives claimed to have seen the Methodist minister on Saturday night after the temperance play. According to them, Judah had been even drunker than he had been during the performance. Cody did not know how much weight to give to their stories. He hated to think that Judah had gone on a bender, but the evidence seemed to be pointing that way.

Nevertheless, *someone* should have seen Judah between then and now. That was what really worried Cody—his brother had simply vanished—and he did not think Judah would have done that of his own accord.

Then his concern really took flight, and he started to worry that someone might have hurt Judah, possibly even killed him during a robbery and hidden the body.

Cody took a deep breath and got hold of himself. Worrying and imagining all sorts of horrors was not going to help one bit. He would keep his eyes open, he told himself firmly, when he went on the nightly rounds with Travis later. Other than that, he could do nothing.

Diagonally across the street in the next block, the front door of the Grand Palace Hotel swung open, splashing light from the lobby onto the boardwalk. Cody glanced toward the bright pool, saw a figure emerging from the hotel, and frowned as he recognized Bethany Hale's tiny form. She was carrying something long that glinted in the lantern light. Cody caught his breath.

Bethany was moving rapidly in his direction on the opposite boardwalk. Cody called out, "Miss Hale!" Quickly he stepped into the street and started hurrying toward her. But he had to pause to let a freight wagon pass and cursed in frustration as he dodged around it. As soon as his view was clear, he saw she was now almost opposite him and was cradling a shotgun in her arms.

Cody broke into a run. He had no idea what Bethany was up to, but he doubted it was anything good. He had not seen her since after Stoddard and Dowling had died in the jail cell on Saturday night, following the fiasco of the play, and had no idea what she had been doing since then. But he knew she was upset and figured that she had been holed up in her hotel room ever since. Evidently she had come out sometime to buy or borrow that scattergun.

Bethany was turning into the Bull's Head Saloon as Cody bounded onto the boardwalk. He called her name again, but although he was certain she heard him, she did not slow down or look around. Flinging open the saloon door, she marched in and raised the shotgun.

Cody pounded down the boardwalk as cries of surprise rang from inside the Bull's Head. Racing into the saloon behind Bethany, he heard her exclaim, "Everyone out! Get out of this den of iniquity while you have the chance!"

Cody stopped just inside the entrance several feet behind Bethany, who was sweeping the shotgun from side to side, menacing the large crowd inside the always busy saloon. He quickly scanned the customers and spotted Joselyn Paige standing at one of the faro tables, a stunned expression on her attractive face. The saloon's owner and his two bartenders held their hands up, their faces clearly showing they thought Bethany was crazy.

Cody glanced at the tiny spitfire in front of him. Her back was rigid with anger, her head quivering. He was certain he knew what had prompted her to take matters into her own hands. She had been sitting in her room brooding about what happened Saturday night until she could no longer stand it and decided that violence would work where her morality play had not.

"Miss Hale, what the devil are you doing?" Cody asked quietly.

She gasped in surprise but did not turn around or lower the shotgun. "I'm doing the Lord's work, Deputy, not the devil's," she hissed. "This saloon must be closed, and I'm going to see that it is."

"By shooting it up?"

"If necessary." Bethany's voice was firm, determined.

"That's not going to do any good," Cody replied, trying to sound calm and reasonable. "You'll just wind up in jail, and the Bull's Head will keep on doing business as usual." He paused, then went on, "Probably they'll be busier than ever. Folks will want to come see the place that got shot up by a pretty little temperance lady from back East."

"You're making fun of me," she accused.

"No, ma'am, not really. I'm just telling you the truth."

Bethany half turned as he took a step toward her. "Don't come any closer!" she warned shrilly. "I'll shoot anyone who interferes with me."

"Now, you don't want to hurt anybody," Cody said soothingly, watching her intently. There was something ludicrous about such a small woman threatening people with a big shotgun, but the buckshot would be just as deadly no matter who fired it. Maybe if he could keep her talking, she would get tired and drop that very heavy weapon.

But she was drawing strength from her beliefs, he realized as he saw how the shotgun's double barrels never wavered. And she gave no sign that she could be talked out of the dangerous turn her crusade had taken.

"I don't want to hurt anyone," Bethany cried. "That's why all of you have to leave now!"

Several customers started to move, edging nervously past her, heading for the door. One cowboy said, "Sure, lady, if that's what you want. There's plenty of other places around where a man can get a drink."

A slight smile played over Bethany's face. "Soon there won't be," she promised. "When I'm done, liquor and its evil will be driven out of this town!"

One of the bartenders spoke up. "Look, lady, you want us to close down, we'll close down. All right? Just stop waving that scattergun around."

"Not yet," Bethany said grimly. "You'll forgive me if I don't trust you, sir, considering the business you're in."

"I don't care who you trust, miss," the owner of the saloon called from where he stood at the end of the bar. "But you can't come in here and threaten my customers like this. Deputy, I demand that you arrest this woman."

"Take it easy," Cody advised the saloonkeeper. Several people were filing past him toward the door, and he used their movements as cover while he edged closer to Bethany. He went on, "Just what is it you want, Miss Hale?"

"You know quite well what I want, Deputy. I want all the saloons in Abilene closed permanently."

"Will you settle for just this one tonight?"

Bethany hesitated. "I suppose I might—on the condition that you promise it will remain closed from now on."

Cody shook his head. "I can't promise that. But I can tell you that there won't be any more drinks sold here tonight. How about that?"

"Cody!" the outraged saloon owner exclaimed. "You don't know what you're saying—"

"You'd rather have a few holes blown in your place?" Cody snapped. "Some folks hurt, maybe?" He waited as the red-faced saloonkeeper sputtered into silence, then he turned back to Bethany. "What about it, Miss Hale? Are you willing to accept that deal?"

"Are you going to arrest me?" she asked.

Before Cody replied, he shot a fast, hard glance at the saloon owner, warning the man to keep his mouth shut. "I don't think there's any reason to do that," Cody said. "There hasn't been any damage so far. As long as we keep it that way . . ."

"What about the business this crazy woman has run off?" the saloonkeeper demanded, ignoring Cody's warning look.

"Count yourself lucky it's not worse," Cody replied

tersely. "Like I said, this is liable to increase your business in the long run."

"All right, that makes sense." The man looked at Bethany. "You're getting off lucky, young woman. You'd better grab this opportunity while you've got it."

For a split second, Cody thought Bethany was going to unload both barrels at the saloonkeeper's arrogant expression. He tensed reflexively, preparing to leap forward to spoil her aim and save her from a murder charge. But abruptly she relaxed.

"The Bible preaches forgiveness, sir, so I shall forgive you for your insults." She took a deep breath and lowered the scattergun.

Heaving a sigh of relief, Cody stepped forward, his right hand reaching for the weapon. His fingers closed over the cold metal, and he twisted the gun out of Bethany's grasp. Turning to the remaining customers, he said, "You heard the deal, folks. You'll have to find some place else to do your drinking tonight. The Bull's Head is closed."

Now that the danger appeared to be over, a few customers grumbled in protest, but they began to clear out. Within minutes, the place was empty except for Cody, Bethany, the owner, and the two bartenders.

"Satisfied now?" Cody asked the young woman.

"No, but I suppose this will have to do." Bethany turned to glare at the tavern keeper. "I warn you, sir, this isn't over. I shall continue to oppose your evil and that of the other saloons in Abilene."

Cody took her arm and steered her toward the door before the target of her wrath could respond. "Come on," he told her firmly. "There's been enough excitement for one night."

Still glaring, Bethany allowed Cody to lead her out of the saloon. When they reached the boardwalk and the door was closed behind them, the deputy paused and broke the shotgun open. He grunted in surprise as he peered into the empty barrels.

"No shells," he commented and then narrowed his eyes at her. "You couldn't have done much damage with this scattergun, Miss Hale. But I suppose you knew that."

"Of course," Bethany snapped. "I didn't come to Abilene to hurt anyone, Deputy. I came to save people from harm."

"Hard to stop folks from doing something they're bound and determined to do." Cody closed the shotgun. "And waving a gun around sure isn't the way to do it. Where'd you get this thing, anyway?"

"It was behind the counter in the hotel. The clerk was nowhere around—"

"So you helped yourself." Cody shook his head and went on, "Well, maybe he'll agree not to charge you with theft. I'll have a talk with him. In the meantime, you'd better go back to your room and stay out of trouble."

Bethany's features tightened with indignation. "Stay out of trouble?" she echoed. "You don't seem to understand, Deputy. I'd fly in the face of Hell itself to end the evil of alcohol! I'd do *anything*!"

The passionate fervor rang in her voice and glowed on her face. Bethany believed so deeply in what she was doing that she would take all kinds of foolish chances. If he had not moved quickly tonight, she might have gotten herself shot by bursting into a saloon with a cocked shotgun.

"I know you think you're doing the right thing," he

began, attempting once more to reason with her. "But there're other ways to go about it."

"Ways that don't work," Bethany shot back scornfully. "You can *talk* to a person until you're blue in the face and try to show them where they're wrong, but when they've been drinking, it's no good. They just keep guzzling that awful stuff until it's too late . . . until they're . . . they're . . ." Her voice trailed off, and a sudden sob wracked her small frame.

Cody stood there awkwardly, unsure what to do. His first impulse was to put the shotgun down and take her into his arms, but considering her moral rectitude, he was afraid she would misinterpret the gesture. So he stayed where he was, waiting in silence as Bethany's crying ended in a flurry of sniffles.

She took a deep breath and said, "I-I'm sorry you had to witness such an emotional display, Deputy. You just can't know how difficult this fight has been. I've tried so hard, and it seems everything I do backfires. The morality play just caused trouble for the town and for your . . . your poor brother."

"Judah's got to take the responsibility for his own problems," Cody said, trying not to sound harsh. In reality, he was more than a little resentful that Bethany had roped Judah into something that had turned out badly for him. But dwelling on that would not do any good now.

"Have you seen him or talked to him since . . . ?"

Cody shook his head. "Nope, he's holed up somewhere, I imagine."

"Drinking, probably."

"Could be," Cody admitted.

"And it's my fault." Bethany shuddered. "Ever since Saturday night, I've been sitting in my hotel room, thinking about everything that has gone wrong. I simply couldn't take it anymore. I had to get out and *do* something, try to atone for my mistakes and get the crusade back on the right path."

"I reckon you'd do just about anything if you thought it would help stop folks from drinking, wouldn't you?"

She nodded solemnly. "That's right. I would."

Cody lightly touched her arm. "Well, now I want you to go back to your room and get some rest. And try not to brood about things. That'll just make them worse."

"I suppose you're right," she murmured, but she did not sound convinced.

When Cody and Bethany entered the lobby, the clerk was behind the desk, and his eyes widened in surprise when he saw the shotgun in the deputy's hand. Cody strode over to the desk and thrust the weapon at the startled man. "Here you go, Claude," he said. "Thanks for the loan of the shotgun."

"What—"

"The marshal and I appreciate it."

"Well . . . sure, Cody, anytime." The man shook his head, content to remain puzzled. Evidently he had not noticed that the shotgun was gone.

Cody escorted Bethany to the foot of the stairs. "Good night, Miss Hale," he said. "Try to get some rest."

"I will. And you'll let me know if you hear anything about Judah, won't you?"

"Sure." Cody nodded. "Don't worry about him, though. He'll be all right."

"I'll pray that's true, Deputy."

Cody waited until she had climbed the stairs and disappeared down the hall before he left the hotel. As he stepped onto the boardwalk, he thought that if he were the praying kind, he would say a few words on Judah's behalf, too. Bethany was probably better at that sort of thing; maybe she could take up the slack for him.

But if Judah did not show up soon, Cody would have to try praying himself.

Cody tossed sleeplessly for most of the night in the little room at the marshal's office. Something that he had seen or heard in the last few days nagged at him like an annoying fly buzzing in his head. He watched the shadows dancing on the ceiling, trying to force the idea into focus. But no matter how hard he tried, he could not pin it down. Added to his concern over Judah was this new worry—whatever it was—and both kept him awake until dawn began to lighten the eastern sky.

He finally dozed off, only to be awakened by the elusive idea a half hour later. Dragging himself wearily out of his bunk, he swung his bare feet onto the cold stone floor, shuddered as a chill ran up his spine, and trudged into the office to start a fire in the stove and put water on to heat for coffee. Then, still half asleep, he pulled on his pants, boots, and shirt and went to the front door.

As he stepped onto the boardwalk for some fresh air that he hoped would clear his muddled thoughts, he noticed that his breath puffed out in a plume of steam. The sun was just rising, and the morning was crisp and cool. Normally he enjoyed autumn mornings like this one; he just wished he had gotten more sleep.

By the time Luke Travis arrived an hour later, Cody felt somewhat better. He had downed several cups of strong black coffee, then strolled to the Sunrise Café and eaten a big breakfast of flapjacks and bacon. When Travis pushed open the office door, Cody was sitting at the desk, methodically cleaning the rifles from the rack behind him.

"Everything quiet this morning?" the marshal asked as he hung his hat on a peg.

"Quiet as can be," Cody replied. He put down his rag and turned in the chair to replace the last of the rifles in the rack. Standing up, he went on, "You need me for anything this morning?"

Travis shook his head. "Nothing that I know about right now. Why? You have something in mind?"

"I thought I'd ride out to the orphanage and see if Sister Laurel has heard anything from Judah. I figure he'd get in touch with me if he was going to talk to anybody, but you never know."

"No," Travis said. "You don't."

Cody reached for his hat and jacket. "I'll see you later, Marshal."

Within a few minutes old Wiley who ran the livery stable had Cody's horse saddled and ready to go. The deputy mounted the pinto and headed west down Texas Street toward the church and orphanage, which were only seven blocks away.

When he reached Elm Street, he saw the children from the orphanage walking to school, bundled up in warm clothing. All of them waved at him as he rode by, and Cody returned their greetings with a smile. He had always enjoyed the children, and the sight of their eager faces on this worrisome morning cheered him. As he drew even with Michael Hirsch, the impish redhead called, "Hi, Cody. Where're you going?"

"To church," Cody replied, then grinned as he saw the surprised look on Michael's freckled face. It *was* a little unusual for him to be going to church, he supposed.

He tethered his horse at the iron rail in front of the church and then, on the off chance that Judah had returned, went inside. Pushing the heavy wooden doors open, Cody stepped into the white, high-ceilinged room, his footsteps echoing in the empty sanctuary. Everything appeared normal—except that Judah was not there.

Brushing aside his disappointment, Cody walked to the parsonage. He found Sister Laurel seated on the floor in the big, sun-drenched parlor with the children who were too young to go to school surrounding her. She looked up from the game they were playing as Cody paused in the doorway, and her bright blue eyes quickened with interest. "You're doing very well, children," she told the little ones cheerfully. "Please go on without me for just a moment." Then she rose and threaded her way among the seated youngsters toward Cody.

Before she reached him, however, he shook his head. "I can tell by looking at you that you're about to ask the same question I was going to ask you," he said softly.

"You haven't seen your brother, either?"

"I'm afraid not."

Sister Laurel sighed. "I've been praying for Judah," she said anxiously. "I'm very afraid for him, Cody."

"So am I, Sister. But there's still no sign of him." He glanced at the children. "How are you getting along out here without him to help? Do you need anything?"

"We're all right," the nun assured him. "The children miss Judah, of course, but they're doing fine. Agnes and I have told them that he had to go away for a while and that he will be back soon. The younger ones can accept that quite easily; the older ones have a bit more trouble with it, especially when they hear things about him at school." She sighed again. "I'm afraid your brother has caused quite a scandal in some circles. As uncharitable as it is for me to say it, I almost wish that young woman had never come to Abilene."

"You and me both, Sister," Cody agreed. "I reckon most of the folks in town feel the same way." Quickly he told her what had happened the night before in the Bull's Head.

Sister Laurel shook her head and clucked her tongue. "Miss Hale has good intentions," she said. "But she has a great deal to learn about people. However, she's still young. Perhaps in time she will learn to temper her passion with reason."

"I wouldn't count on it," Cody muttered disgustedly. "She went into that saloon last night looking like she had a blood score to settle—" He stopped suddenly and frowned. The elusive idea that had bothered him all night was trying to push itself from the recesses of his mind.

"Cody? Is something wrong?"

Cody blinked and peered at Sister Laurel. "I reckon there could be," he said quietly. "I may have just figured something out."

"About Judah?"

Cody shook his head. "Nope, I still don't have a clue about where he's gone. But there's something else I need to check." He started toward the door, then turned to say, "Listen, if you need a hand out here while Judah's gone, just let me know. I'll do what I can."

"Thank you. I'm sure we'll be fine, though."

Cody nodded, put his hat on, and went out quickly to his horse.

As he rode back toward town, he examined the theory that had suddenly formed from the nebulous worries that had rankled him. He did not want to believe it, but some of the facts fit. And he was going to check on some others that might fill in the gaps.

He rode straight to the Kansas Pacific depot. The Western Union office was located inside the big red-brick building, and that was Cody's destination. He took a message pad and a stubby pencil from Jason, the telegraph operator who was on duty, and quickly printed out a message. When he handed it back to the telegrapher, Jason scanned the words and raised his eyebrows. "The Christian Ladies Temperance Society, huh?" he said. "Fixing to join, are you, Cody?"

"It's official business, Jason," Cody snapped. "Just send it, all right?"

"Sure, sure," the operator mumbled. Pulling his key in front of him on the desk, he began tapping out the message.

When he was done, Cody asked, "How long will it take to get a reply?"

Jason shrugged. "Hard to say, probably at least an hour."

"I'll be back."

Cody left the depot and rode around the corner to the marshal's office. Travis, who was seated at his desk, glanced up and frowned as Cody strode into the room.

"Why didn't you tell me about what happened over at the Bull's Head last night?" the marshal asked sharply. "I had to find out about it in the café."

Cody grimaced. "There really wasn't much to it. I was able to head things off before there was any real trouble. Besides, that shotgun wasn't even loaded. She just had it for show."

"That kind of show could have gotten somebody hurt."

"That's what I told her," Cody said. "I don't think she'll be pulling any more stunts like that, Marshal."

"I hope not," Travis grunted. "Seems to me Miss Hale has worn out her welcome in Abilene. Eula Grafton was waiting for me when I got back from breakfast."

Cody frowned. "Mrs. Grafton? What did she want?"

"She'd heard about the trouble at the Bull's Head, too. She wanted to assure me that her society didn't have anything to do with it. In fact, they're withdrawing all their support from Miss Hale. According to Mrs. Grafton, the girl's just hurting their efforts to curb drinking in town with her tendency toward violence. The society wants her to leave."

Cody nodded, not surprised. He wondered if Bethany knew about the change in the local temperance society's attitude. She would view it as another setback in her mission, which was rapidly turning into a one-woman crusade. Bethany would be better off if she just got on the train and returned to Philadelphia, he mused.

If that was where she really came from, Cody added to himself. He might have the answer to that question soon.

He was still in the office less than an hour later when the door flew open and Jason hurried in with a piece of yellow paper in his hand. The telegrapher said,

"Here's the answer to that wire you sent, Cody. It came in quicker than I expected, so I thought I'd run it over here to you."

"Thanks, Jason," Cody said, digging a coin out of his pocket and handing it to the man in exchange for the message. He started reading the words printed on the paper, and his face tightened.

When Jason was gone, Travis looked at Cody and asked, "What wire? What's wrong, Cody?"

The deputy took a deep breath. "I sent a telegram to the headquarters of the Christian Ladies Temperance Society, back in Philadelphia," he said. "I wanted to find out more about Bethany Hale's background."

"Why would you want to do that?"

"Because all along, I've had the feeling that she's been hiding something, Marshal. It's like she's got some sort of personal stake in this attempt to wipe out drinking. Maybe whiskey killed somebody close to her, or something like that."

Travis stood up, his eyes alive with interest. "That would explain why she's so all-fired determined about it, all right," he said. "I reckon that's the answer from the society you've got there."

Cody nodded.

"Well, were you right?"

Cody held the message toward Travis. "I don't know. According to this, the Christian Ladies Temperance Society has never heard of Miss Bethany Hale, and they sure as hell didn't send her out here to Abilene."

"What?" Taking the message from Cody's outstretched hand, Travis read it quickly. "Then she's been lying all along."

"And that's not the worst of it." Cody's voice was

grim. "I remembered something else this morning. Those two cowhands died in the cellblock right after Miss Hale had taken them some coffee."

Travis stared at him, his eyes narrowing. "You think *she's* the one who poisoned them?"

"I don't know," Cody said honestly. "But I sure intend to find out."

Chapter Eleven

———◆———

CODY WAS HEADING TOWARD THE DOOR WHEN TRAVIS'S voice stopped him. "Hold on a minute," the marshal said. "There're a few things you haven't thought of."

"Like what?"

Travis stepped from behind his desk. "What about Abner Peavey?"

Cody frowned. "That's right. Peavey might've died from drinking bad whiskey, too."

"And that was before Bethany Hale showed up in Abilene. That girl doesn't strike me as the sort to go around poisoning people, either."

"She lost her temper and got in a fight with Joselyn Paige, and she stormed into the Bull's Head waving a shotgun around," Cody pointed out. "Stoddard and Dowling said some rough things to her earlier in the evening on the night they died. Maybe she thought she was taking some sort of righteous vengeance on them for helping to ruin her play."

"Judah did more to ruin it than Stoddard and Dowling," Travis said bluntly.

Cody's face flushed with anger. "Maybe so, but there's still the matter of that coffee she gave them."

Travis rubbed his jaw, then nodded. "That's true. And it's suspicious enough that it needs to be checked out. Do you want to do it?"

"I surely do. And I'm going to do it right now." Cody turned and reached for the door knob.

"Hold on a minute. Remember you don't have any proof. It might not be a good idea to start throwing accusations around."

"I'm not going to accuse anybody. I'm just going to see if Miss Hale will answer some questions—like who the devil she really is and what she's doing in Abilene."

Cody went out, almost slamming the door behind him.

He paused on the boardwalk and took a deep breath, trying to force his racing brain to slow down a little. Travis was right; Abner Peavey's death threw a kink into his theory. But it was possible that Peavey had not been poisoned at all. The man might have actually drunk himself to death, just as Travis and Cyrus Worden had thought at first. At this late date, there was no way of being sure. Either way, Bethany Hale could still be responsible for the deaths of Stoddard and Dowling.

Cody did not want to believe that. He had liked Bethany from the start, despite her coolness toward him. Even though she might have unwittingly prompted Judah's relapse into drinking, Cody had not turned against her. But if she had slipped something into the coffee she had given to Stoddard and Dowling, then she was nothing more than a cold-blooded murderer, no matter how obnoxious they had been after the performance of the play.

Cody could not forget the fervor in Bethany's voice as she insisted that she would do anything to further her cause.

Anything . . . including murder?

He walked quickly toward the Grand Palace Hotel and learned from Claude that Bethany was in Room Seven. Cody took the stairs two at a time as he climbed to the upper corridor.

He rapped sharply on the door of Room Seven, so sharply that he scraped some of the skin off his knuckles. He paid no attention to that. A moment after his knock, a surprised female voice called, "Who is it, please?"

"Cody Fisher," he said flatly.

He heard Bethany say, "Oh!" Then, seconds later, she opened the door and looked anxiously up at him. "What is it, Deputy?" she asked. "Have you found your brother?"

Cody shook his head. "No, this isn't about Judah. He's still missing, though, if you care."

"What do you mean, if I care?" Bethany sounded angry now. "Of course I care. I've been worried ever since he—"

"I need to ask you some questions," Cody cut in. "Can I come in?"

"Into . . . my room? I-I'm not sure that would be proper, Deputy Fisher, not without some sort of chaperone." Bethany clutched at the door, clearly disturbed by Cody's grim, insistent demeanor.

"All I want is some answers," he said. "And you may want to answer in private once you hear the questions."

"All right." She stepped back. "Please, come in."

Cody strode into the room and glanced around. The small room was immaculate, but he was not surprised at its neatness. That was exactly what he would have expected from Bethany Hale. He remembered enough of his manners to take off his hat, then turned to face her. She was wearing a green dress that was attractive because of its simplicity. Cody thought she looked lovely—but that did not have any impact on the reason he had come.

"What is it you want to know?" she asked.

"First of all, who in blazes are you?" he demanded.

Bethany bit her lip. "You know quite well who I am, Deputy. I'm Bethany Hale, from the Christian Ladies Temperance Society—"

"No, you're not," Cody interrupted, shaking his head. "Your name may be Bethany Hale, but that temperance society never heard of you."

"Why, that's preposterous! Of course they've heard of me. They sent me to Abilene to help stamp out drinking."

"I sent them a wire and received the reply a few minutes ago. They don't have anybody named Bethany Hale on their membership list, and they haven't sent anybody to Abilene to do anything." He wanted to reach out and grab her shoulders and shake the truth out of her, but he restrained himself. "Now, who are you really, and what are you doing here?"

Bethany stared at him for a long moment, her face going pale. Cody returned her gaze steadily. Finally, she sighed and closed her eyes. "My name is Bethany

Hale," she said wearily. "I've come to Abilene to put an end to drinking—"

"That's a lie!" Now Cody did reach out with one hand and grasp her upper arm. "I told you, the Temperance Society—"

"Damn the Temperance Society!" Bethany cried out, her eyes opening and flashing with anger. Her fierce reaction stunned Cody, making him release her and take a step back as she went on, "Where was the high and mighty Christian Ladies Temperance Society when my brother was drinking himself to death in some back-alley Kansas saloon? I'll tell you where they were, Cody Fisher—they were sipping tea and feeling self-righteous and spouting useless platitudes! They don't understand. You have to meet violence with violence!"

Cody could hear the fury in her voice, and in that moment he was convinced that she was fully capable of killing someone if she believed they deserved to die. Within seconds, she had turned from a petite, attractive young woman into some kind of avenging angel. "And you consider drinking to be violence?" he asked.

"It killed my brother. How much more violent can something be?"

"What happened?" Cody wanted to keep her talking, to give her a chance to calm down a little. He was getting the answers he wanted, but suddenly he was not sure if he had done the right thing.

"Matthew—my brother—started drinking back in Philadelphia. My family is . . . quite well-to-do. My father said that he would not have a drunkard in the house, so he threw Matthew out. I only saw him once more before he left the city. He promised me that he had stopped drinking, but he was too proud to return to Father and beg forgiveness. So he intended to come west, to make a new start for himself. He was coming to Kansas, he said . . ." Bethany's voice trailed off, and a shudder ran through her. Cody kept quiet, and a moment later she regained control and went on, "We received a wire from Abilene about a year ago. My brother Matthew was dead. He had died of pneumonia after he passed out in a drunken stupor in the snow and stayed there for hours before anyone found him. But it was the liquor that really killed him."

Cody shook his head. "I'm sorry. I was already a deputy then, but I don't remember hearing about any Matthew Hale dying last year."

"He was using another name, calling himself Matthew Allen. That was his middle name. I suppose he didn't want to bring any further shame on the family when he got out here and realized that he couldn't quit drinking. But he carried our family's name and address among his belongings. The undertaker wired us . . . to see if we wanted to pay for the burial." Bethany's voice caught again, but she went on hurriedly, "My father refused. He wired back that he knew no one named Matthew Allen. My brother . . . my brother is probably buried in an unmarked pauper's plot somewhere on your so-called Boot Hill. I've looked, but I haven't been able to find the grave."

Cody took a deep breath. He had no idea what to say to her. He had expected some sort of story from her to explain her lies, but not this tragic tale she had just revealed. Despite its melodramatic aspects, it rang true.

"I swore then that I was going to do everything in my power to save other people from the fate my brother had suffered," Bethany said. "I've been preparing ever since for the mission that brought me here. And now you know the truth about me, Deputy."

"What about that Christian Ladies Temperance Society business?" Cody asked.

"I went to them first, to see if I could work with them. But I could tell immediately that they didn't really understand the gravity of the situation. However, I thought if I borrowed their name, so to speak, I might be able to find more support from the local temperance groups. You saw how effective it was here. Mrs. Grafton and her friends couldn't do enough for me at first."

Cody nodded. "Until you started brawling in saloons and threatening people with shotguns," he pointed out. "Then that support disappeared pretty quick."

Bethany lifted her chin. "I'll continue the battle alone, if need be. Abilene is only the beginning, a symbolic starting place because this is where my brother's life ended."

"Some other folks have died here, too." Cody's voice hardened. "What about those cowhands, Stoddard and Dowling?"

Bethany's forehead creased in a puzzled frown, and she gave a little shake of her head. "I don't understand. Do you mean those unfortunate men who passed away while they were in jail?"

"The ones who drank the coffee you gave them just before they died," he said coldly.

The young woman's eyes widened in horror as she realized what Cody was implying. "Oh, no," she gasped. "You don't think that I . . . you couldn't think . . ."

"You said you'd do *anything* to get rid of drinking. I reckon that could include killing a couple of drunks."

"I didn't," Bethany insisted, tears glistening in her eyes. "I swear to you that I had nothing to do with their deaths, Deputy. I only want to help people, not hurt them."

"You lied about who you really are," Cody said flatly. "You might be lying about this, too."

"Oh . . ." Bethany's face became even paler, but then two angry crimson spots flushed her cheeks. Her arm flew up and swung back as she started to slap Cody across the face. His left hand met it easily in a gesture that seemed almost lazy in its deceptive speed. He caught her wrist, his fingers clamping around it like iron and holding it motionless.

"You do lose your temper pretty easy, don't you?"

"You . . . you are the most arrogant man I've ever known!" she sputtered. "If you think I've broken the law, why don't you go prove it?"

"That's just what I intend to do."

"Fine. But until you do, I'll thank you to get out of my room, sir!"

Releasing her arm, he said, "I'm going. But I'll be back. I'm sorry about your brother, Miss Hale, I really am. But that doesn't change anything."

"Don't you even mention my brother! Just get out of here!"

Cody nodded and turned to the door. He half expected her to throw something at him as he left, but she stayed where she was, standing in the center of the room, shoulders slumped, tears running down her cheeks, breathing heavily. Pausing at the door, he took one last look at her, then closed it softly behind him.

The sound of her sobbing followed him as he

started down the hall. At that moment, he hated himself for what he had done. But if she was guilty, he intended to prove it. She had lied to him, lied to Judah, lied to everyone in Abilene; there was no doubt about that. But was she a killer?

Cody hoped that not too many more people would be hurt before he found the answer.

At noon on Wednesday Kermit Barlow, now fully recovered, had just put the big pot of squirrel stew on the table and was stepping through the front door of the family's cabin to call his brother and cousins when he heard yelling coming from the barn. He hurried to the corner of their ramshackle house and looked around it in time to see Denton, Amos, and Jed running frantically from the barn. Denton shouted, "It's gonna blow!"

An explosion rocked the barn behind them. Amos and Jed howled in fear and flung themselves on the ground, covering their heads with their arms. Denton kept running until Kermit leapt toward him, grabbed his arm, and jerked him to a halt.

"Goddammit, what happened?" Kermit demanded, shaking his younger brother.

"The line on one of the boilers got twisted up somehow!" Denton bleated, casting apprehensive glances over his shoulder at the barn. Hissing noises were coming from inside it, and steam was billowing through the open door. Denton went on excitedly, "We didn't notice in time, and the pressure got too high!"

The twins were still cowering on the ground. Amos looked up and cried, "The boiler blowed up, Kermit! It just blowed up!"

Kermit glanced at the barn and spat. "Blowed up real good, from the looks of it," he rasped. "You two get up off the damned ground! We got us some cleanin' up to do."

Pulling Denton with him, Kermit trudged toward the barn. As he passed Amos and Jed, he resisted the impulse to kick them. They slowly got to their feet as Kermit glared at them, then trailed after him to the barn.

Most of the steam had dissipated quickly, rising to the rafters and escaping through the gaping holes in the siding and through the open door. The barn reeked of whiskey.

Kermit stood in the doorway, waving his arms to clear what steam was left from his line of vision, and squinted at the wreckage. They had set up three separate boilers to make as much moonshine as possible, and one of the big metal contraptions had indeed blown up. A huge split ran down one side; the pressure had built to such a point that the metal simply gave way.

"Don't look like the other two stills was hurt," Kermit said. He gestured impatiently to his three relatives. "Get in there and clean up that mess. 'Fore you do that, though, put out the fires under them other two boilers. We sure as hell don't want no fire spreadin' in here."

If that happened, it would be even more disastrous than the boiler explosion. If fire were to reach the barrels of stored whiskey that lined one wall of the barn and ignite them, the blast would be so tremendous that it would put even that new invention called dynamite to shame.

"What are we goin' to do, Kermit?" Denton whined as Amos and Jed extinguished the fires under the two remaining boilers. "We can't afford to lose that boiler."

"Ain't nothin' else we can do right now. It'll take money to get it fixed up, and we ain't got enough, not since we had to get them new axles for the wagons."

Kermit's voice was bleak. This incident was just another in a series of accidents that had plagued the Barlows since their trip into Abilene a couple of days earlier. On Monday night Denton had discovered that several of the barrels stored in the barn had mysteriously developed leaks, and valuable whiskey had seeped unnoticed into the ground. None of them knew how long the kegs had been leaking, but a dozen barrels were empty. Then, at the start of a delivery run on Tuesday morning, the rear axles on two of the wagons had broken. Twenty barrels tumbled out of the two beds and broke open, pouring their entire contents on the thirsty Kansas soil.

When things started going bad, it seemed as if they just kept on going that way.

Denton was still clutching at his brother's sleeve. "We got to do somethin', Kermit," he wailed. "Ever'thin's fallin' apart!"

Kermit jerked his arm out of Denton's grip. "Dammit, I know that better'n you!" he snarled. "Lemme think a minute, why don't you . . ." Suddenly, he turned toward Denton and waved a hand at the barrels. "We been thinkin' too small. I reckon it's time we made a *real* whiskey run!"

The twins, hearing the excitement in Kermit's voice, stopped cleaning up the barn and rushed over to Denton and Kermit. "What do you mean?" Denton asked.

"We been sellin' three barrels here and half a dozen there, makin' lots of trips and movin' plenty of whiskey, but what we need is somethin' that'll pay off big. I think we ought to load up ever' barrel we got on hand and take 'em to Dodge City!"

Denton gaped at him for a moment, then exclaimed, "Dodge City? That's more'n a hunnerd and fifty miles from here, Kermit! It'd take us a week to get there, at least."

"And Injuns 'tween here and there," Jed put in, looking apprehensive.

"And owlhoots," Amos added nervously.

"Yeah, and three times as many saloons in Dodge City as there is in Abilene," Kermit replied, waving off their objections. "You've heard tell what a rip-snorter Dodge is. But I reckon we can sell all our whiskey for a higher profit than we can get around here. Then we can bring the money back and use it to make us a fresh start."

"Well, I reckon it could work out," Denton said dubiously. Amos and Jed nodded tentatively.

"Of course it'll work out," Kermit insisted. "I ain't steered us wrong yet, have I?"

"No, I reckon not. You always was the smart one in the family, Kermit." Denton grinned abruptly. "All right. We'll do 'er. Kansas ain't never seen a whiskey run like the one the Barlows are goin' to put on!"

Kermit slapped his brother on the shoulder. "Damn right! That's the spirit. Now you boys finish cleanin' up this mess so's you can start loadin' the wagons. If you can get 'em all loaded tonight, we can get started first thing in the mornin'.'"

Grinning cheerfully now, Denton, Amos, and Jed began working. As usual, Kermit had come through for them, thinking up an idea to get them out of trouble. Everything was going to be fine, once the big whiskey run had been made.

Kermit stood by and watched, a grin on his face as well—but the expression did not reach his eyes. They were cold and hard and saw things the other Barlows knew nothing about.

It was almost midnight when the door of the Barlow cabin opened slowly and a lone figure slipped silently away from the house into the deep shadows. As the man walked toward the barn, the clouds that had been covering the moon cleared and the silvery light shone brightly on the yard, revealing the unshaven face of Kermit Barlow. He went into the barn and started saddling one of the horses.

Denton, Amos, and Jed were all in the house, asleep; Kermit had checked on each of them before leaving the cabin. They had worked hard all afternoon, cleaning up the mess from the boiler explosion and then loading the whiskey barrels on the wagons. The Barlows owned four heavy vehicles, and each was carrying ten barrels of liquor—forty barrels of whiskey to rescue the Barlow family from the sudden run of bad luck they were having.

Too bad it was not really going to work out that way, Kermit thought as he swung into the saddle and walked the horse quietly away from the farm, heading south.

He had a rifle resting across the pommel of the saddle in front of him, just in case the man he was going to meet tried to double-cross him. Kermit did not think that was likely; after all, he had been dealing with him for weeks. Still, it never hurt to be careful. The plan was speeding up rapidly, and folks had been known to get greedy.

Kermit was greedy himself. That was why he had not considered the matter for very long when the man first approached him with the proposition. The money was good, and it was easy to earn most of the time. Of course, there was the question of betraying his own flesh and blood, but Kermit preferred not to think of it that way.

He was just trying to make enough money so that they could move on to something better, he told himself. Yes, that was it. But it was more difficult to think of it that way when he remembered the three men who had died.

No one was supposed to have been hurt. The Barlows had been putting strychnine in their whiskey ever since the old days in Tennessee. Nothing was better for giving the brew that little extra kick. The stuff was poisonous in bigger doses, but Kermit and his kin had always been careful not to use too much—until the stranger had approached him and offered him money to sabotage his own operation.

It had been the other man's idea to increase the amount of strychnine in the whiskey, just enough to start making people a little sick. But it was not supposed to kill anybody. Kermit figured he had gotten a little heavy-handed a couple of times when he added the extra crystals while nobody was looking.

Well, he could do nothing about it now, Kermit thought as he rode through the darkness toward the spot where he was to meet his mysterious employer. The man always stayed in the shadows and did not let Kermit get a good look at his face, and that was fine with Kermit. He did not need to know whom he had sold out to, just as long as he got paid. And so far there had been no problem with that. He had been squirreling away the extra money under a loose board in the cabin floor, and he had accumulated more than five hundred dollars already. His brother and cousins had no idea he had that kind of money. They would certainly be surprised when he finally broke the news to them. They might be mad at first, too, but Kermit felt sure he could talk them out of that. After all, he was the smart one in the family.

He had been smart enough to cause whiskey barrels to leak and the axles to break and the boiler to explode. The man he was working for had suggested all those tactics, but Kermit carried them out with no trouble.

More than once Kermit had wondered why it would be worth so much money to stop their whiskey production. For that matter, why not just pay them to quit brewing the stuff altogether, instead of working behind the scenes to sabotage the operation? But Kermit did not spend much time pondering such questions. He simply took the man's money and did what he suggested.

The grove of trees where he usually met the stranger loomed up ahead. Kermit reined in fifty yards from the copse and gave a whistle. A moment later a buggy emerged from the trees, rolled slowly toward him, and stopped a few yards away. The vehicle's canopy blocked the moonlight, and the driver's face was hidden in deep shadows. "Good evening, Mr. Barlow," a voice said smoothly.

"Evenin'," Kermit replied. "Well, I done like you said. One of the boilers is busted all to hell. Then I suggested that big whiskey run to Dodge, and the boys finally come around to my way of thinkin'."

"Very good," the man in the buggy said. "Will you be leaving tomorrow?"

"First thing in the mornin'. I figger we'll skitter around Abilene to the north, then when we're west o' town cut south for the trail to Dodge."

"Excellent. I'll have my men waiting. There's no point in prolonging this. They'll stop your wagons sometime before noon and confiscate the whiskey."

"You mean they'll steal it?"

"Exactly," the man confirmed.

"And nobody gets hurt, right?"

"Of course not. My men will have the drop on you and your relatives. You'll have no choice but to surrender the wagons. There won't even be any shooting."

Kermit nodded. "Sounds good. That way the boys'll never know I was in on it."

"Certainly not. No reason for them to know, is there?"

"Reckon not." Kermit cleared his throat. "Uh, you got the money we talked about?"

"Right here." The stranger tossed a small pouch out of the buggy, and as Kermit caught it, the coins inside clinked. "Two hundred dollars in double eagles, just like you requested. I hope you're taking good care of your money, Mr. Barlow."

"Oh, yeah, I got a good hidin' place. The boys wouldn't never think to look under the floor of the cabin." Kermit happily tossed the bag up and down and listened to the pretty clinking sound. Then he grinned as he stowed the pouch under his coat. "Reckon this is the last time we'll be doin' business. Once your fellers take that whiskey tomorrow, we'll be wiped out."

"Yes, but you'll wind up richer in the process." The man started backing up the buggy. "It's been a pleasure doing business with you, Mr. Barlow. Good luck in the future."

"You, too, mister." Kermit turned his horse and kicked it into a trot. He glanced over his shoulder as he rode back toward the cabin, but the stranger had already disappeared.

Some things might not make a whole lot of sense, Kermit thought, but all it took was the sound and feel of gold coins to make everything right.

The man in the buggy drove over the rutted, moonlit trail back toward Abilene, keeping one eye on the road and the other on the shadowy brush that lined it. He was not surprised when a figure on horseback pushed out of the scrubby bushes and trees, walked his horse to the middle of the trail, and paused. Hauling on the lines, the man brought the buggy to a stop.

"Is that you, Rawlings?" he called, his hand hovering near the butt of the gun underneath his coat. Despite the moonlight it was still too dark to make out facial features from this distance.

"Sure, boss," a familiar voice answered. "Who'd you expect it to be?"

The man in the buggy sighed. "Nobody. A man can't be too careful, though."

"Reckon that's true. But you can trust me and my men, as long as you're payin' us." The rider chuckled, then went on in a more serious tone, "You get everything set up with that idiot Barlow?"

"I certainly did. They're starting a whiskey run to Dodge City tomorrow morning with all the liquor they have on hand. At least that's what the other three think. Kermit Barlow knows that you and your men will be stopping them."

The man on horseback laughed, a harsh, unpleasant sound. "I'll bet he don't know you plan for us to kill all four of them. Damned dumb hillbillies!"

"Just be sure none of them lives through the ambush," the man in the buggy said coldly. "Barlow finally let it slip where he's been hiding the money I've paid him, so it won't be any trouble to recover it. I'll do that tomorrow morning after they've gone, while you're hitting them northwest of town."

The rider nodded. "Sounds good. And once they're dead, I reckon you want us to take the whiskey on to Dodge?"

"That's right. You shouldn't have any trouble disposing of it for a good price."

"Got to hand it to you, boss. You've figured out ways to get paid from all sorts of directions."

The man in the buggy took a cigar from his shirt pocket, unwrapped it, and stuck it in his mouth without lighting it. He felt relaxed now and rather satisfied with himself as well. He *had* done a good job of planning this operation, setting up the Barlows and leading them along. They were the biggest obstacle in his path, and he had tricked them into removing themselves. He would make a handsome profit on the deal, too, even with the expense of hiring Rawlings and his hardcases.

"Well, I'd better be going," he said. "Tomorrow's going to be a big day, after all."

"Sure, boss. We'll see you in Wichita next week, like we planned. So long."

The man lifted a hand in farewell as Rawlings turned his horse and rode away. He rolled the cigar from one side of his mouth to the other, then picked up the reins and flicked them, getting his horse moving again.

Outsmarting Kermit Barlow was almost too easy, he thought as the buggy rolled toward Abilene, but a man had to take his opportunities where he found them.

Chapter Twelve

DEPUTY CODY FISHER HAD TOLD BETHANY HALE THAT he would find the evidence to prove she had been responsible for the deaths of the two cowhands. But try as he might, he could turn up nothing solid linking Bethany to the deaths.

He had spent all day Wednesday talking to every clerk and storekeeper in town, trying to learn if Bethany had bought any kind of poison. All of them told him that she had not and swore that had the pretty little temperance lady from the East made such a purchase they would remember it.

Cody then considered the possibility that she had left Abilene to buy the stuff in Salina or one of the other settlements in the area. But after talking with Harvey Bastrop at the railroad station and the men at the livery stables, he was convinced that Bethany had not made use of their services, either. She had been in Abilene all along.

On Thursday morning, after spending two days on the investigation, Cody told Luke Travis about his lack of success. As he wrapped up the report, he said, "All I can figure is that she already had the stuff when she came to Abilene. If that's the way it was, we'll never be able to prove it."

"I warned you we didn't have any evidence," Travis commented. "What's Miss Hale been doing while you were trying to find a trail to follow?"

"Sitting in her room, as far as I can tell," Cody said glumly. "I don't know why she's still here, to tell the truth. It looks like she might as well leave. After all that's happened, nobody's going to take that temperance business seriously anymore."

"Maybe she thought that leaving town while you were poking around would make her look guilty," Travis pointed out.

Cody nodded. "That makes sense . . . if she really is innocent."

"Reckon it's hard for you to accept that possibility, Cody, but I think you're going to have to face it."

The deputy stood up and walked to the window, leaning on the sill and sighing as he looked out at Texas Street. Without turning around, he replied, "I don't mind her being innocent. We haven't gotten along real well—her choice, mind you—but I don't want to see anybody railroaded, either." He turned around and sighed again. "I reckon I ought to go see her, tell her I guess I was wrong about her."

"I was just about to suggest that," Travis said. "If that story about her brother is true, the lady's had enough grief in her life already."

"Yeah." Cody yanked his hat from the peg and then

paused before putting it on. Looking bleakly at Travis, he said, "Her brother dropped out of sight and then died from drinking. I hope the same thing hasn't happened to Judah. It's been five days since he disappeared."

"I imagine Judah's all right," Travis replied. "He's not like Miss Hale's brother. He'll come through, you'll see."

Cody frowned at Travis and started to say something, but the marshal abruptly pulled some paperwork in front of him and picked up his pen. He concentrated on the documents, clearly not wanting to continue the conversation.

"I'll go see Miss Hale," Cody muttered. Then casting a puzzled glance at Travis, he left the office.

The marshal had sounded annoyed at him for bringing up Judah's disappearance. Cody supposed he might have been dwelling on it too much, but after all, Judah was his brother—his only living kin. A man had a right to be worried in those circumstances, plenty worried.

He walked quickly to the Grand Palace Hotel. A cold wind blew down Texas Street, cutting through Cody's jacket. The nights were downright frigid now, and the days had grown steadily colder. The old men who sat on the boardwalk in front of the barber shop were nodding sagely these days and talking about the hard winter that was coming. Cody figured they were probably right.

He went into the hotel and climbed the stairs. He was nervous as he reached the door of Room Seven and lifted his hand to knock on it. He was not used to apologizing to someone he had practically accused of murder. And there was no *practically* about it, he thought; he had come right out and told Bethany that he thought she had killed those two cowboys. He could not really blame her for getting angry at him, especially since he had failed to find anything to back up his charges.

And the worst part about it was that she might still be guilty. Just because he could not prove it did not make her innocent.

He sighed, shook his head, and rapped on the door. He had no choice now except to admit his failure. If she wanted to leave Abilene, there was nothing to hold her.

Cody stared at the unopened door for a minute, then frowned and knocked again. There was still no response. He had not seen Bethany around town during the last few days, but he was certain she was still registered at the hotel. He knocked one more time and waited, then turned toward the staircase, descending it to the lobby.

"Hello, Claude," he said to the clerk behind the desk. "I'm looking for Miss Hale in Room Seven. She's still staying here, isn't she?"

"Oh, sure, Cody," the clerk replied. "But I don't think she's in now. I saw her go out a little while ago."

"Any idea where she was headed?"

The man shook his head. "Sorry."

"But she didn't check out?"

"Oh, no. She wasn't dressed for traveling, and she didn't have her things with her. I'm sure she's somewhere around town."

"Thanks." With a nod, Cody turned and strode out of the hotel.

When he reached the boardwalk, he paused and looked up and down Texas Street. He could always wait and come back to the hotel to see her later, he told himself. But now that he had decided to admit to her that he might have been wrong, he did not want to put it off. Bethany would not have any reason to leave the downtown area; he could take a look around and probably find her without too much trouble.

Cody chuckled dryly. He should probably check the saloons first. She could be making one more try at closing them down.

That proved to be unneccessary. As he walked east along Texas Street, he spotted Bethany emerging from the Great Western Store, a block away on the other side of the street. Cody stepped down from the boardwalk and angled toward her.

She had some sort of package in her arms, he saw as he drew nearer. Whatever it was, it was wrapped in brown paper and appeared to be heavy.

There were steps leading down from the boardwalk at the corner, and Bethany had just reached the bottom of them when she saw Cody hurrying toward her. She stopped and watched him approach, her face expressionless. As he came up to her, he touched the brim of his hat and said, "Good morning, Miss Hale."

"Deputy Fisher," she responded coolly. "What can I do for you? Have you come to arrest me?"

Cody shook his head. "No, ma'am, I just want to talk to you."

For an instant, her icy composure seemed to soften. "Have you heard something about Judah?" she asked quickly.

"I'm afraid not. He still hasn't shown up."

Bethany's expression settled back into the mask she had been wearing at the beginning of the conversation. "Oh. I'm sorry. What was it you wanted to talk to me about, then?"

Cody gestured at the package in her arms and said, "That package looks mighty heavy. Why don't you let me carry it back to the hotel for you, and we can talk on the way?"

Bethany shook her head emphatically. "I'd prefer not to do that, Deputy. If you have something to say to me, I wish you'd just say it."

Cody shifted his feet. "I know, but it's hard for me to stand here and watch a woman holding something heavy, Miss Hale. It goes against my upbringing." He wondered if his mumbling about the package was just his way of putting off the unpleasant task he was facing.

Bethany sighed. "Oh, all right." She glanced across Cedar Street, nodding at the ornate wrought-iron benches that stood near the corner. "Let's go sit down on those benches, and you can tell me whatever it is you're being so mysterious about."

"Fine with me." Cody reached for the package.

Bethany pulled back. "But I'll still carry this, thank you. I'm perfectly capable of bearing my own burdens."

Cody did not doubt that. He walked across the intersection beside her and climbed the steps to the boardwalk. If Cody remembered correctly, the wrought-iron benches had been a project Mrs. Grafton and her friends had undertaken back before the formation of the temperance society. In their opinion Abilene needed to be prettied up to get rid of its cow-town image. The benches had been placed at various spots on the boardwalks around town, and at each end of the seats were matching wrought-iron stands that held flowerpots. The flowers were dead now, killed by the first autumn frost, and the flowerpots would soon be put away until spring. But until the ladies got to them, they were still sitting there.

Bethany settled herself at one end of the bench,

placing the package at her feet. Cody took the other end of the seat, knowing without asking that she would want to keep as much distance as possible between them.

"Now," Bethany said, "what was it you wanted to tell me?"

Cody took a deep breath. "I reckon I might have been wrong about you, Miss Hale," he declared. "I want to get that right out in the open."

"Wrong?"

"I haven't been able to find one blasted thing to prove that you might've poisoned those two cowboys. If you want to leave town, you can go without making anybody suspect you."

"Any more than you already do, you mean." Bethany's voice was tart, but Cody thought he saw her features relax a bit. If she was innocent, it had to have been uncomfortable for her to know that at least one of Abilene's lawmen considered her a prime suspect in two murders.

Cody shook his head. "I can't prove it either way, but I figure I was wrong about you, Miss Hale. I don't think you had anything to do with it." Even as he spoke the words, he realized that he believed them. All along, he had been trying to convince himself otherwise just because the facts had seemed to point that way. But circumstances could be deceiving, he decided.

Bethany smiled slightly, the expression warm and genuine. "I'm glad you feel that way, Deputy. I suppose I was wrong to come into town and lie about who sent me, but everything else I've said has been true. I never wanted to do anything except show people the evils of drinking and try to put a stop to it."

Cody leaned back against the bench. The metal was

cold, and even in better weather the seat was not very comfortable, but at the moment he did not care. He felt a great sense of relief; this conversation had gone better than he had feared it would. Bethany did not seem to be holding a grudge, and he was grateful for that.

"I never doubted your motives, ma'am," he said. "I just wasn't sure how far you'd go to accomplish them. Sorry I didn't believe you right off."

"You had your job to do. And according to Dr. Bloom, someone really *did* poison those men, whether it was deliberate or not."

"The stuff had to be in the whiskey they were drinking when they started that fight," Cody said, casting his mind back to that night. So much had happened—the play, Judah's drinking, the trouble during Bethany's lecture, the ruckus with Nestor Gilworth, the brawl at Earl's place, the painful deaths of Stoddard and Dowling . . .

Travis had tracked the whiskey to the Barlows, but he had been as unsuccessful at finding evidence against them as Cody had been in his investigation of Bethany. Cody did not like it, but there was a very real possibility that the poisonings would go unsolved. Maybe they had been accidental. Nothing else had happened since then; Travis had asked every saloon in town to let him know if anybody got unusually sick from drinking, and so far no one had.

Cody shook his head. "We'll probably never know," he said.

"I'm sorry." Bethany sounded as if she meant it.

Cody forced a grin. "Reckon you'll be leaving pretty soon. There's nothing to keep you here now."

"Nothing except my mission."

He looked dubious. "You'll never get people to stop drinking, Miss Hale. It's just not possible."

"Perhaps not. I will be leaving Abilene shortly." Bethany smiled. "It's possible that a new start somewhere else might prove more successful. But I still have one more thing I want to do here." She stood up. "I really must go now, Deputy. I'm glad we had this talk, though. It's nice to know that you don't hate me."

"I've never hated you, Bethany," Cody said, deliberately using her first name. She blushed slightly but did not object. He was grinning as she started to bend for her package. Moving quickly, he reached it first and scooped it up. "Let me get that for you," he insisted.

"No!" Bethany cried, but she was too late. Cody was hefting the package in his arms.

He could feel the object's shape through the brown wrapping paper and could hear a faint sloshing noise as he shifted it in his hands. A familiar, acrid odor emanated from the package. He pulled back a corner of the paper and had his guess confirmed. Bethany's face was set in anxious lines when he looked at her and asked, "What the devil are you doing with a can of coal oil? Planning to burn down every saloon in Abilene?"

He was joking, but Bethany's voice was serious as she answered, "No, not the saloons—but fire is a purifying agent."

Those words sent a chill up Cody's spine. "What are you talking about, Bethany?" he asked, almost afraid of her reply.

"There's a warehouse a couple of blocks from here on the other side of the railroad tracks where most of

Abilene's saloons and taverns store their extra stocks of liquor. Mrs. Grafton told me about it before she and her friends decided they didn't support our common cause as strongly as I do. It should make quite a conflagration, don't you think? Just imagine, thousands of gallons of whiskey that will never get the chance to corrupt and destroy innocent people."

Bethany's voice had trailed off to a whisper that had gotten softer but somehow more intense as she spoke. Cody stared at her, thunderstruck. She had just come right out and admitted that she was planning to burn down a warehouse with this coal oil he was holding.

"Dammit, you can't do that!" he exclaimed. "It's against the law—"

"I told you once before, there are higher laws than those of the State of Kansas," Bethany replied calmly. "Please give me my package." She reached for it.

Cody half turned. He was still stunned by her admission. Here he had thought that he was wrong about her, that she was not crazy after all, and then to come up with this idea—

"No, ma'am," he said firmly. "You just come along with me. We're going to go have a talk with the marshal."

"I can't, Cody. I . . . I'm sorry."

She moved faster than he expected, scooping up the flowerpot from the stand at the end of the bench and lunging at him. The bulky, paper-wrapped can of coal oil slowed him down as he tried to dodge. The flowerpot slammed into the side of his head, shattering into a hundred pieces and knocking his hat off. Clumps of dirt showered on his shoulder and down the front of his shirt.

Cody felt himself falling, felt the package slipping from his grasp. Bright lights began to flash behind his eyes. He had been knocked out before and knew what was happening to him. Nevertheless he tried desperately to hang onto consciousness. But it was futile.

He landed heavily on the planks of the boardwalk. Somewhere far away, he heard Bethany's voice echoing hollowly as she said again, "I'm sorry."

One last thought flashed through his stunned brain before he fell all the way into darkness—she had called him Cody.

The Barlows had started from their farm early that morning, not long after sunrise. Each man drove a wagon pulled by a team of mules. Kermit was in the lead wagon, with Denton, Amos, and Jed following behind. The heavily loaded wagons could not move very fast. Denton's estimate that it would take them at least a week to get to Dodge City was probably correct . . . *if* they were going all the way to Dodge City. Kermit knew better.

His cohort in the scheme to hijack the whiskey had not told him exactly where the raid would take place, but Kermit suspected it would be soon. He kept his team moving, his eyes constantly scanning the horizon for some sign of the phony ambushers.

His brother and his cousins were in high spirits. They had recovered from the despair they had felt after the boiler explosion, and now they were looking forward to seeing Dodge and collecting a pretty price for the barrels of whiskey that were loaded in the wagon beds. It would have been an exciting trip, Kermit mused. He was almost sorry things were working out this way.

But they would be better off in the long run. The others would just have to understand that when the time came.

Barlows had been making whiskey for as long as they had lived in the hills of Tennessee, maybe longer for all Kermit knew. A man could make a living at it, but that was all. He was never going to get rich brewing and running 'shine.

Kermit wanted something better for himself and his family. When they had come to Kansas, starting up in the whiskey business had been the natural thing to do, and it was about the only thing Denton, Amos, and Jed knew *how* to do. But Kermit had been looking around, and he had a feeling that with enough money to buy some stock, they could become rich in the cattle business. He had seen successful ranchers in Abilene and knew that was what he wanted—fancy boots and a big Stetson and a spread with cowhands to look after his herds. That was a dream a man could hold onto, not something slippery like whiskey and pigs.

The money he had earned in the last few weeks would go a long way toward bringing that dream within his grasp. That would make all the deception worthwhile.

The wagons swung wide of Abilene, keeping it to the south and east. They moved through rolling prairie, dotted with clumps of trees and brush, cut by an occasional creek or gully. Kermit could see quite a distance from the high seat of his wagon, but the men who were being paid to take the whiskey were probably more familiar with this country. They would know the best hiding places, the most likely spots for an ambush.

Still, Kermit was surprised when over a dozen men on horseback suddenly appeared a couple of hundred yards ahead of them. There had been no sign of them until that moment. They popped into sight, probably from the bed of a dry gully, and starting riding toward the wagon at a fast trot.

Kermit hauled back on the lines of his team, calling, "Whoooaaa!" to the rangy mules. Behind him, he heard an anxious shout from Denton.

"Look, Kermit!" the younger brother cried out. "You see those fellers?"

Kermit twisted on the seat. "I see 'em," he replied. His brother and cousins had also halted their wagons. "Don't get all het up. Maybe they ain't lookin' for us."

He looked toward the approaching riders again just as one of the men in the lead slid a rifle from his saddle boot, lifted it to his shoulder, and fired. Kermit saw the flash and the puff of smoke from the weapon's muzzle, heard the buzz whizzing by his head. A split second later, the crack of the rifle came to his ears.

"Goddamn it!" he yelled involuntarily.

They are shooting! There was not supposed to be any shooting. That had been agreed. But now more of the riders were pulling their guns and starting to blast at them.

"Damn double-cross!" Kermit muttered, diving for the rifle that was lying on the floorboards at his feet. He snatched it up and hesitated only long enough to swivel his head and shout to the others, "Get the hell out of here!"

He had no idea why the man in the buggy had changed the plan, but he did not have time to worry about that. Kermit flung the Winchester to his shoulder and began to fire, throwing lead at the oncoming riders as fast as he could squeeze the trigger and work the lever. The ambushers were less than a hundred yards away now, and the air around Kermit's head was singing with slugs.

The bang of another gun came from behind him,

and he glanced back to see that Denton was returning the fire. Amos and Jed were busy turning their wagons around. They were probably every bit as scared as he was, Kermit thought, but they were working coolly and efficiently. Again Kermit felt a surge of pride. They might not be much for thinking, but they were good men to have on your side in a fight.

And that was just what they were in for. The withering rifle fire from Kermit and Denton made the attackers break ranks and swerve away. A couple of the saddles had been emptied, but the ambushers still heavily outnumbered the Barlows.

Kermit looked around again. Amos and Jed had turned their wagons; the teams were pointing toward Abilene now. Kermit made up his mind in a flash, selecting the only course of action that might give them a chance to live through this attack.

"Come on!" he yelled to Denton. "Leave your wagon!" He was leaping down from his seat even as he called out.

"But the whiskey—" Denton started to protest, lowering his rifle.

"I'd rather lose it than eat lead!" Kermit replied. He started to run toward Amos's wagon. "You ride with Jed! You and me'll lay down coverin' fire while we try to make it to Abilene!"

Denton nodded, triggered one more shot at the riders, who had pulled back slightly to regroup, then dropped off his wagon and ran toward Jed's.

If they had saddle horses, Kermit thought, he would order the others to abandon the wagons and light out on horseback. But the whiskey wagons were the only transportation they had, the only hope of escape from the men who were trying to kill them. As Kermit and Denton swung into the beds of the wagons driven by their cousins, the riders charged again, whooping and shooting.

Kermit braced himself between two of the whiskey barrels, and the wagons lurched into motion. He glanced at the other wagon and saw that Denton was hunkering down, too. The kegs not only offered some cover but could be used to steady their aim while they fought off the attackers. Amos and Jed were cracking their whips, shouting, and doing everything to urge the greatest possible speed out of the mule teams.

The animals were not built for speed, but Kermit and Denton were able to shoot accurately enough to keep the riders from getting too close. Bullets thudded into the barrels as Kermit crouched among them. He could smell the whiskey leaking from the riddled kegs as the wagon bounced over the rugged ground.

Fury blazed inside him. He hated nothing more than being double-crossed. If they got out of this alive, he was going to hunt down the man who had set it up. He had a score to settle, and Barlows never left a score unsettled.

But first, he thought as he squeezed off another shot and saw one of the trailing riders sag in the saddle, they had to make it to Abilene.

Chapter Thirteen

───◆───

Cody Fisher blinked and looked up at the whiskered face peering anxiously down at him. "Are you all right, Cody?" the man was asking. "Why in blazes did that gal bust a flowerpot over your head?"

So that was what had happened, Cody thought as the words penetrated the fog around him. From the pain that was pounding in his skull, he figured he had been caught in a buffalo stampede.

He tried to sit up. The world tilted strangely and almost threw him on his face, but the man kneeling next to him caught his shoulder and steadied him.

"Thanks, Fred," Cody gasped, recognizing him as one of the clerks from the Great Western Store across the street. He looked around and saw that several people were standing around on the boardwalk, staring at him curiously.

"I was looking out the store window," Fred was

saying, "and I saw Miss Hale just up and clobber you with that pot, Cody. Why would she want to do a thing like that?"

"Maybe the deputy got a mite fresh with the gal," one of the bystanders suggested with a grin.

Cody glared at the man, then turned to Fred. "Help me up, will you?"

The clerk slid a hand under Cody's arm and helped Cody to his feet. Another man picked up his battered black hat, brushed the dirt off, and offered it to him. Cody took it and saw the huge dent in its crown. The hat had absorbed some of the force of the blow, maybe saved him from worse injury.

Cody pushed out the dent, settled the hat on his head, and winced as fresh pain hammered inside his brain. Trying to ignore the pain, he struggled to remember why in the world Bethany had hit him.

The coal oil—the liquor warehouse—the purifying agent of fire.

It all flooded back to Cody in an instant, and he reached out to grasp Fred's arm. "Which way did she go?" he demanded. "How long ago?"

Fred blinked in surprise. "I-I think she headed north, across the railroad tracks," he gasped. "And it couldn't have been more than five minutes ago. You came to almost before she was out of sight!"

Then I still have time, Cody thought, *time to stop her from getting into worse trouble.*

Abruptly he realized how hard he was squeezing Fred's arm and released the man. "Sorry," he muttered. But he had no time to say anything else. He turned and started running along the boardwalk, ignoring the puzzled cries that followed him.

Cody knew the liquor warehouse Bethany had been talking about. It was on Fifth Street, three blocks north of the Kansas Pacific depot and a good distance from downtown. By the time he had covered a couple of blocks, he wished he had been less impulsive and gone back for his horse. Then he could have easily beaten Bethany to the warehouse. But his mind had not been working too clearly; all he had been able to think of was hurrying after her and stopping her. Now it was too late to do anything but continue on foot.

The boardwalk ended before he reached Fifth Street. Running in the street, Cody swung around the corner and looked for Bethany. He saw the huge warehouse, a massive stone structure with wooden shingles on its roof, looming up on his left. The walls themselves would not burn, but the roof and everything inside would—unless he got there in time.

As he drew closer, he saw no sign of Bethany in front of the building and grew frantic. Would she have gone to the back to set her fire? If Cody remembered correctly, both the lot behind the warehouse and the one across the street were vacant. No one would spot her back here.

His feet hurt from running. And every time they hit the ground, the top of his head felt as if it were going to fly off. But he kept moving. Despite what she had done to him, he did not want Bethany to go to jail.

He reached the warehouse, turned, and ran alongside it. As he whipped around the rear corner, he spotted Bethany, standing near one of the few windows in the building. The glass was shattered, and the coal oil can was lying at her feet. Instantly Cody knew that she had broken the window and then poured the coal oil inside the warehouse. All it would take now was something to light it.

Bethany held a match in her hand.

She cried out as she saw Cody, then hurriedly

rasped the match into life against the rough stone wall. Stretching up on her toes, she thrust it at the broken window.

Cody yelled, "No!" and then dove at her. He was not in the habit of tackling women, but this was no time for manners. His shoulder slammed into Bethany. His fingers closed around her wrist, jerking her hand back. She screamed as they both fell. Cody tried to twist in midair, so that he would not land on her with his full weight. The breath heaved out of his lungs as he crashed to the hard ground with Bethany coming down on top of him. Enraged, she was shrieking and fighting, clawing at him with her fingernails. Cody gasped for air and pushed her away. Then he saw the match lying on the ground a couple of feet away, the flame at its tip still flickering. He reached over and swatted it out.

Bethany had stopped fighting. She lay huddled on the ground, sobbing. Cody rolled over, pulled himself up on his knees, and crouched beside her. "Bethany?" he asked. "Are you all right?"

"Wh-why?" she gulped. "Why did you stop m-me?" Her red-rimmed eyes were filled with tears.

Anger welled up inside him. "Why did I stop you?" he echoed. "To keep you from going to jail, you little fool! It's against the law to burn down buildings."

"It has to be done!" Bethany wailed. "I have to stop people from drinking—"

Cody grasped her shoulders and pulled her to a sitting position. "Not this way!" he grated. "I know that what happened to your brother hurt you. I know you want folks to quit drinking, and you're probably right about that. But not like this! You can't force people to think the way you do, Bethany."

Pain and confusion flickered in her eyes as she

stared at him, trying to grasp the meaning of his intensely spoken words. Suddenly her face crumpled, tears rolled down her cheeks, and she began to sob brokenheartedly. Like a lifeless, broken doll she sagged in his arms. He folded them tightly around her, cradling her as she cried.

"I'm so sorry," she mumbled a minute later. Gently she pulled away from his embrace and swallowed hard, trying to compose herself. "Are you all right? I . . . I didn't mean to hit you so hard. I just wasn't thinking. . . ."

Cody smiled slightly and tried to ignore the painful lump throbbing on the side of his head. "That was a pretty good wallop," he quipped lightly. "But I'll be fine."

"Are . . . are you going to arrest me for hitting you?"

He shook his head. "Nope. I reckon you just got carried away."

"I was insane, just as you said. When you made that comment about burning down the saloons, I thought you had figured out what I was planning. I thought it would be better to go ahead and admit it and try to take you by surprise."

"You did that, all right."

"But I never meant to hurt you. You've got to believe me, Cody," she wailed, and tears began to well up in her eyes.

"I do," he told her gently, hoping to soothe her. "You just take it easy now. My head's plenty hard. And you haven't done any real damage to this building. You can pay to have this window replaced and for cleaning up whatever mess that coal oil made inside. That'll be the end of it. Uh . . . there is just one more thing."

She turned her tear-streaked face to him. "What is it?"

"It might be a good idea if you left Abilene pretty soon, the way you were planning to anyway. I don't like to see a pretty girl leave town, but . . ."

"But I've worn out my welcome," she finished for him. A tiny, knowing smile played at her lips.

"Some folks might think so," Cody admitted lightly and grinned.

Bethany sighed and nodded wearily. "All right, I will. I did want to be sure that Judah was all right before I left, but I'll give you an address where you can reach me. Please, let me know when you find him."

"I will," Cody promised. He stood up and then helped her to her feet. "Come on, now. I'll walk you back to your hotel, and you can start packing."

As they moved around the warehouse and started down the street toward the heart of town, Cody went on, "You didn't really think you could burn down a warehouse in broad daylight and get away with it, did you?"

"I was planning on doing it tonight," Bethany confessed. "But then you saw that I had the coal oil, and I panicked. I thought I had to do it now or give up the idea."

He chuckled grimly. "That would've been the best thing to do."

"I can see that now—"

Bethany broke off abruptly, and Cody's head jerked up. Gunshots were echoing through the streets. "What the devil?" he muttered.

"Someone's shooting!" Bethany cried, whirling around in panic.

"And doing a lot of it," Cody added; his eyes narrowed as he assessed where the gunshots were coming from. When they noticed the gunfire, they had just reached the intersection of Fifth and Cedar; they were standing exposed in the open. Cody realized the shots were coming from the north, but behind them. "Sounds like it's getting closer!"

Slipping his left arm around Bethany's shoulders, he tightened it protectively and pulled her up against the nearest building. Then he rested his right hand on the butt of his Colt and peered out toward the noise.

Suddenly a pair of wagons flashed by, careening down Walnut Street, crossing Fifth two blocks west of Cody and Bethany. Two men were crouched among barrels in the wagon beds firing rifles behind them. Seconds later men on horseback galloped through the intersection, and the riders were shooting as fast as they could at the wagons.

It was a running battle, headed right for Texas Street and downtown Abilene.

"Stay here!" Cody hissed to Bethany and began to pull away from the building.

"What are you going to do?" she cried, clutching at the sleeve of his jacket.

"Innocent folks are going to get hurt if that shooting keeps up," he replied. "I don't know what's going on, but the marshal and I have to stop it!"

Then he broke away from her and started to run, leaving her behind.

For a day that had started out peacefully, Cody thought fleetingly as he hurtled toward Texas Street, this one was sure going to hell in a hurry.

As Cody Fisher disappeared toward the heart of town, the man who had been watching from the doorway of a closed store emerged and hurried across the street toward the warehouse. From where he had been crouching, he could not tell what was causing the uproar that distracted the deputy, but that did not matter. He would not pass up this opportunity.

He had seen Bethany Hale carry the can of coal oil toward the back of the building, and it had not taken a genius to figure out what she was planning.

The idea had been very pleasing to him.

But evidently that blasted deputy had shown up in time to stop her. If he had not, the warehouse would be in flames by now.

Maybe the situation could be still be saved. The man trotted down the alley beside the warehouse and turned behind it. He immediately spotted the broken window and saw the oil can lying on the ground nearby. Picking it up, he shook it and then grinned— nearly empty. He put his nose to the window and sniffed, catching the odor of the coal oil just inside. His grin widened.

He knew a big stock of liquor was stored inside the building. If anything happened to it, the owners of the town's saloons would have no choice but to replace it as quickly as possible; otherwise their businesses would be crippled.

And he would be in the right place at the right time to sell them plenty of whiskey. Everything was working out perfectly. His chief competitors, the Barlows, would be out of business before the morning was over—not just out of business, in fact, but dead. With the liquor in this warehouse gone as well, the Wagon Wheel Distillery would reap a tremendous profit. In reality the company consisted only of himself—the whiskey he sold was bought on the cheap from moon- shiners in Missouri.

The broad grin still on his face, Peter J. Wallace fumbled in his pocket, pulled out a match, and scratched it to life on the rough wall. He made sure it was burning vigorously, then dropped it inside the broken window.

The spilled coal oil ignited with a satisfying *whoosh!* Wallace hurried away, anxious to put some distance between himself and the warehouse before the flames reached the stored liquor.

He could still hear quite a bit of shooting coming from downtown and decided that he would go see what was causing it. Whatever the fuss was, it was going to be overshadowed in a few minutes by a blast that would rock Abilene to its foundations.

Marshal Luke Travis was sitting at his desk in his office when footsteps pounding on the boardwalk just outside told him that something was wrong. He was on his feet and heading toward the door just as it burst open.

"Marshal!" yelled the townsman who stumbled in.

"What is it?" Travis demanded sharply.

"Sounds like a war coming!" exclaimed the man breathlessly. "Somebody's coming toward town and shooting!"

Travis could hear the gunshots now, drifting in through the open door. His Colt was in its holster strapped around his hips. Spinning, he pulled one of the unloaded Winchesters off the rack, grabbed a handful of cartridges from his desk drawer, and began sliding them into the magazine.

The way the gunfire was exploding, it sounded as if a bunch of wild Texas cowboys were on a tear. But the shots were coming from the wrong direction, and of course this was the wrong time of year. This was some new threat, Travis thought as he ran out of the office, the rifle gripped tightly in his hands.

Once outside he saw the pedestrians along Texas Street scurrying for cover. He wondered where Cody was. The deputy had not come back from visiting Bethany Hale. Travis noticed Orion McCarthy emerging from his tavern with a shotgun in his hand. Catching Orion's eye, Travis motioned for him to find some cover; then the marshal ducked to crouch behind a rain barrel at the edge of the boardwalk.

The shots were very close now, coming from the west, so Travis looked to his right down Texas Street. Suddenly he spotted a pair of wagons drawn by mule teams appear at Walnut Street, a block and a half away, and make a sliding turn onto Texas Street, heading toward him. The mules were moving faster than Travis had ever seen such animals run. The careening wagons swayed wildly as they turned, almost toppling over. But when Travis peered through the dust raised by the mules' hooves, he saw that the vehicles were tightly loaded with barrels of some sort. That weight was probably all that prevented them from tipping over. In the bed of each wagon was a man, facing backward and firing a rifle.

Rounding the corner after the wagons were close to a dozen men on horseback, who were peppering their quarry with rifle and pistol shots. The marshal muttered a curse and tried to figure out which side in the fight he ought to support. Then the wagons thundered by him, and he recognized the drivers—the Barlow twins.

But regardless of who they were, Travis saw they were heavily outnumbered, and the pursuers seemed bent on killing them. Travis made up his mind; he would put a stop to this fight and then sort it out later.

Raising the Winchester to his shoulder, he fired and sent a slug over the heads of the riders. Down the street, Orion followed his lead, the booming blast of the shotgun joining with the cacophony of hoofbeats. The men on horseback slowed abruptly as they realized that they were riding into a crossfire.

But they were still shooting. Suddenly a stray bullet slammed into the head of one of the lead mules pulling the first wagon. The animal pitched forward, its feet tangling in the leather traces, and the other mules in the team toppled with it. The wagon jackknifed, its axles snapping with loud pops. The other wagon was following so closely that it had no chance to avoid overturning, even though its driver tried desperately to swerve around the wreckage. That team trampled into the first wagon and toppled with a grinding crash. Barrels and men were flung from the vehicles and flew through the air. In the whirling debris Travis caught a glimpse of Kermit Barlow flailing his arms and legs and screaming as he sailed above the street.

Within seconds, the street was utter chaos. The barrels split and shattered when they hit the ground, spilling hundreds of gallons of whiskey. Injured mules thrashed and shrieked, and guns were still cracking.

Several of the men who had chased the wagons into town began to flee, but the rest kept trying to kill the Barlows. Out of the corner of his eye, Travis saw Kermit Barlow pull himself to his feet and scramble after his fallen rifle that lay a dozen yards from him. Kermit had almost reached it when a bullet slammed into his body, spinning him around and doubling him over. He fell into one of the rapidly forming pools of whiskey with a splash.

Travis could not tell if the other Barlows had been hurt in the crash, nor had he time to check. He fired at the remaining riders who were shooting wildly around them. Suddenly someone was beside him, holding a six-gun and firing at a steady, deadly clip. The marshal glanced over and saw Cody crouching next to him.

Other citizens besides Orion were joining in the fight now. The rest of the men on horseback tried to make a break for it, but they were pinned in. Most of them threw down their guns and raised their hands as bullets flew around them. But one man kept firing. He must have been the leader, Travis thought as one of the man's slugs chewed splinters out of the rain barrel between Cody and him. Travis fired coolly, and the last gunman pitched from his saddle and tumbled bonelessly to the street.

Now that the battle was over Travis straightened his tall frame and glanced at Cody. "You all right?" he asked.

The deputy nodded. "I'm fine. They were throwing a lot of lead around, but it didn't hit much."

Travis jerked his head toward the riders who had surrendered and said, "You'd better go take charge of the prisoners."

As Cody strode toward the gunmen, Travis approached Kermit Barlow's body. He saw that the other three Barlows were gathered around the sprawled figure. Denton had a long, bloody scratch on his face, and one of the twins was cradling a bloody arm that was probably broken. But that appeared to be the extent of their injuries. They had been lucky, considering the violent wreck.

They had rolled Kermit over to get him out of the pool of whiskey. A large red stain was blossoming on his shirt, and his eyes were closed. Denton looked up, saw the marshal coming, and wailed despondently, "They killed Kermit! They killed him!"

Travis looked up and noticed that the townspeople

had begun to gather now that the shooting had stopped. Catching the eye of a curious bystander, he barked, "Go get Dr. Bloom." The man nodded and broke into a run. Travis knew that Aileen, drawn by the shooting, would appear at any moment, but the man could see to it that she came to check on Kermit first.

"Now," Travis said sternly to the Barlows, "what the devil was all this about?"

Before any of them could answer, a huge explosion shook the ground and sent women and children running for cover again. Travis whirled around, instinctively bringing the Winchester up, but he saw nothing to shoot at. Instead, a few blocks north, a column of black smoke was billowing into the air, and flames flickered over the rooftops between Texas Street and the site of the blast. Whatever had exploded over there had become an instant inferno. Even though his ears had been stunned by the blast, he could hear the popping, crackling blaze.

Travis saw Cody leave the prisoners in charge of Orion and a half dozen gun-toting citizens and run toward the boardwalk. Bethany Hale was standing there, and Cody grasped her shoulders fiercely and spoke angrily to her. Travis hurried over and reached them in time to hear Bethany crying, "I promise you, Cody, I didn't! I swear it! I came right here after you left me!"

Behind Travis, the Barlows had picked up Kermit's body and were carrying it toward the boardwalk.

Travis caught Cody's arm and asked, "Do you know what that is?"

Before Cody could answer, a new voice babbled, "It's that liquor warehouse up on Fifth Street! I saw it explode, Marshal. It's going up like you wouldn't believe!"

Travis believed it. Now he understood why the explosion had been so violent. And trying to put out a fire in a warehouse with so much fuel in it would be futile. The fire would have to burn itself out. But the town's fire wagon would need to go to the scene to make certain the conflagration did not spread.

The marshal looked at the man who had spoken and recognized Pete Wallace, the whiskey drummer. His business would probably be booming in the next few days, Travis thought wearily. He was about to tell Cody to organize the fire-fighting effort when a commotion erupted behind him.

"It's him!" somebody howled. "Lemme up, dammit! I'm goin' to kill the son of a bitch!"

Travis turned to see Kermit Barlow, half sitting and struggling in the grip of his brother and cousins. Evidently Kermit had just regained consciousness, but something had galvanized him and given him the strength to momentarily throw off the effects of his bullet wound. His wild, hate-filled eyes stared past Travis.

The marshal turned to see whom Kermit was trying to go after and noticed that Pete Wallace, his normally florid face pale, was slowly backing away.

Travis flicked his gaze back to Kermit. "What are you talking about, Barlow?" he demanded.

Kermit leveled a shaky finger at Wallace. "I heard his voice just now, and I tell you it's him! He's the one who double-crossed us! It was his idea to put that extra strychnine in the whiskey, Marshal, not mine. It'd make folks a mite sick, he said, but he never said nothin' about it killin' 'em!"

Suddenly, Kermit let out a groan and sagged. He would have fallen if the others had not been holding him up. Travis glanced at Cody and saw that the deputy was just as puzzled as he was, but one thing was clear—they would have to have a long talk with Peter J. Wallace. Travis took a step toward Wallace and said, "Hold on a minute, mister."

The whiskey drummer moved more quickly than anyone would have expected. His hand darted under his coat and drew out a derringer. As he pointed the gun at Kermit, he yelled, "You damn pig farmer!"

Cody, the closest one to him, threw himself forward and dove under the barrel of the gun. He crashed into Wallace, wrapping his arms around the man's waist. The impact knocked Wallace off balance, and both of them plunged off the edge of the boardwalk. The pistol in Wallace's hand cracked, but it was pointed straight up and the slug blasted skyward.

Wallace tried to throw Cody off as the deputy pummeled him. They rolled over and over, splashing through one of the puddles of whiskey. Cody punched Wallace in the jaw, but the drummer's knee came up and smashed into Cody's groin. Wallace threw Cody aside and struggled to his feet, moving with a speed born of desperation. Travis snapped a shot at him, but missed.

Instead of returning Travis's fire, Wallace lunged toward the boardwalk. Travis saw too late what the man intended. Bethany Hale was still standing there, having watched anxiously while Cody struggled with Wallace. Now she screamed as Wallace grabbed her and jerked her in front of him.

"Drop it, Marshal!" Wallace shouted, digging the gun barrel into Bethany's side. "Drop your gun, or I'll kill her!"

An eerie silence fell over the curious crowd who had been watching the bizarre scene. Everyone's eyes were on Wallace, who had begun to drag Bethany into the street. Her face was ashen with fear and pain as he cruelly prodded the gun into her side.

It was plain to Travis that Wallace was behind all the trouble that had been plaguing Abilene. He could worry about why later. Now he had to bend down and carefully place his Colt and rifle on the boardwalk.

Clearly the man was crazy enough at the moment to kill Bethany if anybody tried to interfere with him.

"All right, Wallace, take it easy," Travis said in a deliberately calm voice. Out of the corner of his eye, he saw Cody get to his feet and take a step toward them. "Hold it, Cody!" he shouted.

"But, Marshal—" Cody started.

"Wallace has got the upper hand," Travis snapped, cutting off his deputy's protest. Then turning to the drummer, he said, "What is it you want, Wallace?"

"A way out of this town," Wallace replied harshly. "I don't know how everything went wrong, but I'm damned if I'll stay here and hang for something some dumb hillbilly did. Now everybody just back off!"

Travis gestured to the crowd to do as Wallace said. They withdrew quickly to the sides of the street. Wallace backed down the middle, pulling the terrified Bethany with him. Travis glanced toward the boardwalk and saw that Aileen Bloom had arrived sometime during the confusion. She was kneeling beside the sprawled form of Kermit Barlow, who had evidently passed out again.

"You can't get away, Wallace," Travis called after the drummer. "You might as well let that girl go and make things easier on yourself."

Shaking his head, Wallace tightened his hold on

Bethany and grinned—a horrible parody of his hearty salesman's smile. "Everybody stay away or I'll kill her," he warned again.

The two of them were about even with the entrance of Orion's Tavern when Travis saw a figure stepping through the tavern's doorway. The man was moving silently and so rapidly that he was almost a blur. Travis opened his mouth to warn the newcomer to stay back, but it was too late.

Wallace must have heard a scuffing footstep, because he began to whirl around. When he saw the man lunging toward him, he shouted a curse and started to tighten his finger on the trigger of his gun. Bethany, fainting, slumped in his arms.

Moving with blinding speed, the man reached out with his left hand and slipped his little finger in front of the hammer, blocking it from falling, as his other fingers closed around the cylinder of Wallace's gun. Wallace released Bethany and jerked back a step as she crumpled to the ground, but he could not escape the attacker's long reach.

Reverend Judah Fisher's right fist smashed into Wallace's jaw. The whiskey drummer flew backward, leaving his gun in Judah's left hand, and crashed heavily to the street on his back. He tried to lift his head, then moaned and let it drop.

Chest heaving, knuckles swelling, Judah stood for a moment over the man he had knocked out, then turned worriedly toward Bethany. He dropped to one knee beside her crumpled form and, grasping her wrist, patted her hand and called her name.

Up the street, Cody stared at his brother with a stunned expression on his face. "Judah . . . ?" he mumbled incredulously. Then he broke into a run and

raced toward the three figures clustered in the middle
of the street.

Travis followed at a slower pace. By the time he
reached them, Bethany was awake, lying with her head
pillowed in Judah's lap while Cody knelt at her side.
She peered up at the minister and whispered, "Judah
. . . is it really you?"

"It is, Bethany," he told her quietly. "Thank God I
was in time to help you."

"You saved her life," Cody told his brother. "After
nearly getting her killed," he added with a frown.
"That was a fool stunt, Judah. Where the hell have
you been, anyway, and what happened to you?"

"Hell," Judah murmured. "That's exactly right,
Cody. That's where I was."

Travis rested a hand on Judah's shoulder and
squeezed it. "There'll be time to tell everybody about
that later," he said firmly. "Why don't you help Miss
Hale over to the boardwalk and let Aileen take a look
at her?"

Judah lifted Bethany to her feet while Cody took her
arm. Together, the brothers supported her between
them and moved slowly toward the boardwalk. Aileen
was just straightening from her work on Kermit
Barlow as they approached.

"Aileen, why don't you check on Miss Hale and
make sure she's all right," Travis suggested. Cody and
Judah stayed at Bethany's side while Aileen examined
her.

Travis knelt beside Kermit Barlow. His head lay in
Denton's lap, and a rough bandage was taped to his
chest. His eyes flickered open as Travis asked, "Are
you up to talking, Barlow?"

"I . . . I reckon I am if'n it means tellin' you

'bout . . . that no-good skunk who double-crossed me. . . ."

"You mean Wallace?" Travis said, glancing toward the street. Orion and a couple of other men had taken charge of Wallace and were pulling him to his feet and marching him toward the jail.

"Don't know his name," Kermit replied, "but I ain't never goin' to forget the voice. He's the one who paid me to . . . to poison that whiskey, Marshal. But I never meant for anybody to get hurt. He said it'd just make folks sick. He wanted to . . . to ruin our whiskey business."

"And you went along with him?" Travis asked, frowning.

"You don't understand . . . He was payin' me good."

Travis looked at the other Barlows and saw the startled, hurt expressions on their faces. It was plain that they had known nothing about any of this. Travis listened as Kermit Barlow confessed his part in everything that had happened, right down to the attempted hijacking of the Barlows' whiskey wagons during their run to Dodge City.

"Reckon when we . . . when we started shootin' back, those boys took it personal," Kermit stammered. "Never figgered they'd foller us all the way into Abilene. They was sure tryin' to . . . to kill us."

"Yes, they were," Travis agreed grimly. "Why are you telling me all this now, Barlow?"

"'Fore I die . . . I want to know that that son of a bitch Wallace is goin' to get what's comin' to him. He's as much to blame as me for them fellers dyin', Marshal. I couldn't go out . . . without evenin' the score—"

Kermit's head slumped onto his chest.

Travis reached for his wrist to check his pulse, but Aileen's fingers closed around it first. Kneeling beside Kermit, she looked at her watch for a moment, then said, "That's what I thought. He's passed out again, Luke, but he's a long way from dying."

The twins were crying. One of them gulped and said between sobs, "You mean Kermit ain't goin' to die?"

"It's not likely, at least not from that wound," Aileen answered crisply. "It missed his heart and lungs. He'll recover with enough time and rest. Now, if you men will take him over to my office, I'll do a better job of patching him up." To the twin with the broken arm, she added, "We need to set that bone of yours and put a splint on it."

Travis helped Aileen straighten up. "Is Miss Hale all right?" he asked.

Aileen nodded. "She's shaken up, of course, but she'll be fine. She's not hurt at all."

Travis turned, surveyed the scene along Texas Street, and shook his head. He saw dead and injured mules, wrecked wagons, huge puddles of whiskey, and debris from countless shattered barrels. There was quite a clean-up job to be done. The prisoners had been taken into the jail. No doubt the cells were packed to bursting. Cyrus Worden, the undertaker, had arrived in his wagon and was preparing to load the bodies of the hardcases who had been killed in the fighting. To the north, smoke from the burning warehouse still billowed into the sky, and the strident clanging of the fire wagon could be heard as it rolled toward the blaze. Somebody had thought to call it out in all the confusion. Travis was thankful for that.

Curious, the marshal pulled his watch from his

pocket and flipped it open. Hard as it was to believe, a little less than an hour had passed since Cody had left the office to look for Bethany Hale. Travis snapped the watch shut and laughed softly. It was a tired, ironic sound.

That hour had been one of the busiest in the long, violent history of Abilene.

Chapter Fourteen

CODY WAS STARING AT HIS BROTHER, STILL FINDING IT hard to believe that Judah was back and that he had returned at such a dramatic, fortuitous moment. As they stood on the boardwalk with Bethany, Cody said, "You've got a heap of explaining to do, Judah."

The minister nodded. Wherever he had been, he looked none the worse for it—perhaps a little thinner. He was not wearing a tie, either, which was unusual for him. "I do owe both of you an explanation," he said, "and an apology. All I wanted to do was—" A hand came down on Judah's shoulder, stopping his explanation. Luke Travis, a grin on his face, said, "Maybe you'd better let me tell it, Judah. I know how modest you are."

Judah cast a startled glance at Travis, but he remained silent as the marshal raised his voice and addressed the curious townspeople who were on the street. Quite a few of them had stayed and had already begun the clean-up effort.

"Gather 'round, folks," Travis called. "There's something all of you need to know." When a sizable group had crowded in front of the boardwalk, he went on, "Most of you were at that play last Saturday night, and you saw that Reverend Fisher was having trouble with his part. You know he disappeared after it was over, and you've all heard the talk. The gossip has it that the Reverend was *drunk!"*

Mutterings of agreement rose from the crowd. It was scandalous, and the town had buzzed about it for days.

"I know a lot of you thought that Judah was off on a bender," Travis continued. "But you didn't know the real story. That was exactly what we *wanted* you to think."

Now the group listening to Travis gasped startled exclamations. Cody's face wore a puzzled frown, as did Bethany Hale's. The crowd grew larger, its numbers swelled by the arrival of a large group of schoolchildren, shepherded by Sister Laurel and Leslie Gibson. With the uproar the explosion and fire and gun battle had caused, continuing with classes was a hopeless task, and the schoolmaster, Thurman Simpson, had reluctantly dismissed the students.

Judah glanced at his brother, then turned to Bethany Hale, to Sister Laurel, to Michael Hirsch, and to all of his other friends. They looked confused and were waiting for the marshal to continue his explanation of Judah's bizarre behavior.

"Marshal, what are you talking about?" Cody asked.

"It's really pretty simple," Travis replied. "Judah

just *pretended* to be drunk. I was the only one who knew the truth. Judah wanted all of you to see the strongest lesson possible about the power of liquor." He clapped a hand on Judah's shoulder again. "If someone as strong and upright as Reverend Judah Fisher could fall victim to whiskey, then anybody who's not careful could do the same. That's why he pretended he was drunk during the play and afterward. That's why he's been hiding ever since while all of you talked about him and how awful it was that he had taken to drink. But when he saw Miss Hale in danger, he couldn't stay out of sight any longer. He had to give up the game to save her."

Bethany moved closer to Judah and placed a hand on his arm. "Judah? It was all an act?"

Slowly, the minister nodded. "Like . . . like the marshal said. It was . . . a lesson."

"Oh, Judah." Bethany moved into his arms and rested her head on his chest, unashamed now as she embraced him.

Cody shook his head and grinned. "Reckon you fooled us all, big brother. You had me mighty worried. The next time you get a crazy idea like that, how about letting me in on it?" Genuine, justifiable anger edged Cody's voice.

"I won't be doing anything like this again, Cody," Judah told him. "I can promise you that."

Cody turned to Travis. "You knew all along that Judah was all right. That's why you kept telling me he'd be back and that I shouldn't worry too much about him."

Travis shrugged. "I would have told you the truth, Cody, but I had given my word. And you've got to admit, even you thought the worst." The marshal grinned. "Your brother's a mighty fine actor."

"Too good," he commented dryly.

The laughing, talking crowd pressed closer now. Some of them congratulated Judah on his act, while others insisted that they knew he had been faking all along. He stood there smiling and holding Bethany, and somewhat uncomfortably accepted the plaudits of the citizens.

Close beside him, Travis said quietly, "Reckon it's all over now, Judah."

"Yes," Judah Fisher said slowly. "I suppose it is."

But it was not over, Judah thought. There was one more thing he had to do.

By late afternoon, most of the signs that Abilene had been through a small-scale war were gone. The terrified mules and horses were at the livery stable. The wagon and whiskey barrel debris had been removed from Texas Street, and the sun had dried up the puddles of spilled whiskey. A faint odor of liquor still lingered in the air, but it was fading rapidly. The smell of smoke hung over the town, too, even though the fire at the warehouse had died hours ago. The building was gutted, but the fire had not spread.

Marshal Luke Travis strolled along Texas Street, enjoying the peace and quiet. He had been busy all day, helping with the clean-up and straightening out the mess that had caused all the trouble. Faced with the testimony of Kermit Barlow and the surviving hardcases that he had hired, Pete Wallace confessed to committing the crimes in order to take over the liquor trade in Abilene. The man had pretty grandiose ideas, Travis thought. Controlling the liquor in Abilene had only been the first step. Wallace had hoped eventually to run all the whiskey in Kansas.

Any scheming the man did from here on would be in prison, at least for the next several years. Travis doubted that the prosecutor could make murder cases against Wallace and Kermit, since they had not planned that anyone would die, but they would have to pay for the accidental deaths. In addition, Wallace would be serving time for the destruction of the warehouse and the attempted murder of the Barlows, not to mention the kidnapping of Bethany Hale. Travis was just glad that only three people had been unfortunate enough to get hold of the whiskey that contained the fatal amount of strychnine. It was only by chance that Kermit and Wallace had not killed more people.

Travis paused in front of his office, glanced again at the sun-bathed street, and then went inside. He found Judah Fisher waiting for him.

The minister stood up as Travis came in. "Hello, Luke," he said.

"Judah." Travis nodded. "Something I can do for you?"

"I'd say you've already done a great deal for me," Judah replied. "More than I can ever repay."

"I don't know what you're talking about, Reverend." the marshal answered.

Judah squared his shoulders and looked Travis in the eye. "I'm talking about the way you lied through your teeth this morning to save my reputation."

"I just told folks what they needed to hear."

"Yes, but you know I really was drunk, that I really did go on that bender you said I faked. If it hadn't been for you, Orion, and Miss Paige hiding me and helping me dry out, I'd still be drunk."

"You don't have to worry about Orion and Joselyn

saying anything," Travis assured him. "They're good folks, and they don't want to see anybody hurt."

"I know that," Judah admitted. Then he drew a deep breath and went on. "I should be thankful to the three of you. I *am* thankful. But the idea that from now on I'll be living a lie . . . Well, that *bothers* me."

"Listen, Judah," Travis said, his voice hardening. "You've licked whiskey again, haven't you?"

"You know I have. And this time, it's for good."

"Then what good would it do for anybody to know you really fell off the wagon? The way it is now, the whole town is talking about the way you made them think, about the lesson you taught them. That's a good thing, isn't it?"

"Yes," Judah agreed grudgingly. "I suppose it is."

"Then don't call it living a lie," Travis said. "Call it living a lesson."

Judah met his steady gaze for a long moment, then smiled and stuck out his hand. "Thank you, Luke," he said softly.

"You're welcome, Judah," he whispered as he shook the minister's hand and grinned. "Now, tell me. What's the story with you and that temperance gal?"

Judah laughed. "Miss Hale and I are good friends, but I think that's all, Marshal. She's already told me that she plans to leave Abilene. She'll be taking the eastbound train tomorrow morning."

"Going back home, is she?"

"For now. But she hasn't given up on her mission. She'll be coming west again, I'm sure."

"Back here to Abilene?"

Judah just smiled. "I suppose we'll have to wait and see."

* * *

Early the next morning Cody Fisher was walking down Texas Street. He was on his way to the Grand Palace Hotel to say good-bye to Bethany Hale and see if she would let him accompany her to the train station. Then he noticed a wagon pull up in front of the Sunrise Café, and he thought he might have to be delayed.

Denton, Amos, and Jed Barlow were hopping down from the wagon.

Cody strolled over to them. "Morning, boys. What brings you back to Abilene?"

"We been up to see Kermit," Denton replied.

"How is he?" Cody knew that, while Kermit Barlow recuperated from his gunshot wound, he would be staying at Dr. Bloom's, with guards on duty around the clock. When he had recovered sufficiently, he would go to the jail to await trial.

"Oh, I reckon he'll be all right. He sure is mighty sorry 'bout ever'thin' that happened, Deputy."

Cody nodded and glanced over at the wagon. "Where'd you get this? I thought both of your wagons got busted up yesterday."

"This's one of the ones we left out on the prairie when we lit out for town," Denton replied. "Them fellers was too busy chasin' us to go back and get 'em."

Cody frowned. "So you've still got whiskey to sell after all."

All three of the Barlows shook their heads. "We done poured it out," Denton declared solemnly. He seemed to have taken over Kermit's job as spokesman for the group. "We don't want nothin' more to do with makin' and sellin' whiskey. We's honest, respectable farmers now."

"We're raisin' pigs," one of the twins said. Cody

was not sure which one he was, but he had his arm in a sling.

"Yeah, I know," Cody said. "So what are you doing here at the café?" Even as he asked the question, the answer came to him.

The other twin reached into the back of the wagon and brought out a large ham. "Since we's upright citizens now, we've done decided to come courtin' Miss Agnes after all," he announced, then glared defiantly at Cody. "And if'n you don't like it, Deputy, that's too bad. We figger it's time to let the best man win."

"And that'll be me," the twin with the broken arm added. With his good arm, he pulled a large package wrapped in brown paper from the back of the wagon and scoffed, "Bringin' a ham to a gal! Ain't that the stupidest thing? Ever'body knows you go courtin' with *bacon!*"

"Ham!" his brother insisted. "That's the way to a gal's heart!"

The other twin glared at him. "We'll just see!" He turned and broke into a run toward the door of the café, carrying the package of bacon.

"Hold on there, dammit! Not fair, not fair! It was my idea—"

The door of the café slammed behind both of them, cutting off the argument. Cody glanced through the window and caught a glimpse of Agnes Hirsch's horrified face before she turned and darted into the kitchen.

Denton jerked his head toward the café. "Ain't you goin' to get in there and stand up for your rights, Deputy? I thought you and that redhaired gal was sweethearts."

Cody shook his head and tried not to laugh. Agnes was just going to have to cope with this by herself. "I know when I'm licked," he replied, throwing his hands up in defeat. "I'm not going to try to compete with a couple of smooth operators like your cousins."

"They are a pair of sweet-talkin' romantic devils, all right." Denton grinned. "And you ain't got no pigs, so—"

"What's the point of trying?" Cody agreed. "So long, Denton. You boys stay on the straight and narrow, you hear?"

He turned and headed toward the Grand Palace, a broad smile on his face.

Bethany was just stepping through the hotel's front door when he got there. Close beside her was Judah, his arm linked with hers. Cody shook his head slightly. It looked as if he was too late, and besides, he did not even have any pork with him, he thought wryly.

"Good morning, Cody," Bethany greeted him.

Cody touched the brim of his hat. "Hello, Bethany. Morning, Judah. Reckon you've come to see Miss Hale off."

"That's right," Judah replied. "We've already sent her luggage to the station." He looked more like himself this morning in his sober dark suit and string tie.

"Why don't you come with us, Cody?" Bethany asked. "I'd like to say good-bye to both of you."

He shrugged. "Sure, why not?" He fell in step on the other side of Bethany. The three of them strolled down the boardwalk, but none of them spoke.

The silence became a little awkward, and Cody was glad when they reached the Kansas Pacific depot. As they emerged onto the platform where the train was waiting, Bethany turned to face them and said, "Thank you for everything. You've both been so nice to me . . . nicer than I've deserved."

"Nonsense," Judah said heartily. "You were simply acting on your beliefs in everything you did, Bethany. There's nothing wrong with that."

"As long as you don't get carried away," Cody added.

Bethany smiled. "I suppose you're both right." She stepped over to Cody and rose on her toes to brush her lips against his cheek. She murmured, "Good-bye, Cody."

"Good-bye, Bethany," he replied softly.

Then she turned to Judah, abruptly throwing her arms around his neck and planting a kiss on his lips. Cody saw his brother's eyes widen in surprise, but that did not stop Judah from returning the kiss and hugging Bethany tightly to him for a long moment. When she finally took her lips away from his, she said, "I've got to go now. But . . . I'll be back someday."

"Good-bye," Judah whispered. He found her hand, let his fingertips trail over hers as she turned away and walked briskly to the car. Bethany did not look back as she climbed aboard the train.

Judah drew a deep breath and blew it out as Cody grinned. "Quite a gal, isn't she?" Cody commented.

"Indeed," Judah agreed. "The most frustrating mixture of beauty and stubbornness I've ever encountered."

"Amen to that." Cody laughed. "Although I reckon you ought to be saying that, not me. . . . You really think she'll be back?"

"I'm sure of it." Judah smiled faintly. "One of these days, some poor unsuspecting drunk is going to be set upon by that lovely little fury. And she'll make him see the error of his ways."

"Yeah. At gunpoint, more than likely."

Cody and Judah turned and walked off the platform as the train whistle blew. The locomotive lurched into motion and the wheels began to turn as the train rolled out of the station.

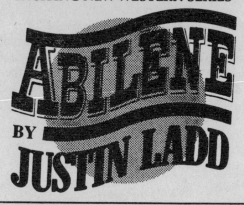